DISCARDS

DISCARDS

ALLAN DAVIS

IGUANA

Publisher: Meghan Behse
Editor: Toby Keymer
Front cover design: Ruth Dwight, designplayground.ca

ISBN 978-1-77180-492-9 (paperback)
ISBN 978-1-77180-493-6 (epub)

This is an original print edition of *Discards*.

Chapter One

Salty

From the shelters and the streets, we hear the muffled wails of hidden remorse in a penance we will never understand.

June 2004

In early May, Salty got on the night shift driving a bulldozer for AMC construction. They were building a new highway through Mennonite farm country, 150 miles northeast of the city. Salty found a trailer park not too far from the construction site with hookups for his thirty-eight-foot Trailmaster and space to park his Dodge Ram pickup. It had his name on the side: "Harold 'Salty' Saltzmanous: Renovations." That business had gone bankrupt the year after he had bought the truck, which he still owed money on.

As he was signing the bankruptcy document, his wife, Lee Ann, had said, "Every time I look at that stupid truck I remember how much money your construction business lost. I hate that truck."

Salty thought more or less the same thing every time he looked at *her*, how much of his money she drank away in whatever bar was closest to whatever trailer park they were staying at. She's stupid, but I don't hate her, he had thought.

At forty-three she still looked okay, except now she needed those Styrofoam push-up-the-sags bras to match her tight blue jeans and six-inch heels and all the stuff she put on her eyelids after she'd drawn on the fake eyebrows.

All that makeup was what had given him the courage six years ago in the Wagon Wheel Bar to ask her to join him for a drink. It was like she was wearing a sign: "Ask me to join you for a drink." In the morning, she didn't look too bad without all the makeup. Salty thought, "That's how women are these days. They dress up like hookers and get into the drinking and get taken home by some guy and they both get drunker than skunks and next, well, it's not her fault, even though she had her hand in his weeds playing with his dick all the time they were sitting at the bar. Because in court, it turns out, she's a decent young woman just trying to get by."

It was Nikki's, not the Wagon Wheel. That next morning, while Salty was still sleeping, she had sorted through the tiny kitchen of his thirty-two-foot Prowler and, standing barefoot at the stove, made him a decent breakfast. Any bar pickup he'd ever had hadn't hung around to make him breakfast. So, she must be a decent young woman doing her best to get by.

A decent young woman who thought that now, after six years of trailer parks, she deserved better. How she said it was, "Our daughter deserves better. What is she going to do all day while you're sleeping? This trailer park is all old people. There's no children for Sylvia to play with. What am I going to do all night while you're working? There's no mall near here, no movie theatre, nothing. I'm sick and tired of living in this stupid trailer and looking at all these ugly, stupid trailers."

So Salty phoned his younger brother, Frank, who lived with his wife and two children in Mt. Forest, ten miles from the construction site. Frank said, "There's a farmhouse for rent just outside the town limits. It would be an easy walk into town for Lee Ann. It's next door to a Mennonite farmer, Eli Martin, who's got three kids Sylvia's age."

Salty checked it out. It looked pretty good.

It worked out pretty good too. Eli and his wife, Mary, helped Salty and Lee Ann carry their stuff into the house. The three Mennonite girls were dressed in pale-blue print dresses and little white bonnets like in that story, "Little Bo-Peep." They stood out of the way next to the gate of the barbed wire fence that separated the two farms.

After that, every day from that day on, the oldest girl, Rachelle, would meet Sylvia at the gate. Hand in hand, they would set off across the field. They would stop on the way for a handshake with Eli's sheepdog, Amos. Then, after getting permission from Amos, they would pat each of the seven woolly lambs before continuing along the path between the two houses. In Eli's yard, they would play among the chickens that wandered and pecked in the grass, and in Eli's barn with the cats and the kittens that hid and hunted in the hayloft.

"I like it here," said Salty. He was sitting at the kitchen table, midway through a twenty-sixer, midway through a mid-June day. "I could stay here forever."

Lee Ann said, "You could stay here forever? Look at the windows. They're going to be drafty in the winter. And did you look at the furnace? It's an old boiler piece of junk coal-to-oil conversion. It'll cost a fortune to heat this place. And back off on the drinking, you have to work tonight."

Since there seemed to be something wrong with everything Lee Ann looked at, Salty never took her complaints seriously. Six days a week he was either working or sleeping. A shot of rye and a beer chaser would take the edge off her sharp voice when he was home all day Sunday.

On Sunday afternoons, Salty liked to stand at the gate to watch Amos, stretched out flat, chin resting on front paws, minding the sheep. Sometimes Salty would go halfway across the field and sit with a bottle of Canadian Club on the one big boulder in the otherwise rockless field. Eli would join him and they'd sit together, passing the bottle, watching the sheep.

"If one wanders off," said Eli, "strays away from the others, Amos's head will come up. He will come to attention. If that sheep does not return to the flock within five minutes, I've timed the dog, it's like he's got a watch on his wrist, he'll get up and trot over to steer the stray back where it belongs."

Salty liked Eli because he was soft-spoken. There were long pauses between his thoughts before he moved them into words. Lee Ann did not like Eli because he called Mary "the wife," as though she was the same as "the dog" or "the horse."

Salty passed the bottle to Eli.

Eli was saying, "Sometimes a sheep wanders off and gets lost, not one of these, mind you. Amos is a good sheepdog. But it happens. A good sheepdog knows it's his fault and it's his responsibility to find that one sheep that's slipped away on him. He knows it's his duty to bring it back. Sheepdogs have been known to search for weeks, sometimes dying on the roadside, searching for that one lost stray."

Eli passed the bottle to Salty.

Eli said, "Amos has this habit, I don't know where he learned it, every time you come up to him, he sits down and holds out his paw for a handshake."

Eli squatted on his heels and leaned his back against the rock. Salty tried the same but he was too thick-legged. He sat instead, legs stretched out.

Eli said, "They're bred to look after sheep, but they look after people too. I sometimes help with my cousin's produce deliveries to the market in the city. The vendor's name is Ron. He told me about a sheepdog he had a few years ago. Ron was working all kinds of crazy hours, but the dog always knew when Ron would arrive home. His wife said the dog would get up and wait at the door. It had nothing to do with time; the dog just knew, like he had one of those flying drone things telling him what time Ron left the market and what time he would walk in the door."

Eli ran his hand through the twitch grass, pulled up a long stalk, and began to chew on the soft end. Salty did the same. It tasted sweet.

"He took his kids camping. He put the kids in one tent with the dog, and him and the wife in another. In the middle of the night, the dog routed the kids out of their sleeping bags and made them get out of the tent. Twenty minutes later, a tree came down on the tent. There was no wind and no rain. But the tree was rotten inside and down it came."

Eli removed his fedora hat to scratch his balding head. Salty had no hat to remove, but his thick black hair, turning grey on the sides, did enjoy a scratch.

"Some dogs are smart like that, but none are smart as a sheepdog. Ron told me about a man and his sheepdog standing at the corner; a different dog. Him and the dog were standing on the corner outside the market. The dog started to worry and fuss until the man moved away, and two minutes later a drunk driver smashed into the pole where the man had been standing."

Salty offered Eli a cigarette. He shook his head no. Salty put them away. He settled himself against the rock. It was a perfect sunny day with the green fields and the white sheep spread out before him and a bottle going back and forth between the two men.

"Something I've noticed," said Eli. "People are like sheep. What one does, the other one does. They copy one another. Their minds imprint like geese. But every so often, one will wander off, away from the flock, and become lost, like those homeless people living in shacks in Silver Park down in the city. They say some of those homeless men are escaping the law. They go down there, change their name, lose their identity, and disappear. They even got a tattoo place down there that burns off fingerprints. I sometimes drive past Silver Park on the way to the market. I say to myself, 'These men are lost sheep with no sheepdog.'"

Salty thought for a moment, remembering. "I had a buddy, Fred, he's dead now. He used to live near Silver Bridge. It crosses the Silver Ravine, which divides the city in half, The Rose on one side, The Thorn on the other. Fred and me and this girl Helen went to school together. We were farm kids and rode the bus together. Helen and Fred got married and bought a fixer-upper about a block from Silver Bridge. He was a carpenter, so he converted the garage into a workshop to do his carpentry. Helen is still there, probably."

"All kinds of crazy things happen down there on the Thorn side," continued Eli. "One guy murders another guy and throws him into a dumpster. Fifteen-year-old girls get pregnant and throw the babies into a dumpster. They've lost their way. They need the number one sheepdog to shepherd them back home, if you know what I mean."

***

Salty spent the July 1st holiday helping Eli rebuild his porch. When they opened the floorboards, they found a barn cat with a mangled hind leg hiding between the joists. It had been attacked by something, a fox, probably, and was hiding away to die a slow death. Eli's wife wouldn't allow guns on the property, so Salty went home for his old lever-action Cooey twenty-two, a rifle he'd got from his father when Salty was fifteen, growing up on a beef cattle farm near Teeswater, not that he used the gun anymore. It was a keepsake, like an old bicycle from when you were a kid. He put the cat out of its misery.

Salty would not take any money for helping Eli. So, the following Sunday, as Salty sat on his porch enjoying the quiet of the countryside with a glass of Scotch, he heard a clop-clop in the gravel and he turned to look. Eli was climbing out of his buggy. He had a live, reddish-brown chicken tucked under his arm.

Eli said, "Life hasn't been too good to this chicken. It was a good layer, but now it's lame in one leg and this eye here is blind. The other chickens pick on her, so that's why her comb is all scabby tatters. So, the wife says, 'Give it to Salty. It'll make a good Sunday dinner.'"

Salty had to admit, "I never killed a chicken before."

Eli handed him an axe from his buggy. "Three steps. One: hang the chicken upside down to drain the blood into the head. Two: lay the neck across the chopping block, like across that stump over there. Three: chop off the head. It's easy, as long as you do the hanging upside down part first. That is why it's rule number one."

Salty accepted the chicken and the axe.

"She's a Rhode Island Red," said Eli.

Eli climbed into his buggy. He picked up the reins and turned around, and the horse set off down the lane at a returning-home trot. Salty remembered going to the sulky races at the Teeswater Fair. The track horses were all Standardbreds, like Eli's. That was probably where he got that horse.

Salty gently placed the chicken in the grass where it sat quietly, its head swapping from one direction to the next as its good eye tried to sort out the details of its new situation.

Salty poured himself another drink and sat down on the porch step to watch the chicken as it got to its feet and took a few careful steps, favouring that one leg. Salty did not want to kill anything that had been picked on. With the cat, there was no choice. But this chicken was a little different. After a few days wandering undisturbed in the yard, its leg and its comb and maybe even its eye might get better.

Salty sipped at his drink. He thought, I'll build her a little house, with a nest to lay her eggs in. Maybe I'll get a couple more chickens, friendly ones that won't pick on her.

Salty said to Lee Ann, "That chicken reminds me of Frank."

"What about Frank?"

Salty noticed she seemed a bit prickly when she said that. "Frank was picked on when he was a kid."

She gave him a suspicious look. Or maybe it was a guilty look. Whatever kind of look it was, Salty took notice.

Little brother Frank. Salty was only one year older, but by fourteen Salty was big and sturdy, already filling out. Frank was small and skinny. Salty remembered his mother driving twenty miles to the nearest Walmart to buy them jeans: Salty was size husky; Frank was size slim. His mother had taken a picture of them in their new jeans. Frank still had it. The picture was big and little brother heading off, Salty's fifteen-foot bamboo fishing pole slung over his shoulder, Frank, his little helper, trailing along behind to the river to grapple mullet and suckers out of the fast spring runoff below the dam. Salty did the grappling. He still had that three-inch, three-pronged hook in his tackle box. But not the fifteen-foot pole.

Salty poured himself another Scotch. He said to Lee Ann, "We can keep her as a pet. Five minutes for a chicken is like five years for a person. She's got her whole life ahead of her."

As far as Salty was concerned, this chicken could wander and peek in the rented farmyard for the rest of time. "We can call her Rhoda."

Lee Ann said, "You'll offend Eli if you don't eat the chicken, and I don't want a chicken wandering around dropping poop everywhere for Sylvia to step in like over there in Eli's yard. And you better sober up before you try to kill that chicken. You'll cut your own head off is what you'll do."

He finished his drink.

"If you don't want to kill it, take it back to Eli. Ask him to kill it for you."

That is what she said. But the way she said it sounded more like, "If you're not man enough to kill it, take it back to a real man to do the job."

So, Salty picked up the axe and the chicken. He walked with the chicken under his arm, a fresh drink in one hand, and the axe in the other. The tree stump was ten feet down the lane. He stared at it as he walked along. One clean chop and the chicken would flip and flap and flop and die. That would be the end of it.

He sat on the stump. "I'm sorry, Rhoda." She was sitting quiet in his arms, her one good eye staring up at him not saying much of anything but looking hopeful that he would not chop her head off.

Salty did not want to hang her upside down. He wanted her to die peacefully, not knowing what hit her, believing he had done her no harm. But when Salty tried to lay her neck across the stump with the blind eye facing him so she couldn't see he was the one chopping off her head, she started to squawk. He raised the axe, trying to time a swing to the movement of the head, blind eye up. But as the axe came down, Rhoda twisted her head to look straight at him with the eye that could see.

Down came the axe. Into the grass dropped the chicken.

But the cut was not clean. Up she got, head dangling, wings flapping her in circles, wobbling and teetering across the grass to the lane where she stopped, her good eye swiveling around in her upside-down head trying to figure out what was what.

Salty remembered Sylvia was in the house. They'd been to Walmart and he'd bought her a new pale-blue dress like the little Mennonite girls wore. And he'd bought her a Ronald McDonald doll. She should have been sitting on the living room carpet dressing the doll. Salty knew Lee Ann would be sitting on the chesterfield watching "The Young and the Wrestlers." Salty thought she would be keeping an eye on Sylvia to make sure she didn't come into the yard while he was killing the chicken.

But Lee Ann must have fallen asleep watching the TV, and Sylvia had come out to see what was going on. She stood in the lane, halfway between the house on one side and the fence on the other, staring at the chicken. The chicken's head stopped circling long enough for its good eye to see an upside-down girl in a blue print dress. The chicken's brain must have thought, "This little girl would be Eli's youngest daughter if she were right side up."

Off across the yard went the chicken, headed for back home, straight at Sylvia.

Sylvia tried to run to the house but the chicken, running in a wobbly circle, cut her off. Sylvia ran the other way, towards the gate of the barbed wire fence, the chicken right behind her. Unable to open the gate, Sylvia tried to climb the barbed wire fence. But her new blueprint dress caught in the barbs. She managed to rip herself free and make it to the top. Balancing with one hand on the post and one foot on the top wire, she tried to jump to the other side. But her dress pulled her into the barbs as she fell.

When Salty drew back the axe and swung sidearm into the post, the wire snapped into coils. He swung again and sparks flew as the strands wrapped themselves around her. He dropped the axe and waded in, the barbs biting and snapping at the bare flesh of his arms as he tried to free her from the hopeless tangle he had created. He ran to his pickup for his wire cutters. Sylvia wrapped her arms around his neck and hung on as he cut her loose.

Her new dress, shredded to pieces, had shielded her body. But her left cheek was ripped open, skin dangling like the chicken's head, as he carried her to the pickup.

"You're like a bull," said Lee Ann as they returned from the hospital. "You're like a bulldozer. You don't think. You just charge in and send everything flying. Why don't you think first?"

Salty pulled up the laneway and got out of the pickup.

"Why didn't you just take the chicken back to Eli? You're so stubborn. Or why didn't you wait till you were sober? But, oh no, you wouldn't listen."

Lee Ann carried Sylvia into the house. Salty followed her in for his twenty-two that he had left in the kitchen closet. He knew the chicken was dead by now, but he wanted to kill it again, as though he believed one shot through the chicken's head would make it dead enough that he would never have to think about that chicken again. He spent over two hours cleaning up the mess, scruffing away the drops of blood in the laneway so they wouldn't get stepped in, washing gobs of blood off the face of the stump, and cleaning red clots out of the bark with a scrub brush and soap and water. Then Salty picked up the chicken by its scaly feet, stiff as yellow sticks now, but head still dangling, eye still staring at him, and he threw it into the garbage.

Back in the kitchen, he washed and bandaged the four gashes the barbed wire had ripped on the inside of his left arm. Then he poured himself half a water glass of Canadian Club with a Molson Ex chaser.

Chapter Two

Salty

Salty arrived home from his night shift, eyes sore from the dust and the lights, body tired and dirty from eight hours on the bulldozer. He left his mud-covered work boots on the mat at the door. First thing, he went upstairs to check on Sylvia. She was lying on her back, hugging her Ronald McDonald doll to her chest, sound asleep from the painkillers. Her cheek was sewed up with twelve stitches that looked like tire treads in snow.

Salty went downstairs. He sank down at the kitchen table and opened a beer to chase down the remainder of the bottle of rye he'd been drinking on the bulldozer. The radio was playing his favourite song, "Long May You Run." He picked up his guitar. Quietly so as not to wake anyone, he strummed backup for Neil Young. He got up and took out the bread and the meat slices for that night's lunch. Ham, not chicken. Lee Ann would not pack his lunch, not because she thought he should eat lunch at lunchtime, not midnight, but because it reminded her he carried a lunch bucket and not a briefcase to work.

He'd said, "I'll pack my lunch in a briefcase."

"The thermos won't fit."

In the cupboard behind the butter dish, he noticed a letter with his name written on the envelope: Harold. It had been hidden behind the MixMaster next to his almost-full bottle of Scotch. But when he reached for the Scotch, he knocked everything over. Lee Ann would have had something to say about his clumsy construction worker fingers.

He sat at the table and drank the rest of the beer and opened a second to chase down the Scotch. "Don't drink from the bottle," she'd say. "And your hands are filthy," she'd say. So he got up to get a glass. He sat down. Then he got up to wash his hands. He did not want to use dirty construction fingers to open her clean white envelope.

She's not clean and white now, he thought, climbing the stairs. Sneaky bitch, he thought, opening the bedroom door. Lee Ann was asleep, her long black hair spread over the pillow. He sat on the edge of the bed. Asleep she looked younger than forty-three. He wondered why she had not removed her blue sweater and jeans and makeup before climbing into bed, falling into bed, it looked like, or why she had not taken off the gold locket that snapped open to a tiny picture of Sylvia.

He shook her awake and handed her the letter. She did not have to read it to know what it said.

She sighed, "I'm sorry, Harold. I've been trying to tell you. Things haven't been good for us... I don't know... one thing leads to another..."

No one called him Harold, not even himself. He almost looked around to see if someone called Harold was in the room with them.

"It just sort of happened."

She sounded little girly, like a twelve-year-old caught smoking pot. He went downstairs. In his mind, "Long May You Run" was still playing. He opened another beer and poured a double shot. By now he was drunk enough to think a crazy thought: I'll shoot the bitch with my twenty-two.

He stared at it propped up in the corner by the back door. If it hadn't been for killing that chicken, he wouldn't have thought that. If it hadn't been that the loaded rifle was there in the corner where he could see it instead of locked in the closet where he should have left it, he wouldn't have thought that.

But it was no more than a thought. Killing a chicken had been hard enough. He could never kill a wife, even if she had persuaded his little brother Frank to sleep with her.

Not knowing what else to do, he called Frank. Frank said he would come right over.

Salty sat at the kitchen table with his drink. He thought about little brother Frank, standing off to one side, careful to stay out of the way of Salty's three overhead swings with a quick point halfway through the fourth to get the three-pronged grappling hook out across the rushing river surface to the middle where the water was deepest. Longer lines were too hard to swing. Shorter lines would not go far enough. Using the leverage of the bamboo pole, Salty could feel the movement of the hook as he tugged the line with steady jerks, one, two, three, careful to keep it from snagging on the bottom. The out-of-season trout he threw back. The suckers and mullet he kept. Together, Salty and Frank sold them door to door to the old ladies on Main Street to feed to their cats. Well, not really together: Frank didn't like to touch the fish, and didn't like their smell. So yeah. He was a bit of a sissy.

Frank will be on the road by now, thought Salty. It's a twenty-five-minute drive.

The Main Street ladies would say, "What have you got for us today, Salty?" Already at fourteen that was his nickname.

"And how is wee Frank today?" They would have to bend a little to see wee Frank peeking out from behind big Salty.

Frank would be on the road, but wee Frank will want to take his time getting there, trying to think what to say to big Salty. That was how Salty still saw him in his mind, still wee Frank. That's why Salty couldn't blame Frank. That, and the fact that Lee Ann was a pushy bitch who got wee Frank into her bed to get even with Salty for who knows what; he was never too sure.

Salty got up. He went into the living room to look at the framed picture of Lee Ann on a sailboat, hanging on to the rail, smiling into the wind. This picture was hanging on the wall. The picture hanging in his mind was Lee Ann on that stool in Nikki's, hanging on to her beer glass. Salty hadn't said, "How's it going? My name's Harold." He'd said, "How's it going? My name's Salty."

On the opposite wall from the sailboat picture, next to the big mirror she'd got at a garage sale in Teeswater, was a picture of Salty and Frank in Dr. Reed's old rowboat. Salty was holding a five-pound largemouth bass, Frank was holding the equipment. One of the old ladies they sold fish to had taken the picture with a Polaroid camera. Frank was so interested in the picture coming to life before his eyes that the lady had had the photo framed for him. But Frank didn't want it because he didn't like how the eye of the fish had stared at him as it lay flipping and flopping and dying in the bottom of the boat, like the eye of that chicken had stared at Salty as it flipped and flopped and died in the dirt. Salty had teased Frank for not liking the eyes staring at him. Salty wished now he hadn't done that.

Salty went back to the kitchen, poured another drink, and sat at the table. He knew Frank would take his time getting there. Maybe he wouldn't come at all. Maybe he was sitting at home at the kitchen table remembering how the old ladies called him "Salty's little helper."

"Did you help Salty land that big fish, Frankie?"

Wanting to help Salty was why Frank had tagged along wherever Salty went. Because he wanted to be big like Salty, who had never once wondered how small he must have made Frank feel.

Helping Salty would have been how this affair got started. Lee Ann would have phoned Frank and invited him over for a drink. She'd have complained about living paycheque to paycheque, skipping from trailer park to trailer park so the bill collectors wouldn't catch up with them. Frank would have listened patiently, nodding in agreement. Lee Ann would have faked a few tears, but not so many that they smeared the eye stuff down her cheeks. Trying to feel as big as Salty, Frank would have taken her in his arms. Lee Ann would have faked a big, dry-eyed cry. She would have poured them each another drink. That's probably how it went.

Salty could feel the eye of that chicken looking up at him from that stump like the eye of that fish had looked up at Frank from the bottom of that boat like the eye of Lee Ann had looked up at him from the bed when he gave her the letter.

The day after that Polaroid picture got took by the old lady, Salty's swinging line had snagged the grappling hook into Frank's thin shoulder. Salty had cut the line and together they had walked to the Main Street Medical Clinic where the doctor cut it out. Frank hadn't cried. He hadn't even complained. The doctor had handed him the hook. He'd said, "No more fishing with Salty for the next two weeks.

In fact, I think you should give up fishing with Salty altogether. Play baseball like the other kids your age."

Frank had given the hook back to Salty and together, like nothing had happened, they'd gone door to door with their suckers and mullet. Frank had told their mother it was his fault. He hadn't wanted Salty to lose his fishing privileges.

Salty should have said, "No more fishing with me, Frank." Instead what Salty had said was, "Let's see if I can catch another largemouth before the water gets too warm. "

Frank hadn't looked too sure about that.

Salty had said, "There's not many days left, Frank. Soon the water will be too slow and the bass too lazy to bite, and their flesh too soft."

Frank had stared down at his feet, wearing his afraid-to-say-no look. Salty should have said, "You're right, Frank. I should go on my own."

Instead, Salty had said, "We'll cut down the ravine and follow the shoreline to the millpond and borrow Dr. Reed's rowboat."

Frank had hung his head and in a whiny voice that annoyed Salty said, "We shouldn't be stealing his boat."

Salty said, "Dr. Reed, he's ninety-nine years old. He's not interested in his old rowboat. Besides, his house is on the top of the ravine and the boat is hidden by trees and the path to the dock is too steep for him to climb. Maybe he's older than ninety-nine. Probably he doesn't even remember he's got a rowboat."

As usual, wee Frank had carried the stuff: a fiberglass rod with a Mitchell spinning reel in one hand, the tackle box in the other. Frank rowed while Salty, standing in the bow, cast into the shade of the trees close to the shore. He had reminded himself to pay attention to where Frank was and where his triple-hook Shad Topwater was. But after half an hour of casting, the boat drifting lazily in the early-morning June sun, Salty's mind had begun to wander, drifting with each cast towards the bank, thinking that even if the bass weren't biting, a day like this with no wind would not be wasted.

Salty took another drink, remembering in exact detail that it had been a perfect day to practice his cast with that lure. It gave him the exact weight to carry the line to within a few inches of where he wanted it settled. That day he had drawn back his rod and cast. He had waited for the line to sail out ten feet above the water and then drop where he had intended with a plunk, gentle as a grasshopper falling off a tree branch. When no line had appeared and no plunk came back to him, Salty had glanced around, realizing he had felt a tug at the tip of his rod as he cast.

Salty had rowed back to shore while Frank, wiping at his tears to keep the salt away from the hook, sat in the bow, holding the dangling line so it didn't weigh on the hanging skin. By the time they had reached shore, Frank's shirt was soaked with blood.

Frank told his mother it was because of the blackflies. He'd felt a sting on his cheek. His hand must have gone up to swat, accidentally catching the line and driving in the hook, ripping open his cheek. The stitches looked like tire treads in the snow.

Salty poured another drink. The clock on the kitchen wall above the refrigerator said it was almost four. He took his Player's from his plaid shirt pocket.

First Frank's cheek and then Sylvia's cheek. First the chicken's blood and then Sylvia's blood. First Lee Ann with Salty and then Lee Ann with Frank. Salty remembered one time him and Frank had gone to the fortune teller, Madame Kratz, at the Teeswater Fall Fair. She had told Salty that bad luck followed itself in threes. To stop this from ever happening, she had sold him a lucky rabbit's foot with a lifetime guarantee. Salty didn't know what had happened to it. Wait, yes, he did. It had started to smell like rotten fish so his mother made him throw it into the garbage. Just like he'd thrown the chicken into the garbage.

The clock on the kitchen wall now said 4:10. Frank wasn't coming. He must have thought if the grappling hook had gone into his shoulder, and the Shad Topwater had gone into his cheek, what would the Lee Ann hook go into?

After the hook in the cheek, Frank had developed a stutter, as though the barbs had gone all the way into his mouth and damaged the muscles of his tongue. At school, the kids made fun of the stutter so that, instead of Frank following Salty around, Salty followed Frank around, making sure no one picked on him.

"I can fight my own battles," Frank had said to Salty.

Frank had fought his battles by keeping to himself. He stayed in his room. He played computer games while the other kids played baseball. To avoid stuttering, he didn't talk much. He finished high school. He studied computers at college. At twenty-two years old he was what he looked like, a computer geek.

He still looked like that, coming up the path in his cargos and blue tailored shirt, his right shoulder leaning a little like it was used to carrying a briefcase, not a lunch bucket.

Salty butted his cigarette. He said, "How's it going, Frank?"

Chapter Three

Salty

In the mirror hanging across from him on the dining room wall, Salty could see sitting at the table a sad-looking Salty, broad-shouldered, face tanned except for the thick scar across his forehead that he'd got when he drove his pickup into a tree. The skin had always been one shade lighter along that crease. At the end of the table to his right sat a frightened-looking Frank with short brown hair parted nice and neat on his left side, his arms and face pale from working inside, the thin scar from when Salty sliced the stutter into his tongue one shade lighter than the rest of him. To Salty's left sat an angry-looking Lee Ann with long hair pulled back in a ponytail, her arms and face as light as Frank's, the same colour, in fact, except for her lips. They were red from the lipstick she hadn't taken off from the day before. There the three of them sat, two white, one dark, a reminder to Salty that he was the black sheep in this family picture.

Lee Ann's left hand was fidgeting with the gold locket that had Sylvia's picture in it. Lee Ann broke the silence. "Three months, if you must know. That's how long Frank and I have been sleeping together. Three months at first and then we stopped and then we started again three weeks ago."

Salty was looking into the mirror and thinking about the number three. He'd opened Frank's cheek with a lure that had three hooks. He always swung his three-pronged grappler three times. He should have cut off the chicken's head with three steps. And he'd hooked Frank twice, and this was the third.

There they were, the three of them, with three empty glasses, one, two, three. Salty watched himself stand and pour three drinks: Scotch and sodas.

Lee Ann's voice was higher than her usual bitchy. "Wherever I was, stuck in some God-forsaken place in that stupid trailer, Frank would drop by."

Frank had that same didn't-want-to-say-no look on his face as when he'd got hooked with the Shad Topwater.

She continued. "Do you blame me? Look at how we live. One job after another. Now we live in a falling-down farmhouse. Where will it be next? A motel? You don't think past tomorrow. You drink away every paycheque. You don't plan ahead. Like the way you killed that chicken, too stubborn to take it back to Eli. And look where you left that rifle, right here in the kitchen where Sylvia can find it."

Salty got up to put it into the closet where it belonged.

"Did you unload it? You didn't unload it." She grabbed the barrel of the rifle. "Let Frank unload it. That way, it'll be done right."

When Salty wouldn't release the grip on the gun, Frank said, "Give me the gun, Salty. Now's not a good time to be fighting over a gun."

Frank said this without a stutter. He said it better than Salty could. He pronounced the words clearly, unlike Salty, who would have said it slurring from the Scotch.

Frank said it again. "You've had too much to drink. You can't think straight when you're drunk. Give me the gun before there's an accident."

So now Frank could think straighter than Salty.

Frank put his thin hand on Salty's thick arm. Frank's fingers were delicate, good for careful work, like putting away a loaded gun. Salty's fingers were thick, his palms calloused, his hands clumsy, his arms strong, not good for careful work, like putting away a loaded gun.

Salty said, "I can put it away myself."

Like a dry branch breaking, the rifle snapped. At first, Salty thought his grip on the stock was so strong he'd cracked the wood. Then Lee Ann released the barrel of the gun and settled on her knees and then flopped over on her side. Blood was turning the front of her sweater from blue to red. Frank knelt beside her. With fingers delicate from fixing computers and hands soft from working on keyboards, he tried to find a pulse, first in her wrist, then in her throat.

Time of death, thought Salty, his head like that chicken's circling upside down from the whiskey: Three minutes after five a.m., July 13, 2004.

His brain stopped turning and his eyes fixed on Lee Ann, whose eyes were fixed on him. They seemed to be saying, "Now look what you've done." Frank was standing next to him, staring at him, his eyes asking, "Now what do we do?"

Salty removed the locket from Lee Ann's neck and stuffed it into his pocket. He emptied her pockets, rolled her up in the living room carpet, and, while Frank looked on, loaded her into his pickup.

Salty said, "Tell your wife that me and Lee Ann have gone. Tell your wife you'll be looking after Sylvia until we get a place to live. That is what you will tell her. In the meantime, I'll take Sylvia over to Eli's until you get it straightened out at home."

Frank looked lost. He looked like he was back at fourteen years old, doing whatever Salty said. Frank left and Salty sat down to finish his drink before going upstairs. Curled up with her Ronald McDonald doll sound asleep from the painkillers, Sylvia would not have heard the gun. He got her dressed and carried her in the crook of his arm across the field to the neighbours'. He knew the Martins would be up, already beginning the chores. As he walked, Sylvia's little hands with the chubby little fingers traced the scar along his forehead. "Now I'm going to have one too," she said. She looked at the barbed wire gashes crisscrossing his left arm. "But you're going to have more than me."

The three Mennonite children, in little blue print dresses and white bonnets, stood in the yard lined up in a row, watching him coming across the field. Sylvia wanted to wear a blue print outfit, and that is how he had dressed her. He set her on the step. The mother, also wearing a blue print dress, stood in the porch doorway.

"Frank says he'll be over for her at lunchtime," Salty said.

Usually, Sylvia would run off with the smallest of the three girls. Usually, on his way back home, partway across the field, near the big rock, when he turned around to look, she would be gone, into the barn to play with the kittens. Or, when he looked back from the gate, she would be playing dolls with the two little girls on the side porch. Arriving home, standing at the kitchen counter mixing a drink, looking out the window, he would see all four of them out there together in the field, patting the lambs that Amos brought over. As far as Amos was concerned, now he had four more lambs to look after.

But this day Sylvia did not want him to go, and she did not want to be left, and when he looked back he saw that she was holding out her arms to him, not wanting him to leave her there, and he could see that she was trying not to cry because it pulled on the stitches in her cheek. But he left and walked away and when partway across the fields near the big rock he looked back he saw that Mary had taken Sylvia inside and shut the door. Then he saw that Amos was standing, ears forward, staring at the shut door. Salty could not hear Sylvia crying, but he knew by the way Amos was shifting his feet, glancing from the closed door to the lambs and back to the door, that Amos, hearing those cries, was struggling to decide, should I stay where I am or should I go and bring her back to my flock? Salty thought, I should go over and explain to Amos that Sylvia would be leaving today, but don't worry, she'll be well looked after by Frank, so don't go looking for her.

But Salty turned away and he did not go over and tell Amos. Instead, Salty packed his clothes and his guitar and a full bottle of Scotch. He glanced at the carpet rolled up in the back of the pickup to make sure it was still there. He drove through the farmland to Highway 26, tipping back the bottle as he went. Finally, he arrived in the city. He drove through Rosemount where the rich people with the custom-built houses and tailor-made suits lived. He crossed Silver Bridge and stopped in Thornton, the inner-city slum where the poor people lived. He dumped Lee Ann into the biggest industrial dumpster he could find, dumpster 2020, in an alley behind Colonel Wong's Southern Fried Chinese Chicken. He climbed into his pickup and passed out.

Chapter Four

Salty

At first, Salty couldn't remember what had happened. He didn't know where he was; parked on a busy city street, yes, but in what city, and how did he get there? To his left was some kind of park with benches and shrubs and, right in the middle, one tree. And one water fountain. Straight ahead, at the top end of the park, was a ravine. Crossing it was a steel girder bridge. He could hear the back and forth of the traffic. Beyond the bridge, a path led through trees and brush to a cluster of shacks further up the ravine. To his right were storefronts: The Albion Pub, Soapy Suds Laundry, Dixie's Donut Shoppe, and Colonel Wing's Southern Fried Chinese Chicken.

Then Salty remembered the dumpster. Then Salty realized he was in the inner-city slums known as The Thorn. Then he realized he was looking at the Silver Bridge. Then he remembered his dead buddy Fred had lived two blocks away.

He heaved himself out of the front seat of his Dodge Ram. He found his half-full bottle under the seat. He crossed the street and settled himself on a Silver Park bench. He drank from his bottle and chain-smoked from his package of Player's as bit by bit the pieces of the night before returned.

He lit his last cigarette and smoked it to the filter. He decided. He would drive to the nearest police station and say it was an accident. But the police would say, "If this was an accident, why did you not phone us when it happened? Why were you trying to cover it up?"

"Well, I was panicky. I didn't know what to do. I didn't want to get my little brother Frank into trouble."

But then he thought, what if the dumpster has already been dumped? Even if someone had seen him, they would think he was just throwing away an old carpet.

He remembered it was dumpster number 2020. He got into his pickup and followed the garbage cans to the end of the alley. Dumpster 2020 was gone. The number he was sure of, but maybe not the location. He drove to the end of the alley and turned onto Sheldon Street and looped around the block. When he noticed the sign for Colonel Wing's Southern Fried Chinese Chicken, he stopped. He thought the sign had said Colonel Wong. When he looped the block again, he realized there were two: Wing's and Wong's.

For the rest of the day he zigzagged through the maze of alleys and streets until finally, not knowing what else to do, he arrived at the front door of Helen's house. Salty didn't know her all that well but they'd gone to school together and Salty had been Fred's best man at their wedding.

He sat in his truck, gathering the courage to knock on her door. Helen had not liked Lee Ann, he knew that much. Fred and Helen and Lee Ann and Salty had spent drunken weekends camping together in Grand Bend until Helen told Fred no more weekends with that tart Lee Ann. Helen didn't like Salty much either. She'd be liable to say to him, "Are you knocking on my door to ask for directions to the nearest liquor store?"

He didn't have the strength to come right out and tell her why, just like he didn't have the strength to go to the police station and admit he'd sunk another hook into brother Frank's life. That's how Salty saw this mess: his fault, not Frank's.

Helen answered almost right away. She'd probably seen him sitting in his truck. She said, "Look what the cat dragged in."

She led him into the kitchen. She must have been folding her dinner napkins. Their holders were waiting in a basket in the centre of the table. She poured him a cup of coffee. She said, "You're looking pretty rough, Salty."

Salty was not good at talking. He was slow with words. Lee Ann would say, "For Christ's sake, get to the point." But Salty had already sort of thought it through. He said, "Remember when we were in school how we looked after Frank?"

"Has something happened to Frank?"

"Remember the first day of school you walked with him to his grade one class, holding his hand the whole way? Like you were the big sister he never had?"

"Frank was afraid of the other children. He didn't like those games they played at recess. Why are you bringing this up?"

"You'd take him off to one side and play with him, away from the other children. At birthday parties, you went with him and did the same. Like the big sister he never had."

"He never had much of a mother, that's for sure. Somebody had to help out. The other farm kids his age were big. He was such a little squirt. He'd sit in the corner and mouth the words to 'Happy Birthday' because he was too shy to sing out loud. So what? What's happened to him?"

"I never told you. Two summers ago I ran my pickup into a tree."

"So now you're going to tell me you ran over Frank? God help you, Salty. Is he dead?"

"I had quit drinking. I worked all summer on the bulldozer. I came home after dark every night and every Friday gave Lee Ann the paycheque to deposit at the bank. At the end of the construction season, the bank account was empty. Lee Ann had spent all summer drinking and smoking pot with some guy she'd met in the Tim Hortons. So I said, what the fuck, I might as well be the one drinking away my paycheque."

"So you got drunk and ran over wee Frankie?"

"Sort of."

"Sweet Jesus, Salty."

While Helen listened to his story, she folded the napkins. They were the same pale-blue print as Sylvia's dress. She folded them neatly and flattened each one on the tabletop and took a round wooden holder from the basket and put each napkin into one of them. Then she took each napkin out again and unfolded it and flattened it and folded it and slipped it into its holder. She did this until he had finished talking.

Then she said, "Frank's wife is a strong person. She will do what's right for Sylvia."

She started with the napkins again. Salty watched her fingers remove each from its holder, unfolding it, refolding it, sliding it back in. Finally, she looked straight at him. "Lee Ann has gone to landfill, which is where she belongs. I can't believe I'm saying that about anybody but it's true. She was drunk at your wedding and came on to Fred. I couldn't believe it. At her own wedding, for God's sake. Fred blamed her for your drinking problem. Fred said before you met Lee Ann you were a steady worker. After you married her, it was job to job, never settling in one place. It broke his heart the way she treated you. She has no family, none that we know about; no one will come looking for her. If you disappear, no one will think anything of it. Your parents are gone, you have no family other than Frank. If you disappear, she'll have disappeared with you."

"And if someone at the landfill finds her?" asked Salty.

"Frank is your witness; you are his witness. It was an accident. Besides, bodies go to landfill all the time, no one knows the difference."

"What about Sylvia?"

"She's better off with Frank. We both know that."

Her fidgeting with the napkins reminded him of Lee Ann's fidgeting with the locket that was now in his pocket. He took it out and snapped it open and showed Helen Sylvia's picture. "She's just turning six."

Helen stared at the picture. "She doesn't look like Lee Ann. She looks like you, Salty."

Salty looked at the picture.

Helen said, "I know what you're thinking. Don't think it. What kind of life can you give her? You leave her with Frank and you disappear."

She lined up the napkins in their holders in front of her. She said, "Fred made me these napkin holders. I'd been after him for years to make me a matching set. So this one day, out of the blue, he went into his workshop and made this set. He burned my name into this one and his name into this one. The day after he gave them to me, he was killed."

She put them aside. "Remember the time you and me and Fred went to the Teeswater Fair? You got Fred a T-shirt by ringing the bell with the sledgehammer. Then we went to Madame Kratz, the fortune teller that was one booth over. She lives next door now. I go on a regular basis. She remembered that for the three days the fair lasted, you and Frank arrived at sun-up to search the property for money fallen out of people's pockets. She asked me, 'Where were the parents of those two boys?' I said I didn't know. We were just kids. Where were your parents anyway?"

Salty shrugged. "Farmers. Too busy to know what their kids were doing."

"Madame Kratz will probably remember you. You should go for a reading. There's a sign hanging in her reading room. It says, 'Your destiny is open but your fate is sealed.' Sometimes it's better to do nothing than to do something. Sometimes it's better to leave your destiny up to fate. Sometimes it's better to wait and see what your future holds."

To Salty, how she said the words "fate," "future," and "destiny" made it sound like they were, well, not real people, more like spirits you couldn't see but were there, watching you. Eli would see it something like that too. Salty didn't know how to see it, but dealing with what you couldn't see, in his case a dead body buried in a landfill, seemed better than dealing with what you could see, in his case a dead body lying in front of them.

Helen put the napkins aside. She said, "You'll get what's coming to you. But I haven't forgotten how you looked after Frank when we were kids. Well, you snagged him with a fishhook a couple of times, but that's just how it goes sometimes. And I know Fred would want me to do whatever I can. For the time being, you can stay in his workshop outback. It's got its own washroom in there, and electricity that he hooked up illegally to our breaker panel. It's got a closet in there. I sold all his power tools, but his hand tools are still there. There's a box or two of his clothes. He was a big bugger like you. I'll give you a hot plate. There's an old couch in there too. If you need money, sell your pickup. When that money's gone, I want *you* gone. This is a short-term arrangement. There are oddball people all over the place in this area. As long as you don't come knocking on my door, no one will notice you. Short term."

Chapter Five

Salty

Salty sold his pickup to a used-car dealer. He couldn't remember for how much. He walked three blocks to the liquor store. He didn't know how many days later it was that he woke up in Fred's backyard workshop sober and broke. He wasn't too sure what had happened to the money. But after turning his pockets and Fred's shed upside down, he decided he must have spent it. Gone.

Under the workbench, he found half a bottle of clear liquid with no label. He unscrewed the top. It smelled like some kind of homebrew. He took a sip. It brought tears to his eyes. He took a drink. Pretty good, he thought, taking a long pull.

Taped to the bathroom mirror he found a note:

Dear Salty,

Remember you were the best man at our wedding? You were so drunk you dropped the ring and we couldn't find it. The next morning, after you had sobered up, I said, "Do you remember what you did with the ring?" You said, "What ring?"

Last night when I looked out my kitchen window, I saw you stumbling up the lane, a bottle in each hand. The tens and twenties were dropping out of your pocket onto the gravel. A tall homeless man carrying a banjo was following along, picking them up.

When I was sure you were passed out for the night, I went into Fred's shop, which, thanks to me, you are now temporarily staying in. For a short time, let me remind you. I gathered up what money

you had left. I won't say how much. I will once a week leave you
fifty dollars for food until it runs out. When the money is gone, I
want you gone with it.

Helen.

Now Salty remembered: on his second day in Silver Park he had
stumbled across Mr. Bones near the subway entrance. He was playing
his banjo and singing Willie Nelson songs. Mr. Bones looked and
sounded like Willie Nelson. Salty had gone back to the shed for his
guitar. Him and Mr. Bones together had done pretty good: after two
hours twenty dollars each, which they spent on homebrew.

Salty sat down with his bottle of homebrew. Now he remembered:
A three-point knock on the back-alley door behind Dixie's Donut
Shoppe on Sheldon Street, three doors down from Colonel Wing's
Southern Fried Chinese Chicken, would get him a bottle of Curveball.
A four-point knock and four dollars would get him a bottle of
Majestic Diner. Same thing, five and five for a bottle of Kawasaki. The
unlabelled bottles all looked the same, but the brew was not. The one
that was right now clearing his hair-of-the-dog mind had a gold cap,
which meant it was Curveball.

Now he remembered. Mr. Bones had showed him all the places
to eat for free: Mondays, Wednesdays, and Fridays were "Dinners for
the Homeless" in St. James's basement. Tuesdays and Thursdays were
"Light Up My Day" suppers at the Light for the Lost Mission.
Breakfast every day was at St. Joe's. Lunch was at The Daystar Men's
Shelter. All free. Pretty good.

Helen's fifty dollars a week was looking pretty good.

When Salty opened the shed door to have a sober look at the
back-alley view from his doorstep, he saw that Helen had left him a
box of Fred's clothes with a note: "You can take these with you when
you leave."

Pretty good.

Until in one pocket, he found Fred's birth certificate: "Frederick
John Grafton." This made Salty nervous. He thought pretending to be
a dead man, living in a dead man's shop, wearing a dead man's
clothes, and using a dead man's stuff seemed to guarantee a fate and

a destiny of ending up a dead man. Salty put Fred's clothes back in the box and put the box back on the doorstep with a note: "Not good for my future."

***

For the cool June nights, Salty slept under the blanket Mr. Bones had found on a park bench. It was heavy wool, almost the same shade of green as the carpet he had wrapped Lee Ann in. One dark night, the rain drumming on the shed roof woke Salty up. He could hear in the rush of the water off his roof and past his window the voice of Lee Ann coming from under the blanket saying, "First a trailer park, then a falling-down farmhouse, then a back-alley garage. Next comes the streets, with you going through the garbage like a raccoon in a dumpster."

Before he dropped the blanket into the dumpster by Soapy Suds, he checked that it was not number 2020. But from then on, waking up sober in the dawn of a windless morning, Salty would hear in that same voice that same number coming to him like a back-alley ghost standing at his window looking in, saying 2020. So, from then on, the first thing he did every morning was walk to the McDonald's on the other side of the bridge. At the counter, he bought a cup of coffee and asked for the complimentary paper. Every day to reassure himself that the year was not 2020, he read the date at the top of the newspaper. Then to reassure himself Lee Ann had not been found, he searched each page for stories about discovered bodies. He read about the body discovered behind the bushes in the ravine. He read about the body discovered frozen in a freezer in a warehouse on Fleet Street. He read about the body washed up on the shoreline of Cherry Beach. But his body never made the news. No policeman ever rang his doorbell, not that he had one, and no cousin ever asked about Lee Ann, not that she had one.

Never mind, never mind, a left turn from the alley onto Bridge Street, and a short walk through Silver Park, and a right turn with a short detour past Colonel Wong's — he was the brother of Colonel Wing — took him straight to the back door of Dixie's Donut Shoppe for another three-dollar bottle of Curveball.

Never mind, never mind. Days drifted his weeks into months. His hair grew long and his beard shaggy and his clothes ragged. Mr. Bones took him to the Black Widow Tattoo Parlour to get his fingerprints turned into a different squiggly. He didn't sign up for the $205 government homeless allowance with the extra $200 special diet allowance certified and signed by Dr. Singh. You had to give ID for that.

Never mind, never mind. Sitting with his bottle of Curveball on his doorstep like a hermit living in a mountain cave by the forest with the birds and the bees, Salty now lived like a hermit in a laneway shed with the squirrels and the pigeons. At every free meal at whatever church or whatever shelter, before he picked up his knife and fork, Salty did not say, "Thank you, Helen. All that's missing are the cloth napkins and holders." He said, "Thank you, Frank. You will be a better father to Sylvia than I could ever be."

Sylvia. Made by Lee Ann and Salty on that trailer park Trailmaster workbench. Napkin holders. Made by Fred on this back-alley garage workbench. The napkins: pale-blue print, like Sylvia's dress. Helen had pronounced "holder" like "older," which every day Sylvia would be getting. Never mind, never mind. She'll be well looked after by Frank.

Salty went to Home Depot and picked out of the garbage a few pieces of four-by-four pine. He sat on his park bench. The whittling of the wood began to take the shape of a fish. Salty had not intended to whittle a fish, but there it was, like one of those suckers, resting on the river bottom, gaining strength for its trip upstream, hoping that no fisherman's grappling hook would yank it out of the water to feed to some old lady's cat, or worse, to leave on the riverbank to rot and stink.

Salty knew the stink of rot. In an alley or a laneway, he would smell it and he would turn and there would be a dumpster. Some had numbers, some didn't. He never found dumpster 2020. But he knew the day would come that he would find himself in the year 2020. Every day he saw in the complimentary newspaper at McDonald's that the number was getting closer. Every day he got the feeling that his upstream current was getting stronger. Every rainy day when he looked into a back-alley puddle he saw that he, Salty, although now almost unrecognizable, would one day look up and there blocking his path would be both the year 2020 and the dumpster 2020.

He knew this because tucked away in his pants pocket was Lee Ann's locket with the picture of Sylvia that he looked at every day. He saw that every day her numbers were adding up to another birthday. Sometimes, when he snapped the locket open, he saw not a little girl Sylvia but an adult Sylvia. He wanted to stop looking at her, and he wanted to stop carrying her around. But he couldn't. That would be like abandoning her again.

Salty did not sit on the park bench that faced Colonel Wing's Chinese Fried Chicken sign. It had a picture of a reddish-brown chicken on it which reminded him of Rhoda. He refused to look at it. But one day, all the other benches taken, Salty had nowhere else to sit.

He said to his eyes, "Don't look at that sign, eyes."

But no sooner had he got settled on the bench when a tall man in a baggy shirt and pants sat down beside him. At the exact minute Salty glanced up, his eyes fastened not on the intruder but on the one good eye of the chicken that was looking straight at him, saying:

"My name is Father Sutcliffe. I've just taken over at The Daystar Men's Shelter."

The priest looked like a homeless man pretending to be a Father Sutcliffe, like Mr. Bones pretending to be a Willie Nelson, like Harold Saltzmanous pretending to be a Salty.

"I have a message for you from Helen. Your brother Frank has been sick, bedridden in fact."

Salty remembered the door across from his bedroom opened to Frank's room, which was smaller than Salty's. It had a single bed, a dresser, a closet, and there against the wall under a window, an old wooden desk. Frank had set up his computer on that desk. Frank tidied his room every morning without being told. Salty never tidied his room. Frank had sat at that desk and calculated on his computer how many germs lived in Salty's room.

Father Sutcliffe said, "Helen said to tell you. Your brother Frank has passed away."

It took Salty the length of three long pulls from his bottle to come up with the question. "What about Sylvia?"

Father Sutcliffe hesitated before saying, "Helen said to tell you Frank's wife didn't want Sylvia. Eli's wife had been diagnosed with pancreatic cancer a few weeks earlier and couldn't take Sylvia. Sylvia went into foster care the day after you left."

Salty went back to his shed. He sat on his couch. He lit a cigarette. He looked at the fish sitting on the shelf above the workbench, staring at him. He thought, except for their size, they all look about the same. Each new fish he hooked, they all turned out versions of the fish before. Each time he hooked Frank, it turned out a version of the time before.

Salty tap-tapped on Madame Kratz's front door. He was ushered into her parlour. The purple curtains were the same as at the Teeswater Fair, but the spooky light which had hung from a tent pole overhead had been replaced by three candles at the centre of a table. Salty sat opposite her. He remembered her head-down slow-card shuffle, no poker-dealer high-speed finger-tricking like in the casino tent next to the High Striker.

She hunched over the cards, turning them in slow concentration, reminding Salty of Eli picking up a handful of soil, holding it in his palm, reading in it what it should grow.

She spread six face-down in front of her. She flipped them over. She closed her eyes. Salty felt chills go up and down his spine. She said, nodding her head, "The triangular three is following a most interesting chain of events that wants to lead you backwards in time, Salty."

"What does that mean?"

She reached out and turned a fourth face up. She placed it in front of him. The picture could have been of almost anything.

"Do you hear it, Salty?"

"Hear it?"

Madame Kratz seemed to be listening to something far off. She sat back, scowling at the card. She said, "It must be that little girl next door I'm hearing."

She got up. She had almost disappeared through the purple curtain when she turned. She said, "That's all for today, Salty. "

"That's it? I just got here."

"You wanted to know your fortune. I just told you."

Chapter Six

Sylvia

June 2020

Sylvia's first assignment for the School of Social Work's Family Theory 101 course had been, "In one page, 250 words, explain why you want to be a social worker." The prof's comment at the end of the page had been, "Sylvia: Wanting to re-write your own story through other children is not a good reason to go into social work. You are motivated not by compassion but by anger you have spent years repressing."

She had answered, "Because from personal experience I have anger at the system, I will have compassion for the children caught in the system."

Woken up by her mother's angry shouting, Sylvia had climbed out of bed and crept to the top of the stairs. Uncle Frank was there. Her mother and father were fighting over a gun. When she heard the shot she ran back to her bed and hid under the covers. Then, when she heard Uncle Frank say in a loud voice, "She's dead," Sylvia got out of bed again. She had not wondered about the meaning of "dead." She had wondered why Uncle Frank, who always talked so quietly you could hardly hear him, had shouted.

She had watched them load the rolled-up carpet into the back of the pickup. She had gone back to bed to wait for her father to come up and explain what was going on. But the painkillers were strong and she fell asleep and was barely awake when her father dressed her and carried her across the field. She was too groggy to understand what he said to Eli Martin, something like "Look after Sylvia until Uncle Frank comes." It sounded like he was talking to Amos, saying something like, "Look after Jumpy Sheep until Uncle Sheep comes."

Jumpy had been her favourite lamb. He liked to jump over the big rock her father and Eli sat on to drink their whiskey.

Uncle Frank never came, but a social worker did. She listened to Eli explain that he wanted to keep Sylvia, but his wife had only a month earlier been diagnosed with pancreatic cancer.

One of Sylvia's first "foster sisters" was called Justine. She had visits from her parents every other weekend, either taking turns or arriving together. Justine had been taken from her mom and dad by the police because they were drug addicts. But at least they were not dead.

By the time Sylvia had figured out what "dead" was and how her mother ended up that way, she had decided that she did not want any visits from her father. She would stay in foster care until she aged out of the system.

Another foster sister, Meghan, wrote her father letters which she never sent because she didn't know where he lived. She called him Shadow Man. "Dear Shadow Man. You don't come to my birthday parties, you don't come to see my teacher on parents' night, you don't ask to see my report card. Don't you wonder how that makes me feel?"

Meghan called her mother Ghost Woman. "Dear Ghost Woman. You didn't come to my piano recital. You've never sent me any Christmas cards. Don't you wonder how that makes me feel?"

Sylvia used to imagine writing Uncle Frank a letter: "Dear Uncle Frank. You never came. The person who came was a woman with sheep-coloured hair. She said, 'We'll have this little lamb back with her family in no time.'"

She was right about the "no time."

Her first foster family gave her their last name, Evans. But then they split and Sylvia went back into foster care, one family after another. The only constant was the social worker, Janine, who had been abandoned into foster care and become a social worker so that she could help other foster kids. Now Sylvia realized that would have been a better way of putting it, instead of "I want to rewrite my story."

Stray children, Janine had called them. "The only way to survive," said Janine, "you let the tears come and then you let them go." The "them" was the biological parents.

So now, in the middle of May 2020, fourteen years later, Sylvia was startled to see a Mennonite farmer, a neighbour of Eli Martin, the man said, standing in the doorway of Sylvia's university dorm. Sylvia knew Eli would have greeted her with something like, "Hi Sylvia. I wouldn't have recognized you. You're all grown up now!"

But this man had never seen her before, and she had never seen him. He wore the plain clothes of the Mennonite farmer. He removed his dark and dusty fedora. He had a receding hairline which seemed to extend his thin, pointy nose, unlike her father's, she now remembered, which was somewhat flattened, like a boxer's.

Everyone had called him Salty. He had looked like a Salty, the bearded captain standing in his wheelhouse on the back of the frozen fish sticks package. This man looked like a clerk from a Charles Dickens novel. He was clean-shaven, stooped, and now, standing in her doorway nervously fingering his hat, looked like he wanted to deliver his message and be on his way.

The man's eyes met hers and then shifted briefly to the scar along her left cheek, then shifted away, obviously embarrassed at being caught staring. Sylvia was used to it. Usually Sylvia covered it with makeup, but this was early in the morning. No doubt Eli had told him how she got the scar.

He said, "My name is Meno Martin. I live one concession over from Eli."

The man held up the notepad on which was written in large print her name and address. He said, "I deliver vegetables to the Saturday morning farmers' market down here in the city. I've got a bad back so sometimes Eli comes along to help with the lifting. On the way home, we drop off the stuff we don't sell to Father Sutcliffe at The Daystar Men's Shelter in Silver Park, in The Thorn. Eli carries in the boxes. He saw a man sitting at a table in the kitchen with some of the homeless. After we left, Eli said, 'That looked like Salty Saltzmanous. I recognize that nose, like a boxer's.'"

Sylvia knew her mother was a Ghost Woman. But for a long time, Sylvia believed her father was not a Shadow Man. He was looking for her and he would find her and he would come for her and she would refuse to see him. Simple as that.

The man at her doorstep continued. "Eli said two police detectives were poking around the house next door, where you used to live. Eli told them your mom and dad disappeared and you went into foster care but he had no idea where you ended up. But after the police left Eli remembered the social worker had given him her card. So he phoned her and was given your social worker's number. Her name was Janine. She said you hadn't seen your father since the day you got left at his house. Eli didn't want to get involved in any police business, but he did want you to know he saw your father. Eli said, 'Sylvia's father got lost by the wayside. She'll want to help him.'"

Her lips tight with anger, Sylvia answered, "I am the one who got lost by the wayside. The day after I was delivered to my foster parents' door, I fell down the stairs. I cried all night because my father wasn't there to help me up. Almost everything in foster care is a variation of a fall down the stairs with no father there to help you up."

Sylvia knew Meno would not understand what she meant. She said, "He disappeared a long time ago. I didn't hear from him so I convinced myself I wanted nothing to do with him."

Meno Martin looked shocked. "You don't want to get back together?"

"I was abandoned into foster care," she said. "*Trapped* in foster care is more like it."

He seemed confused. He frowned at the notepad and checked the number on her door. He returned his notepad to his pants pocket. She knew what he was thinking: how could she not want to help her father?

He glanced up the long line of bedroom doors to the exit sign at the end of the hall. "These are all separate rooms?"

"Yes." Sylvia thought, he must believe all these rooms are for abandoned kids. So let him think it.

"Does that exit take me to the front door?"

"It does, yes."

He returned the fedora to his head.

Sylvia added, "Foster care is a mess of abandoned kids."

He looked up and down the long empty hallway again. He seemed to be trying to understand her story.

"Aren't there laws about abandoning kids?"

"Laws, yes. Morality, no. Abandoned kids become nobody's children. Strays. I ended up a stray."

"So... Now that you know where he is, what will you do?"

"Why should I do anything?"

His expression went blank. Sylvia knew that, had he been standing in his farm laneway gazing across his fields, his expression would have been full of understanding of what he was seeing. Had he been looking at his plain house and his plain wife and his plain children, his expression would have been full of comprehension of whom he was looking at. But Sylvia could see that what he was looking at and what he was seeing made no sense to him.

He shuffled a few steps along the hall, wanting to be on his way. "I told Eli I would drop by and tell you."

"I have learned to be self-reliant. I worked my way through undergrad as a waitress. I got a scholarship for my MA in social work. I've gone this far without his help, so I have no intention of helping him now."

The man was halfway to the exit when she called, "One other thing: how is Uncle Frank?"

He hesitated. He turned. In the shadows of the hall, she could not see his face to know whether he had heard the question or was searching for an answer.

"You didn't know? Your Uncle Frank, he died a long time ago."

Sylvia's memories of Uncle Frank were vague, except that he was a little man, made smaller next to her father. She shrugged. "I don't care if he died. He abandoned me too."

Then out popped another question she did care about. "And what about Amos?"

Meno said, "I don't know any Amos."

"Eli's sheepdog. Amos, his name was. Every day I would go to the field to pet him. Sometimes, I sat in the grass and Amos would put his head on my lap and I would tell him stories about myself, and when I stopped talking he would nudge my knee, wanting to hear more. But I couldn't play fetch the stick or take him to my house because he was looking after the sheep."

Meno nodded. Finally, something he could understand. "Eli's dog, yes. He disappeared two days after you left. You left Thursday. The dog spent all day Friday looking for you. Eli loaded the truck for the market in the city at four on Saturday morning. When Amos still couldn't find you, he must have thought you'd gone with Eli. Amos disappeared that Saturday, gone to the market to find you."

Sylvia felt the tears welling up.

His voice changed from uncomprehending to understanding. "Amos was an amazing dog."

Sylvia wiped away the tears with the back of her hand. "He'd walk with me to the gate into our yard to make sure I got there safe. He thought I was one of the lambs." And then she added, "He wouldn't have abandoned me, that's for sure."

She watched Meno walk down the line of doorways and disappear through the exit. She went into the bathroom and examined herself in the full-length mirror. She stepped closer to the glass and stared at her scar, a thin white line running from her ear almost to her mouth. Thankfully, it had been fading as she got older, so, with makeup, it was visible only when looked at closely in direct sunlight. But now, brought back sharp and clear by that knock on the door, it was as red and angry as the day she got it.

She said to her face in the mirror, "This scar is all he left me. I will not allow him to slice me open again."

Chapter Seven

Roof

Detective Ron Roof and his partner, Eric Dickie, had been assigned to the Cold Link Unit. It had a 1-800 number on a website with a nice slogan: "The dead may be silent, but those who know the truth are not."

Roof was explaining their assignment to Dickie as they drove across the bridge to The Thorn. "Letters have been written to the church pastors in the Silver Park area stating that the support for the homeless was greatly appreciated, no other institution in the Silver Park area was doing as much for these men as the church. Blah blah blah. However, some of these men are wanted felons, no kidding, hiding out among the homeless to escape justice."

Roof parked the unmarked Chevy in front of Soapy's Laundry, across from Silver Park. They crossed through the traffic and sat on the closest bench. It was ten o'clock in the morning. The sun was high above the bridge warming things up after a chilly June night.

This was Roof's first time in the area. The park was a one-block square patch of grass bordered by Russell Street at the south end, King Street on the west, and Sheldon Street on the east. The north end of the park extended under the bridge, through the Silver City shacks, and up Silver Ravine, which continued in a network of trails through woods to the 401.

Roof said, "So here is our first anonymous tip that came in on the answering machine from a nice old lady suggesting we might be interested in a homeless man living in Silver City by the name of

"Caps." His wife's name was Rosey Paterno. Sure enough, she's on the cold case file."

Roof read the printout to Dickie. "Rosey Paterno disappeared fifteen years ago. Height five foot four inches, brown eyes, 140 pounds. Rosey and her husband, Howard Paterno, disappeared on the same day. Find Caps and you will find Howard, and then you will find out what happened to Rosey."

Dickie studied a grainy picture of a stout woman in a baggy T-shirt and track pants. "She looks like the envy of the trailer park."

Roof shuffled through the papers. "Here's the second one from the same old lady. Lee Ann Saltzmanous, who probably was the envy of the trailer park. Husband Harold Saltzmanous."

Dickie studied the picture of the middle-aged woman in jean shorts with frayed hems and a see-all tank top standing next to a Mennonite farmer in front of a farmhouse.

"They had a history of living in trailer parks before they both disappeared on the same day from their rented farmhouse. The landlord called the police because of the blood on the kitchen floor. They tried to track down the child but she was lost in the foster care system."

Dickie said, "This one of Lee Ann paints a good picture. The farmer in his fedora hat and work pants standing next to what looks like a trailer park hooker. Who is the farmer?"

"It says here Eli Martin, who lived next door. He says he wanted to take the kid but his wife was sick with cancer. So, they phoned Children's Aid."

Dickie said, "Saltzmanous is not a common name."

"I had a buddy with that name. I think it's German. Hungarian maybe. Polish. Lots of Polish farmers came to that area after the war."

***

By late morning, Roof and Dickie had interviewed three homeless men in the park who said they had never heard of Caps or Harold. Roof and Dickie wandered up the ravine to the shacks of Silver City. Roof counted ten one-room structures made from two-by-fours, glue board, plywood, and whatever else you might scavenge from construction sites. But each was sitting on a wooden platform that, Roof's eye told him, was level and square. He guessed that each would have about eight feet of headroom at the ridge of each asphalt-shingled roof. Some had flower boxes under their windows. A few had Christmas wreaths hanging from their doors. A few had been painted, not matching colours mind you, probably whatever colour they had picked out of the garbage.

The man who answered Roof's knock on the first door had no teeth but had a full head of grey hair. "Never heard of anyone called Caps or Harold."

The shack was so thick with cigarette smoke that Roof could barely see the other man stretched out sleeping on a living room chair next to a kitchen table. "What about him?"

"He's never heard of anyone called Caps or Harold."

They knocked on the doors of the other ten shacks, but only the fourth was answered. By the look in his eyes, his head was spinning too fast for his ears to keep up with any questions. Roof said, "This isn't much different from working community housing."

Dickie said, "These shacks are well built. Someone down here has some skills."

Roof and Dickie wandered along Bridge Street looking for a lunch place. Dickie pointed to a light-up sign with the "B" missing from Albion Bar and Grill. Dickie walked right in, but Roof had to wait at the door until his vision adjusted to the dim light of a narrow, brick-walled room with five empty booths along one wall. Roof's eye doctor had told him his night vision was deteriorating. No more night shifts. Which was why he was looking for homeless drunks in the daytime. But, he thought, better than desk duty.

They sat at the bar. The bartender reminded Roof of a Siberian foot soldier, mean-looking and broad shoulders with a wide chest for pinning medals on.

From the chalkboard menu hanging on the back wall Roof ordered a beer and a hamburger. He had lived on hamburgers and beer for years until his doctor told him his constant hiccups were from indigestion caused by, yes, a diet of hamburgers and beer.

"So how do I get rid of the hiccups?" he had asked.

The doctor stared at his computer screen the way he did when he was reading what he should write a prescription for. He said, "Drink a glass of water upside down."

Dickie ordered a glass of milk and a ham sandwich.

Roof showed his badge to the Russian. "We're looking for a man called Harold Saltzmanous."

Roof liked to watch the eyes when he showed a picture to someone. If they barely glanced at it, that meant they did not know the person. If they looked longer than a few seconds, they probably did.

The bartender barely glanced at it. "The homeless don't come in here, they drink homebrew."

"They make it themselves?"

"The Natives make it on the reserve and bring it down here with the cigarettes. I think it comes from Cape Croker but I don't know for sure."

Roof showed a second picture. "Her name is Rosey Paterno. We're looking for her husband, Howard Paterno, who might be using the name 'Caps.'"

The Russian shook his head.

"How about this woman?" Roof showed him Lee Ann Saltzmanous with the Mennonite farmer.

His look lingered. "Not too bad. Why are you looking for her?"

"A suspected homicide."

"From how many years ago?"

"About fifteen."

"The other day I was walking along and what looked like a pile of rags on the sidewalk stands up and it's Juicy with her cart full of bottles. She sort of looks like someone I knew from high school. But I guess what they looked like then would have no resemblance to what they look like now. The one to ask is Father Sutcliffe at The Daystar."

***

After their lunch, they walked the two blocks to The Daystar, a well-kept Victorian wedged among similar turn-of-the-century houses that were not well kept.

"This would be a good time to buy," said Dickie. "When they clean this area up, these houses will be worth a fortune."

"You can't clean up the area unless you move the people who made it this way. You can build them new houses and in ten years they'll have turned the new houses into slums. The poor are poor because they want to be poor."

"No one wants to be poor. They just don't have what it takes to be not-poor."

Roof said, "The proof is right here. The people living here are poor. The person running this place, the priest, is not. Look at his property. The porch is so freshly painted I can smell it, and the Welcome sign on the front door is brand new."

Roof knocked on the door.

They introduced themselves to the priest, who was dressed in jeans and a T-shirt that said "Staff" on the front. He led them past a long wooden dining room table with eight matching chairs into the kitchen that was clean and tidy. There were no pictures on the walls and no knick-knacks on any shelf. The stove and refrigerator were old, and the small wooden table with four matching wooden chairs looked like it was from the Salvation Army.

"Do I know a homeless man called Caps?" repeated the priest. "That is confidential."

"How can that be confidential?" asked Roof.

"Anything they tell me is confidential."

"In confession."

Father Sutcliffe held his palms up in a priest-like gesture. "A Holy Ordinance takes precedence over any city ordinance. This is my church, the street is my confessional, the park bench is my altar."

Roof said, "And that's why God made park benches?"

"It's called priest-penitent privilege. I'm not sure of the wording, but it falls under the heading of Wigmore Criteria."

Roof was thinking that it fell under the heading of "baloney." He said, "The city will soon be moving these men into public housing. Whoever Caps is, he will soon be identified through social assistance."

"I doubt it. The men carry no identification. They are anonymous and they wish to remain anonymous. The city wants them to apply for public housing but doesn't seem to understand that if the application requires a name, a SIN, and date of birth, the homeless won't apply."

The priest opened the cupboard above the kitchen sink. He pulled out a coffee tin. From another shelf, he brought a filter and put it into the coffee maker. "This is Columbian. I get it from The Coffee Corner, which is across the bridge. They donate ten percent of their earnings to—"

Roof said, "Don't bother trying to change the subject. Before DNA testing, a person could change his name and reappear as someone different. Now a hair left behind from twenty years ago can connect any one of these men to whatever it is they're running from."

Roof showed the priest the picture of Lee Ann Saltzmanous. He said, "Husband's name is Harold."

The priest did not look at the picture. He measured out the water from a gallon jug. "I don't use tap water. It makes a big difference to the taste." The priest measured out three cups and pressed the button to start the brew.

Dickie said, "Smells delicious."

Roof pulled out a chair and sat at the table. "There's nothing like a good cup of coffee to drink while we sit at the table and listen to the information you are obliged to give us. For example, the moonshine they drink. Where does that come from?"

"Not my business. I am in charge of their spirit but not of their spirits."

"I like that," said Dickie. "Spirit and spirits. Is that from the good book?"

"Everything I am is from the good book."

Roof persisted. "I was raised a Catholic, Father. It seemed like every step you take into scripture is into quicksand. No solid footing, a book not of truth but of quicksand. The more scriptures we quote the deeper we sink. A few straight answers might prevent you from sinking, Father."

"I know about sinking. I was in the navy. My job is to save those who are sinking. If I sink with them, so be it."

Roof tried again. "The RCMP has published its own good book, Father. It's called *The Missing Link*. It's available in libraries and book stores and on Amazon. You might want to get yourself a copy. Look closely at the faces of the missing men in the pictures. Read the section on obstruction of justice. Then read about the reward money for information leading to the arrest of the missing links. Missing links never stay missing."

The priest smiled. "Then you don't need my help."

Roof answered, "The reason we are here, Father, is for your help. We are looking for Howard Paterno and Harold Saltzmanous. They have one thing in common: each is suspected of killing his wife."

The priest poured the coffee.

Dickie stirred in the milk and sugar. "While you are listening to their confessions, Father, did you feel that the wives deserved what they got?"

"I do not decide guilt or punishment."

"But Father, it seems to me you're deciding now."

The priest looked thoughtful. "The fact that we each have a conscience capable of giving us both guilt and punishment is proof that God exists and that it is He who is passing judgment. The highest court of justice is the court of conscience."

Roof said, "Not everyone has a conscience."

"I think you're talking about CEOs and politicians, not about the homeless."

Leaving the coffee unfinished, they shook hands. Roof and Dickie returned to the unmarked car. They crossed the bridge, Roof driving, Dickie examining the pictures. "This one of Lee Ann and the farmer: in the background of the bottom-left corner there's a red pickup. It looks like yours."

Roof glanced over. "That's an old Dodge Ram."

"We'll need a blow-up to know for sure, but I think it says the words 'Saltzmanous Construction' on the door panel. Those shacks were built by someone with construction skills. Find out who built them, and you find Harold Saltzmanous."

Roof pulled over to the curb to look.

Dickie said, "It says here in the print-out that Harold Saltzmanous drove a Dodge Ram."

"That's a Dodge Ram alright. But those wheels are custom, not stock. They're special order. Remember the ads? Driving a Ram makes you feel like a man."

"I was never into trucks."

"Well, you are now."

Chapter Eight

Jake

Jake parked the Humane Society truck in an open spot in front of Soapy Suds. He was showing his new partner, Colin, a big kid with a soft body and a British accent, the Silver Park area. Colin was about the same age as Jake was when he had started.

"Those are four of the Silver Park homeless." Jake gestured to the men sharing a bottle in the shade of Silver Park's one big maple tree. "They drink homebrew that comes from the Cape Croker First Nation reserve. The Native woman who sells it says she makes it herself, but she doesn't. They have outlets all over the city, franchise operations, the same as they have franchise operations for Native cigarettes."

Jake pointed to beyond the high bridge spanning Silver Ravine. "Further up are the tin and plywood shacks of the men who won't stay in the hostels. Silver City, they call it."

"Why is everything called Silver?"

"Tim Silver was a rich businessman from The Rose. He ended up a drunk down here in The Thorn. But he got himself together and made it back across the bridge and got rich again. When he died, he left all his money to support the two local homeless shelters, the Outreach on Sheldon and The Daystar one block over. The men living in Silver City use The Daystar address so they can get their homeless cheque under the Reaching Home Program."

Jake continued, "But not for much longer. The city hired social planners to do a study on Silver Park, now known as the Homeless

Hub of Canada. The homeless are now called the Fringe Dwellers. The study has recommended moving them into public housing on the Eastside. But there is a lot of opposition to the public housing from advocates for the homeless. Their spokesman is Father Ronald Sutcliffe, the street priest from The Daystar. He has discovered some old city ordinance that allows any church to offer sanctuary to anyone who wants it. His idea of "sanctuary housing" is to turn the Silver Ravine over to the homeless.

"Why don't they pass a law banning homelessness?"

"City officials are trying to. They want to pass an ordinance banning 'sanctuary housing.' Father Sutcliffe claims the church has the right to preach and pray and administer to the needy according to what the needy need, not according to what city hall thinks they need. Father Sutcliffe cites the human rights code that specifies no government can force anyone to live in a building they don't want to live in, which is what the city is trying to do. So on and on they go with nothing much ever accomplished."

Colin said, "So what dog are we here to catch?"

Jake pointed. "See that black and white sheepdog with the homeless man with the white cane? That dog arrived here about fifteen years ago."

"That's the dog we're going to catch?"

"The man he's with is called Caps. He lives in a shack in Silver City. The big guy there with the long hair and beard who looks like a mountain man is Salty, the man from the mountain. He sits on the bench and carves fish out of scrap lumber he picks up at Home Depot. He's got a locket on a gold chain that he carries in his pocket. He takes it out sometimes to look at it. There's a story in that locket, I bet."

Jake pointed. "That little man over there with a too-big baseball hat sleeping on the far bench? You can't see it from here but the hat says 'City Works.' He's on permanent disability from the city's Public Works department because of a bad back he got from leaning on a shovel all day. That's how he describes it, anyway."

Jake pointed again. "Over there, the one going through the garbage, is Beets, from Newfoundland. And over there, the tall guy who looks like Willie Nelson, is Mr. Bones. The younger one with the ponytail is Donkey Man. He's got snakes tattooed on his arms. He likes to bully the homeless, and the homeless are easy targets."

"So let's get the dog."

Jake continued. "Father Sutcliffe doesn't look like a priest and he doesn't have a real church. The Daily Star did an article about him in the paper, about the homeless priest and how The Daystar is his church and all these men are his flock. The Globe did one too, with a picture of him in front of the local library. They called him 'the librarian of discards' because his favourite line is something like 'each of these men is a story in a discarded book.'"

Now, having set up the situation, Jake asked the question: "What do think, Colin? What we have here is not one stray but six. What are your feelings towards these six strays, each of them a story in a discarded book?"

Colin said, "Caps, Salty, Pavements, Beets, Mr. Bones: are they all chums?"

"Chums? I don't think the word 'chums' suits them. But yeah, in a way, you might say that."

"Why the nicknames?"

"I don't know. I've heard them talk about going to The Black Widow to get their fingerprints changed, which means they're running away from the law. But the nicknames are a subculture thing too. Even among themselves, there's a class distinction. The ones who live in shacks are the Fringe Dwellers, but the ones who sleep in the rough are the Outreachers, the beggars on the corner with their hand out."

"But now there's DNA testing."

Jake nodded. "The RCMP has published a book called *The Missing Link*. They're offering a five thousand dollar reward to anyone with useful information that might link the homeless back to any of their unsolved cold cases. The officer assigned to this area is Detective Roof."

Jake smiled. "'Roof' is a good name for someone investigating the homeless."

Colin asked, "What about the sheepdog? Are we going to catch him? Isn't that why we're here?"

Jake became thoughtful. "We used to put down the unadopted strays in the death chamber. It would hold five medium-sized dogs. The only time I did the put-down was about fifteen years ago. We had four mongrel crosses that we'd been holding for about a month. We'd just picked up that sheepdog. We were over-crowded. My boss said to put in the sheepdog. I shoved the four mongrels into the chamber. I paused at the fifth, the sheepdog. He'd been hanging around the park for about three days, friendly as could be, visiting with everyone, not a mean bone in his body. He had this habit when you came up to him, he'd sit down and hold out his paw for a handshake."

Colin had his hand on the door handle. He seemed anxious to go.

"So, there I was and there he was, waiting for me to put him into the gas chamber. I looked at the dog. It seemed to know what was about to happen, but it just sat sort of staring into my eyes. I knelt beside the dog to scratch its ears. 'I'm sorry,' I said. 'I just started this job. I got to do it.'"

"The dog lifted his paw, sort of a final handshake. As gentle as I could, I edged the dog into the chamber and I shut the door. I went to the panel on the wall. There's a black button that you press to start the gas."

Jake hesitated. "At this point, Colin, what would you want to do? I did not say have to do. I said want to do."

"I would do my job. I would press the button. What did you do?"

"I pressed the button. I stood there with tears in my eyes crying like a baby as the carbon monoxide seeped into the chamber. I went into the office to watch the clock tick away the five minutes. But at three, I couldn't sit any longer. I went back to the panel and turned off the gas. The dogs were all lying down dead. The sheepdog lay closest to the door where I had left him. When I reached in to lift him out, his head stirred. He sat up and licked my hand, like to say thank you. There must have been just enough oxygen leaking in around the door seal to keep him alive."

Jake turned to look straight at Colin. He asked the question. "What would you do next?"

Colin shrugged, "Put him back in for another five minutes."

Jake said, "Hmm. Like a cold cup of coffee into a microwave."

"That's my job."

"Yes, that's your job. If you were a policeman, what would you do to these five homeless men?"

Colin shrugged again. "Arrest them for vagrancy. That's my job."

Jake said, "Those are not the right answers, Colin."

Colin looked surprised. "So what did you do, with the dog, I mean?"

"I picked him up and carried him outside into the fresh air and I sat down and hugged him and cried my eyes out." Jake wiped at his eye. "We're not allowed to adopt dogs as long as we work for the shelter. I would have quit my job just so I could adopt that dog. But my wife and both my kids are allergic. Finally, I found an old guy all by himself in his apartment who wanted company. Every day I thought about that dog, wondering how he was making out. Sheepdogs are working dogs. They love to work, not lay around in someone's apartment. Sure enough, within a week, there he was back again."

"I got out of my truck and called to the dog. He came right up to me, wagging his tail, glad to see me. I knelt down and we shook hands. I wrapped my arms around him and hugged him like he was one of my own kids. I looked into his eyes. I whispered into his ear."

Jake wiped his hand across the other wet eye. "This is a rough area to work. The streets running off Sheldon and Bridge, well, this whole area, is all run-down absentee landlord houses. Parents get pets when they can't even look after their kids. Neglect, abuse, it breaks my heart. But not near as much as almost gassing that dog."

Colin said, "But we can't allow the dog to run free."

"We have a saying: 'While the social workers weep for the poor and bleed for the children, the Humane Society catches their dogs and put them to sleep.' It breaks my heart."

Colin opened the door, anxious to get on with it.

"Aren't you going to ask me the dog's name?"

"What for?"

"I call him Whisper. That's what Caps calls him. That's what the homeless call him."

Colin scowled. "Whisper? That's a peculiar name for a dog."

"This is a peculiar dog. When you look into this dog's eyes, they speak to you, but not in words you can hear, more like in whispers. Happens all the time between people, you know, you look into someone's eyes and they speak volumes. But not in words."

Colin shrugged, "I guess."

"A few days later, Caps appeared in Silver Park. He was stumbling around, half-blind from diabetes. Right away Whisper started to look after Caps, like a trained seeing-eye dog, guiding him across the street, over to The Daystar for lunch, whatever. That was fifteen years ago. He's been looking after Caps ever since."

Jake continued. "I've had job offers to transfers to easier areas where people look after their pets, like across the bridge in The Rose. But I say no. I've got to stay here and make sure no Humane Society employee puts Whisper into the gas chamber."

Chapter Nine

Pavements

The "Tuesday Evening Films" poster Pavements stuck on the door of the All Saints Church's basement had a picture of a monkey asking, "Where do we come from?" At the bottom, it said, "The Truth About the Missing Link." Pavements had helped the church lady, Gloria, set up the folding chairs and the coffee table. On the front step of the church, he had set up the fold-out wooden sign Salty had made. It said "Free Movies Every Tuesday. Everyone Welcome."

Only the homeless came, not for the movie but for the free coffee and donuts that got laid out halfway through, help yourself from the table by the exit door. Last movie night, Caps had put down about six donuts and had gone into a coma, and Father Sutcliffe had to give him a shot.

Beets had been drinking Kawasaki all afternoon so his boiled beets nose had red warts on it. He was looking around as he helped himself to the coffee. "Where's the fucking donuts?"

Gloria said, "I'm sorry. No more donuts. But there's sandwiches."

"Why not?"

Pavements said, "Are you fucking stupid? Last week Caps went into a coma."

Beets looked over at Caps, who was sitting with his sheepdog in the front row, two feet from the screen.

A fat church lady came over. She said, "I'm a new volunteer. My name is Cynthia."

"I'm Pavements."

Pavements offered her a cough drop from the package he had picked up off the floor a few minutes before.

She smiled, "No thank you."

Father Sutcliffe came over. "Glad to have you onboard, Cynthia. I'm Father Sutcliffe from The Daystar. This is Pavements. Over there is Mr. Bones and Beets and Salty. The rest are from the Outreach."

She said, "I've not heard of the Outreach."

Pavements said, "The real name is The Harbour Light. They call it the Outreach because everyone there is an Outreacher, you know, reach out your hand for spare change."

Cynthia was looking around, her nose wiggling like a rabbit's. The church basement always had a musty smell leftover from the morning daycare, so you couldn't smell the Outreachers as long as you didn't stand too close to one. The other church ladies were used to it. They always smiled and acted glad to see everyone no matter how bad they smelled. "How are we today, Beets. How are we today Caps," as though the ladies were the ones seeing double.

Pavements noticed that from a side view, Cynthia, wearing a nice dress, her hair shellacked into spins and waves, looked like the picture of the Queen on the twenty-dollar bill. Cynthia looked like she got picked up out of her palace and set down in this room full of cavemen, which was what the movie was about. Cavemen didn't grow from monkeys into people; God created people with no connection to monkeys.

Cynthia said, "How come they call you Pavements?"

Pavements's City Works baseball hat rode on his ears because his bald head without any hair on it was too small to fill the space. He knew PeeWee would have been a better name. Or Toonies because of his side-hustle. He'd buy a carton of Native cigarettes brought down from the Cape Croker Reserve and sell them loose one at a time to the high school kids coming across the bridge to the library. A toonie for a loosie. That's how he'd say it. But he liked telling his pavement story every time someone asked him.

Pavements showed her his hat. "I worked for the city, thirty years fixing pavement. Every day I fixed pavement. It got so I could taste it. That's why my teeth are turning black and crumbling in my jaw, from fixing pavement."

"Oh, my," said Cynthia.

"My wife, Celia, couldn't stand the smell of pavement."

"Oh my goodness."

"One day, I hear a knock on the door. I'd just finished off a bottle of White Truck Red and was feeling friendly so I let the two Jehovah's Witnesses in. They travel in pairs, like ducks. The man was wearing a suit. He said his name was Philip. The woman was wearing a blue skirt and blouse."

Cynthia said, "If you're a Witness you have to do the door to door."

"They told Celia about when the world was going to end and gave her a magazine. Next day, when I came home from work, I found Celia laying on the bed studying *The Watchtower*. She was reading about the same stuff as this movie's about, Eve being the mother of everyone."

"Yes, they believe in creationism, the same as me."

"Next day, when I came home from work, she says, 'You're getting kind of red-faced from drinking White Truck Red. From now on, no White Truck Red with dinner. I poured it down the drain.'"

Cynthia nodded. "Well, it's not good for you to drink too much."

Pavements stopped talking while he rolled his cough drop around to his back teeth before crushing it to nothing as he took out another one from the package that looked like it had been stepped on a few times.

He offered her one. She said, "No thank you."

"Next day, when I came home from work, she says, 'I want you to come with me to our next meeting at the Kingdom Hall because you're an atheist and won't be saved when the world ends.'"

"Yes, that is what they believe."

"I wouldn't go. So next day she says that she can't stay married to someone who smells like pavement and she wants a divorce."

"She came right out and said she wanted a divorce because you smelled like pavement?"

"She'd been leading up to it. Like how it got started, I'd come home from work and say, 'What's for dinner?' She'd say, 'Pavement'"

"Why would she say that?"

"She'd say, 'Because that's what you smell like. When I sit down with you to eat my dinner that's what it tastes like. Pavement.'"

"That's an awful thing to say. It was from your job."

"Every night I'd ask her what was on television? 'Pavement,' she'd say. 'When I sit down with you to watch television, the smell of melting pavement is in my head. In bed, I can feel my brain melting an asphalt trickle into my throat and into my mouth and into my pillow.'"

Pavements put another cough drop into his mouth.

"A tragic story. And now you're homeless."

"And it's not my fault."

"No, it isn't. So what happened next?"

"I had a bottle of Crown Royal hid in the furnace pipes in the basement, so I went down to the basement to listen to my Van Halen CD. The whole band looks like monkeys wired for rock and roll. They should have put them in this movie."

Cynthia said, "My goodness. Isn't that interesting. The same man who made this movie made one about primates having the capacity for music. His name is Dr. Edgewall. I heard him interviewed on CBC. He said most research discoveries happened by accident, an 'oh boy' epiphany moment when a light in the brain turns brighter."

"How did it do that?"

"This is how it happened. He said formerly it was believed that only man was wired for music. He went on to tell the story of how one day he took his twelve-year-old granddaughter to the zoo. She had forgotten her headphones and was playing her music a little too loud and swinging in time with the tunes, you know teenagers. They were at the monkey cage. Dr. Edgewall noted that the monkeys started dancing and moving with the music, the same as his granddaughter. When she switched to Elton John's Favourite Hits they swayed gently back and forth, like this."

Cynthia weighed a good two hundred pounds, and her fat, jiggling in time with her dancing, made Pavements step back like he was seeing an eighteen-wheeler coming down the road at him.

"Next day, Dr. Edgewall videotaped the monkeys dancing to some heavy metal, Kiss I think. When he compared the behaviours and gestures of Kiss dancing to the monkey's dancing, he saw that they were identical."

"Strike me dead," said Pavements. He had sucked his second cough drop into nothing and was now rolling around and sucking into his third, or maybe it was his fourth.

"So now his research took a new direction. Now he stood, CD player and video camera in hand, studying the dance steps of each of the primates: chimpanzee, gorilla, orangutan, baboon."

"Strike me dead," said Pavements, imagining Cynthia dancing with the orangutans.

"Dr. Edgewall was trying to determine which of the primate dancers most closely resembled rock band behaviours. After each of his trips to the zoo, as he sat at his desk with his video recorder piped into his laptop paying close attention to the audio track, he discovered that for every different song, the primates made different primal grunts in distinctly different keys. They were singing in their own primate language, not much different from the language of the rock bands."

"Did they form a band and do gigs?"

Cynthia's smile showed a row of straight white teeth.

Father Sutcliffe, who had been standing there not saying anything, interrupted, "Do Dr. Edgewall's theories support evolution, Cynthia?"

"It turned out it was all a hoax made by some group called MAG, short for Moms Against God. So no, creation not evolution. Eve is still the mother of us all."

Pavements said, "You mean Eve is the mother of Beets?" He pointed to him drooling into his coffee. "He looks like a missing link. And look at those Outreachers. Gulping down their sandwiches like baboons at the zoo. They're the missing link."

Cynthia pointed to the poster. "See? The monkeys have no thumb. We have a thumb. That is the big difference."

Pavements stared at his thumb as though this was the first time he'd seen it.

He said, "The Outreachers have a thumb. So what they're saying is, first there was monkeys and apes and then evolution grew them a thumb and then moved their tonsils around so they could sing. In the movie, it said the jaw bone got smaller and the brain got bigger so they could figure stuff out better, good enough to form a group, add to that you got a thumb to play a musical instrument. Ask Salty. He plays a guitar. You got to have a thumb to play a guitar. But see, the Outreachers aren't smart enough to figure anything out and they sure as fuck can't sing, but they got thumbs. So, they're the missing link."

Cynthia said, "I'm sure they aren't the missing link."

"Oh no? You oughta see them at lunchtime at The Daystar. They belch and grunt and smack their lips and pick their noses. None of them have more than six teeth and their brains aren't big enough to learn how to fetch a stick. But they got a thumb and they sure as fuck know how to use it to open a bottle of Curveball. They're the missing link, no doubt about it, sitting right over there, monkeys with thumbs."

Cynthia was shaking her head. "No. It's not that simple. That is the point of the movie. You could clean up a Neanderthal and give him a shave and dress him in nice clothes, but he could not walk down any city street unnoticed. It would be obvious. We are a different species. What the movie is saying is each new wave of primate species was the cousin of the preceding species. Homo erectus DNA was passed on to the Neanderthal. But that doesn't mean Neanderthal DNA was passed on to people. People, us, we are a separate species created by God as custodians of his creation, including the homeless."

Pavements said, "What's a Neanderthal?"

"According to the movie, cousins of nomadic Homo erectus hunters and gatherers who were their forebearers."

Pavements said, "That's what I'm saying. The Outreachers are hunters and gatherers. They go hunting for garbage cans and gather what they find inside."

"But they aren't cousins of Neanderthals. They are a different species created by God."

"Well then, he should have made them so we could tell that they're people. Or he shouldn't have gave them thumbs. He should have made them so they walked bent over bare-knuckled so we would be able to recognize them as not-people. One or the other."

Cynthia said, "I'm sure they're doing their best."

Pavements was staring at his thumb, wiggling it back and forth in swings and side shuffles. "I'm going to tell my wife, Celia, the reason God gave me this thumb was to open bottles of homebrew."

Cynthia looked interested. "Homebrew? What about homebrew?"

Pavements was turning his thumb in circles, first one direction, then the other.

Cynthia said, "It looks like you're giving that thumb a cardio workout."

"Sometimes the Outreachers mix Curveball with shaving lotion. Or brake fluid, or furniture polish, or varnish, or rubbing alcohol, or Windex, or windshield washer fluid. You know, whatever they find in the grey bins. Those bottles all got lids you have to squeeze and turn at the same time. So you need a good thumb for that. One for each hand."

"They'll poison themselves!"

"No, they won't. That's what I mean. Their hands are like people's, but not their stomachs. An Outreacher can eat anything. I saw one once. He had found a Tupperware container like my wife Celia used to sell at parties. First, he ate the food, then he ate the Tupperware container."

The other church lady, Gloria, was dimming the lights to get on with the movie.

***

The morning after the movie, Pavements bought a bottle of Curveball with the money he'd earned from his "toonie for a loosie" side-hustle. He was in the library washroom drinking it when Beets, his red nose boiled up to the size of a baseball, wandered in. Pavements and Beets finished the bottle and then went to sit in the soft chairs and read magazines. The people sitting there got up and moved away and stepped to one side, the way you would if you came along a dead cat on the roadside.

Pavements thought, the ones reading the magazines must be thinking there's no roadside here, so where is that smell coming from? Is it this or is it that? Well, fuck me, it's Beets. The library should either stop him at the door or adjust the ventilating system to trigger the minute he walks in. Or set the overhead fire sprinklers to give him a bath coming through the door like at the carwash. But if they did that Beets would phone the newspaper. The newspaper would fix his picture so his nose didn't look like a beet with warts growing on it and write it up about the homeless being banned from a public place.

Pavements went over and asked the lady at the desk and then went straight to where she had pointed to the section called, "Anthropology." A black lady pushing a cart full of books had come over to Beets, who was one shelf along. She must have said something about his smell. He said, "Mind your own fucking business. You smell like a whore with the monthlies."

She was in such a hurry to file away the book she was carrying that she put it upside down on the shelf where Pavements was looking through the titles.

Pavements said, "You filed it upside down."

She didn't come back to fix it.

"She's not long out of the jungle herself," muttered Pavements. He pulled out the book and turned it right-side up. But he didn't put it back on the shelf. He started to leaf through it. He said to Beets, "This book is called *The Missing Link*. But it's not like in the movie. It's like police stuff. It's cold case missing links."

Pavements sat in the chair under the window and began to flip through the pages.

Chapter Ten

Pavements

Pavements was looking through *The Missing Link*'s introduction.

Strike me dead. It was about cold cases from a long time ago that the cops couldn't solve. But with DNA testing, it said, dried spit on a toothbrush from 1950 would be a case maker. The reason the cops had put out the book was to get the general public involved. That's how they said it. The general public, like himself, Pavements. Like if he found sweat on the collar of a shirt stored away for years in one of those zip-up things, he should turn it over at the nearest cop shop and he would get a five-thousand-dollar reward.

Like that time to get enough money to buy a bottle of Kawasaki, Pavements had turned over to the Village Seconds Ladies Wear the bag Celia kept her wedding dress in. Celia was pissed off about that. She said she didn't care about the bag but he should have took the dress out first. She was saving it for if ever they got back together.

On page five it explained that a reward of five thousand dollars goes to anyone from the general public for information leading to the arrest of the people listed below. Then it gave the information and pictures of the missing, feared dead, people, mostly women, one picture of an aboriginal girl, another one of a fifteen-year-old kid from down east.

Strike me dead. Look at the body on this one: Lee Ann Saltzmanous disappeared from a rented farmhouse in June of 2004. Foul play was suspected because of blood on the kitchen floor and the wall. No body and no murder weapon had been found. Missing link:

husband Harold Saltzmanous, who also disappeared in June of 2004. The couple had left behind a five-year-old daughter who was taken into foster care.

There were other pictures: Lee Ann Saltzmanous standing at the door of a trailer, smiling into the camera, her spaghetti top strike-me-dead bulging out like twin moons rising from a red sunset. Fuuuck. Pavements calculated how she would go from the ground, up two steps and into the trailer. First, those twin moons would go through the door. Then, her head would go through the door. Then her butt, not too bad, would go through the door.

Another picture of the clapboard farmhouse. Then two more; one was a close-up of the blood on the kitchen wall and the other of the blood on the kitchen floor. Then Pavements noticed a carving of a fish on a shelf above the table. He carried the book to the front window for better light. Pavements had asked Salty one time, "Why do you carve fish?" Salty had said, "They're like me, always swimming against the current."

Pavements went back to his chair. With a name like Saltzmanous, what would your nickname be? Smith becomes Smitty, Saltzmanous becomes Salty. Then Pavements noticed the locket around Lee Ann's neck, tucked in there between — oh boy, she'd have to bend over to see her feet. How could she keep her balance carrying around those two Dolly Parton beauties?

Salty sometimes took a locket like that out of his pocket and snapped it open to look at the picture inside.

Five thousand dollars. Pavements copied down the 1-800 number.

Pavements continued to leaf through the book until he noticed a photograph of a thin little man wearing overalls and a plaid shirt. The fat woman beside him was wearing lipstick thick as red mud, and a white and pink outfit that looked like stupid. Under the picture, it said, "What happened to Rosey?"

Pavements thought, Well, Rosey. You can only put so much rosy lipstick on a pig. So, get rid of all the makeup.

Then Pavements read the sign in the background: ANNUAL SQUARE DANCE COMPETITION. And just a minute: Further down was a reprint from a police file:

Sudbury, Ontario: Missing Person
Address: 406 Bluewater Street Date of Birth: July 10, 1960
Hair blonde, eyes blue, height 5'10". Missing since Aug 10, 2000.
Remarks: Last seen at 10 a.m. leaving the Bluewater Cafe, where
she worked as a waitress.
Missing Link: husband Howard Paterno.

Then Pavements remembered: in his shack, Caps had a bronze statue he'd won, him and his wife, square dancing. Sometimes sitting on his bench he'd try to blink into focus pictures of him and his wife square dancing.

Pavements worked through the pages, but no other photo or name jumped out at him. He returned the book upside down on the wrong shelf for later reference. He settled himself into one of the comfortable soft chairs by the magazine rack to think about that reward money. From the library telephone, he dialed the 1-800 number. A man's voice said, "Press 1 for Alberta, press 2 for Manitoba, press 3 for Ontario." A second voice shouted a rough "Detective Roof. Leave a message."

Pavements hunched his shoulders around the phone and in a hoarse whisper said, "I've been studying your Missing Link book. I have a lead for you. He lives in Silver City and goes by the name of Caps. In order to protect my identity so I can continue to work undercover on the missing link cases in Silver Park, I can't reveal my real name and will keep it to myself. I dress like the homeless, no one can get the drop on me, but for identification purposes, I can be found in Silver Park wearing a City Works hat. Deliver to me the five thousand dollars in a plain brown envelope."

***

Mr. Bones worked different patches of different cement on different days. Today was Monday. Pavements walked the two blocks from The Daystar to Bridge Street and found Mr. Bones on the corner, playing his banjo and dancing his soft-shoe "Mr. Bojangles." Usually, Caps was with him dancing squares and collecting the money, but not today. Pavements sat on the curb to wait for Mr. Bones to finish his song.

When Mr. Bones was done, Pavements said, "What's Salty's real name?"

Mr. Bones often had trouble recognizing people, not because he was going blind like Caps, but because he had eyebrows so long they hung down into his eyelashes, rearranging themselves and everything he was looking at with every blink. It took a lot of blinks before he could figure out who you were.

Mr. Bones said, "I've been looking for Caps. I wrote a song: 'Following Roads That Go Nowhere.' It's only got three chords, good for Caps to dance his squares to. We were going to practice today. We're going to work in a routine of matching steppers like they did in the fifties."

"What's Salty's real name?"

"We make a good duo. Caps with his sunglasses blind as a bat with his head wandering around like Jeff Healy and me tall and thin looking like Willie Nelson."

Mr. Bones sat on the sidewalk, his banjo across his knees, while he counted his money.

Pavements said, "What's Salty's real name?"

"Don't know."

Mr. Bones got up to play another set. Pavements crossed the street to his park bench. His wife Celia appeared, her shoulder bag in one hand, a Walmart bag in the other. She was putting on weight, it looked like, getting almost square-looking. She sat beside him. But not too close. Celia said. "I went to the library to see if you were there. They gave me a note from the head librarian."

She brought out what looked like an official letter. "It says here you give off 'odoriferous fumes' that are very off-putting."

"Off-putting?"

"I'll not have you smelling like a bum as well as looking like a bum." She handed him a bag with a Speed Stick deodorant.

"It's Beets who's off-putting, not me."

"The letter says it's you."

"Show me where it says that."

She showed him.

"That's not me. That's Beets. He smells because he has to wear bladder pants like diapers. He gets a special government allowance for that but he can't afford to buy them."

"That's because he spends his money on bootleg liquor."

"Beets quit drinking. He put the plug in the jug."

"It says here you and Beets were drinking homebrew in the washroom."

"It was Beets's homebrew, not mine."

"You just said he quit drinking. If he's got money to buy homebrew he's got money to go to the drug store and buy his bladder pants. And it says you were the one with the homebrew."

"Show me where it says that."

She showed him.

Pavements read what it said. He stretched his arms out across the backrest. "Well, I don't care. I'm coming into some money soon. Then things will be different."

This statement surprised Pavements. It came out in words but the thinking part hadn't come first. He just said it: I'm coming into some money soon, like a voice out of nowhere, like when Beets would be walking around, shaking his fist and shouting, and then he'd look around to see who was shouting.

Celia gave one of her sighs. She left, her stalky legs bunching her skirt up around her broad butt because she was walking lopsided from carrying the weight of the Watchtowers in her shoulder bag.

**

When the head librarian came over, Pavements said to her, "I wasn't drinking homebrew in the washroom. And it's Beets that smells like a loaded diaper, not me."

"That's nice, Pavements, good for you, but have you noticed when you sit down here everyone leaves? Clean yourself up and have a shower and come back. If you look half-decent, you can stay."

"My wife brought me this Speed Stick."

"I know. I was talking to your wife. I told her you're taking an interest in reading. Why don't you ask her to bring you more clean clothes that you can put on after you've taken a shower and used your Speedstick. And there's a free dental clinic down near the bridge if you want to get your teeth fixed. Something to ponder."

"Ponder?"

"It means to think about."

***

Pavements had sold all his side-hustle loosies and was on his way through the park, up the alley, and into the underground parking of the apartment building on Bridge Street to look for change that dropped out of people's pockets when they got out of their cars. Whisper, Caps's dog, was there, sniffing the parked cars, looking like he was checking out the travels that had been taken by the treads of the tires. Strike me dead. The cops have picked up Caps already. Whisper is trying to find the cop car that took Caps away.

Pavements said to the dog, "They won't put a blind man in jail. He'll be back for supper."

When the underground parking bay doors rattled open Whisper left, probably heading across the park and up the ravine to see if Caps had made it home for supper.

In the clothes drop-off box in front of the Sally, Pavements found a pair of pants, almost new. And two kitchen knives. He held the pants up against himself. Fit pretty good. The knives looked new. Things were looking up: a new pair of good pants and two good knives for the new kitchen in the new apartment he would get with the five thousand dollar reward money which was coming hand delivered by a certified detective with enough left over for new teeth to replace the ones that had rotted from fixing pavement.

Chapter Eleven

Salty

Salty was sitting on his Silver Park bench in the shade of the bridge drinking his bottle of Majestic Diner. He was wondering if Madame Kratz would come over and read for him the messages coming from the criss-cross of those iron bridge beams linking in groups of three, one side to the other with that beam in the middle pointing like a sundial straight up into the sky.

The city had installed a hotline telephone on this beam so that, instead of jumping, you dialed a 1-800 number. When Pavements had tried it, not the jump but the number, he got put on hold for twenty minutes before he got tired of waiting. The next time he tried it, he got Richard in Malaysia who couldn't speak English.

On the same bench two bottles later it was evening, almost dark. Salty seemed to have lost track of what had happened between those two bottles, although he could remember something about Caps, who had wandered onto the bridge, had been being picked up by the police. The back-and-forth car lights on the bridge were making moving pockets in Salty's blurred vision. As he sorted through the shadows, he saw a sliver of white moving along on the bridge, and then he saw it was a cane, and then he saw it was Caps. The police must have let him go.

But where was his dog? Salty hadn't paid much attention to this dog other than to see that it looked like Amos. But all sheepdogs looked the same. Last week, Caps had sat in the grass with his dog while Salty and Mr. Bones fixed Caps's leaky roof with brand new twenty-year-grade black shingles they had stole from a city improvement site. Beets and two Outreachers had come along to help with the shingling and were good workers, until the passing of the Curveball got to them and they fell asleep under a tree halfway through Beets's story about his aunt who had Alzheimer's and wanted to marry her dog that looked something like Caps's dog. That's why Beets liked to tell the story.

Caps could not have found his way to the bridge without his dog. And without his dog, he should not be on the bridge. Or maybe, thought Salty, Caps had on purpose gone up on the bridge because they had picked up his dog, and without his dog, something else was on his mind, like jumping.

Salty thought, I should go up there on the bridge and say, How's it going, Caps? Something like that, and then say, Let's get off the bridge and go back to your shack and finish off this bottle of Curveball.

Something like that.

The thought of "finish off" got Salty wondering whether the cops had taken Caps's dog to the Humane Society to be put down. Salty was thinking, if they'd caught him, they'd do it, so I better go up there and say to Caps, just making conversation, This is a long bridge, Caps, if you're thinking about crossing it, okay. But jumping off it is not okay. So, let's go you and me and find out about your dog. He's around here somewhere. Or let's go back to your bench, it's not that far of a walk, about a hundred yards, shorter than the fifty yards from the top of the bridge to the dirt, if that's what you're thinking. Or, if that's what you're thinking, phone Richard at the 1-800 number. Maybe he can speak English now.

But then Caps left the rail and was walking away from the bridge and down the grade and up the ravine, heading to his Silver City shack. Salty relaxed and took another drink. He settled himself on the bench and thought about all the things that might have happened if Caps had jumped. The police would come. They would stand there looking down at him lying flat on the ground. They would think he lived in a shopping cart. They would think he slept propped up against a brick wall in an alley. They would think he kept himself alive by picking through the garbage can he woke up next to.

Pavements would look down at Caps and say, Well, strike me dead. It's my old buddy Caps. Me and him and Beets, on rainy days, we'd sit warm and dry in his shack drinking Curveball.

Beets would look down at Caps and say, now we can get our donuts back.

***

The next morning, Salty went to the annual Father's Day lunch put together by the kids from St. Luke's Light For the Lost. They had "Teenies for Jesus" written in black letters on the backs of their white T-shirts. They laid out the sandwiches and the soup. They walked around smiling and introducing themselves, serving the homeless like it was The Beggars' Business Banquet. Each beggar left carrying a little Father's Day box filled with mints and chocolates and a jar of orange marmalade.

After the banquet, Salty noticed Caps going through the garbage behind Colonel Wong's Southern Fried Chinese Chicken. Salty looked around. Still no dog. Salty returned to his bench, in one hand a full bottle of Majestic Diner, in the other hand his box of mints and chocolate and orange marmalade. Sylvia had liked spreading orange marmalade on her toast. It looked like sunshine, she would say, licking the sunshine off her fingers.

Salty noticed that the sunshine time on the Silver Park sundial said high noon. When he glanced up at the middle beam of the bridge, he saw that its shadow was not leaning this way or that way, but stood straight up. Salty thought that if he was right now sitting on the river in Dr. Reed's rowboat he would be casting into those shadows under that bridge while Frank would be trying to stay away from that Shad Topwater zinging like a low-flying bee past his ear. Maybe the fish hook in his cheek was punishment for stealing the boat. But Salty had stole the boat, not Frank. Frank sleeping with Lee Ann was Salty's punishment for the fish hooks and the boat-stealing. Salty knew his punishment for abandoning Sylvia was yet to come.

***

The purple beads on Madame Kratz's wrists clattered like teacups as she lit the candles with a long stick match. Her fingernails were the same shade of purple as her shawl, which looked like it was made from the same material as her entrance curtain, its crack tied together by beads matching the ones around her neck swinging back and forth as she bent over and dealt the cards.

She leaned over to study them.

She said, "It's not that the fall takes a long or a short time, Salty. It's that thought travels faster than the speed of the fall, ten times faster than the speed of light or of dark, in all directions at once. It can re-live the span of a life in less than a second. Words travel by thoughts, but thoughts travel by perceptions that instantaneously cross like strong winds through anything in their path. Through eight-inch thick walls into my candlelit reading room they come to open closed lids and pull what's inside out and lay it down in my cards."

"What does that mean?"

The shadows were moving back and forth across her face with the movement of the candle flames. Salty remembered the night before, how for him the shadows had moved back and forth on the bridge, so he knew something important was coming.

She turned over another card. "Something to do with past and present, how they travel around, and stop when they arrive at now."

He waited on the edge of his seat as she rearranged the cards.

"What is this? It looks like a dog. And in this card, I see the girl."

"What does that mean? What girl?"

She continued to examine the cards. "I'm not liking this." She put the cards away. "No more today, Salty. I'm not feeling well."

"But what does that mean?"

"My job is to read the cards to you. Your job is to figure out what I've read."

She got up and disappeared through the purple exit as if she had left the stage and had left Salty alone in his front-row seat with nothing to watch.

***

Salty took a shortcut through the alley to the back door of Dixie's Donut Shoppe. He bought a bottle of Curveball and returned to the park to find Caps sitting out of the sun in the shade on the bench closest to the bridge, sobbing into his bottle.

"What's going on, Caps?"

"Maybe Jake is off sick. Maybe that other dog catcher put my dog in the pound."

Salty figured they had the dog in the pound for sure now. Then he figured maybe not, so he said, "He's around here somewhere. I'll find him for you."

Salty checked all around, up and down. He came back, saying "As soon as he turns up, I'll bring him to you. Go home and lay down. I'll come by with another bottle after a while."

Caps got up and stumbled off. Salty watched him go, one slow step at a time, feeling his way with his cane. Salty felt like he was looking over Madame Kratz's shoulder at her cards with a picture of Caps on each one. This card here, he'd lost his hardware job. This card here, his wife had left him. This card here, he'd lost his house. This card here, him in his shack with all the cards laid out for him to look down at and see how much he'd lost.

Salty opened his bottle and took a long pull.

The next thing he noticed was that Caps had found his way up the bank to the bridge. Salty lost sight of him for a moment behind the screen of girders, then he saw him in the middle of the bridge walking along almost normal, as though he could all of a sudden see where he was going.

Salty knew that Caps had pawned his watch when he went blind, but with that marmalade sun slightly off-centre overhead, Caps would not need eyes that could look over at the Silver Park sundial to see that it said about two o'clock. Usually by this time of day Caps would be resting on his bench, home-brewed-Majestic-Diner drunk. By around three o'clock on the sundial, he would be floating so high up from Majestic Diner that he could look down like from the back of one of those sparrow hawks, listening to its *chip-chip* that would remind him of the *click-click* of his wife's heels on the square-dance floorboards. By four o'clock, he'd be under the bridge, sitting in the grass holding his old photo album cards on his knee and looking at his square dance pictures right-side up, upside down, didn't matter, because he'd finished his second bottle and his fortune-teller card memories of failings and stupidities that had ruined his life would be marmalade sunspots of do-si-do square dancing, him and the wife.

But now Caps was not on the back of any sparrow hawk. He was at the centre post of the bridge, sitting on the guard rail, having a last drink. Salty could see the glint of the sun on the bottle. Salty could see that Caps was leaning over, looking down.

Salty was thinking, I better get up there quick and get him off the bridge and help him back to his shack to sleep it off. I will leave him the rest of my bottle so when his purple curtains open later on he's got a drink to get him back to this day's square dance. He will finish the bottle and then he will get up and go to the corner and pan until he has enough for another Curveball. If Mr. Bones is there with his banjo, they'll work the corner together, Mr. Bones calling the dance and Caps stepping the squares until they have enough for a bottle each. Then Caps will return to his bench and drink half. Then he will climb halfway up the bank and he will stop for a rest and a drink, this time on a different bench. By this time, Caps's bottle will be almost gone and the day almost gone and he'll be leaning back, content for the rest of that evening to sit there and blue-sky a future for himself and his dog.

Caps's bottle had a red cap. He was drinking Kawasaki. Add a bottle of Kawasaki to a long list of too many bad cards and no dog and almost blind eyes and you've got Caps hanging off the iron struts of the bridge he should be floating over.

Salty squinted into the sun. He rubbed his eyes, trying to get Caps into focus. Sure enough, there was Caps, leaning way out, looking down. No one on foot hurrying across the bridge from the commuter station bothered to stop. No one on the bridge would be interested in Caps, unless it was a passing church lady, give him some soup and a boloney sandwich and away he goes to sleep it off in an alley, and if he turns up next day at the church, how are we today Caps, and give him another baloney sandwich.

But no church lady was crossing the bridge. Everyone was rushing through their own thoughts of hurry hurry past Mr. Bones on this corner and Pavements on that corner and Beets on some other corner and across the bridge into their Happy Father's Day Saturday lunch with their children. They didn't know that between Caps's ears was a deck full of failures too heavy to carry without the help of his dog. They didn't know that the cards being turned into memories in Caps's mind today didn't get put back face down into the deck and put away for the day like usual. This day they had turned themselves face up and stayed that way. It was like they'd gathered and organized and formed a union and taken control and under their control Caps without his dog was bankrupt.

Salty squinted into the sky. Through the marmalade glints of sunlight Salty thought he could see Madame Kratz, seated on the rail next to Caps. She had pulled out the deck full of failures that Caps carried between his ears and was laying them down face up for Caps to look at on his way down. Salty got up, his hand shading his blinks into that marmalade sun, trying to clear the sticky away from his vision.

This is what Madame Kratz had warned him about, that thought takes you all over the place, preventing you from getting into the now. If he had not spent the last twenty minutes drifting around in drunken thinking, he'd be up there on the bridge.

Then Salty saw high up against the blue of the sky the wings of a hawk begin to fold. He saw them tuck themselves away in slow motion, settling themselves into place the way the wings of Rhoda the chicken had settled into place as she gave up and died. Salty blinked again and looked again. Now Caps was slanted forward, arms outstretched in a pre-flight lean before beginning his drop to the dirt.

Then Salty saw on the far side of the park the dog racing full tilt along the concrete sidewalk, dodging between legs, last-minute swerving into the traffic, finally sliding to a scrambling stop to seize hold of Caps's pant leg. Now the walkers stopped. They gathered around. One man held the dog while a second pried open the locked jaw.

The minute the walkers let go, the dog leaped from the concrete to the rail and launched itself airborne. At a run, Salty headed to where Caps would land. He braced himself and held out his arms.

Partway down, Caps turned himself over to reach up to the dog which was stretched out reaching down for Caps. If the bridge had been higher or the fall longer, or thought slower, or time kinder, the dog would have caught up with Caps. He'd have caught hold of him and laid him down peaceful and gentle in the grass and waited there beside him for Caps to get up and give himself a shake and sit down on the nearest bench for a drink.

Blinded by the sun, all Salty could see was their outlines slipping back and forth, in and out the sun's glare. Salty heard one body hit the ground with a thud. He felt the weight of the other body in his arms. The dog scrambled out of Salty's grip and ran to Caps, who was lying face up.

Salty couldn't move. He couldn't figure out how this had happened. He thought, if I hadn't spent the last eight hours drinking, I'd have gone straight to the right spot and stopped it before it got started. *Because you were drunk*, Lee Ann was saying, standing there beside him, looking down at Caps, who Salty heard say, "This is how it goes, Salty. Like tumbler pigeons, the home-brewed soar down Silver Ravine and across Silver Park until one day their bottle is empty and their worn-out wings fold into weak flaps and they drop, sometimes on a bench, sometimes into the grass, sometimes into the dirt."

Salty looked and he saw that Caps was staring up at him. He knelt down.

"Problems with the wife, memories, regrets, so you drink and after two or three you feel better and you keep on drinking and keep on thinking everything is good and then you wake up lying in the alley and all your problems are lying on top of you except now you got a bigger problem to think about. You jumped off the bridge."

Caps continued. "It's a long way down from that bridge. It takes a long time. You got lots of time to think. The list of all the people you wronged, all the mistakes you made, plays through your mind like a square dance on rewind and you think, this time when I sober up I'm going to get every step straight. First off, I'm going to put the plug in the jug. Then, I'm going to get my shit back on track. Then I'm going to…"

Caps's blind eyes suddenly unclouded themselves, cleaned away by the sun it seemed, and he looked up at the bridge and with cured sight he said, "But there's one problem. All the other mistakes I can fix, except one."

Caps pointed to the bridge overhead.

He sighed and closed his eyes. Salty thought he was dead, but as Salty was getting up, Caps grabbed his hand and into his ear he said, "The dog goes to you now. He done for me the best he could. Now let's see what he can do for you."

A man carrying a tennis racket had come running from the courts at the other side of the park. He pressed two fingers against Caps's neck and he pulled back one eyelid. He shook his head. "Nothing I can do," he said.

The sirens and the blue-and-red lights of the ambulance were coming across the park. By the time they had lifted Caps onto the stretcher and driven away, the dog had disappeared.

Salty spotted him behind a parked car, then lost him, and then a few yards up the street saw him, just a glimpse before he disappeared behind Colonel Wong's Southern Fried Chinese Chicken. Salty called to him, but the dog turned and headed the other way, stopping every few seconds, head cocked. He's following the ambulance siren, Salty realized, heading for the hospital.

Salty went as far as the traffic light and, not waiting for a change, hurried across the street and down the sidewalk. Halfway along the block, Salty turned into the alley which ran behind the hospital. But the dog wasn't there, not behind, in front, anywhere.

Salty sat down in the alley dirt. He remembered Eli's story about the sheepdog spending weeks searching for that one lost sheep, finally dying of starvation and exhaustion on the roadside.

"That is what will happen," said Salty to no one in particular.

Chapter Twelve

Sylvia

The Thorn library's location was perfect. Sylvia could take the College streetcar to Bridge Street, cut through the park, and there it was. The problem for some people was that on cold, rainy days when the homeless came into the library to shake themselves off and find a warm seat, it got kind of smelly. One shabby red-nosed man in particular liked to sit in one of the three living-room-style chairs next to the magazine rack. This meant that the other two were always available, if you didn't mind the smell, which Sylvia didn't because the lavender of the makeup covering her scar also covered the smell of the man.

The premise of her sociology term paper on mixed housing in the inner-city apartment building was that the poor would be happy to live with the rich, but because of lifestyle differences, the rich would not be happy living with the poor. This was just a variation on the homeless deserve decent housing, but not in my back yard.

She checked out her books and headed for home. Partway across the bridge, Sylvia noticed a group of people had gathered at the rail. In the park below, she saw a big man with long hair and a bushy beard, one of the homeless, she gathered, who looked familiar; not his rough appearance, but his manner, the way he pushed aside the half-dozen people who had gathered around, almost knocking everyone over, so he could kneel beside a black-and-white dog and hold it until the paramedics had put an injured man on a stretcher and loaded him into the ambulance. It bumped its way over the curb and disappeared.

Sylvia continued to her dorm room. While she was making her microwave supper, she turned on the TV. "This just in," said the nice-looking, grey-haired TV newscaster. "Another man has jumped off Silver Bridge. According to the police report, he had no family and no name other than 'Caps.' He had been living in a shack in the Silver Ravine."

The next part was an interview with a priest called Father Sutcliffe, who was standing in front of his mission, The Daystar. He referred to the homeless as "Fringe Dwellers." He said that Caps was almost blind and got around with the help of a stray dog. But when the Humane Society took his dog for not having a tag and not being on a leash, knowing he couldn't survive on his own, Caps took his own life.

The reporter asked, "Couldn't he have gone into a men's shelter?"

The priest was soft-spoken, like the Mennonite farmer. At this question, there was a long pause before the priest said, "The shelters don't allow dogs. But this was not just a dog. This was Caps's hold on life. Without his dog, life was not worth living."

Then the TV showed a picture snapped by someone's cell phone of the bearded man, arms up ready to catch the dog. The priest explained, "The sun was impossible to look into. Salty caught the dog by mistake."

Sylvia thought, Salty because he likes salt? Salty because he's cantankerous? Or Salty because his last name is Saltzmanous?

***

The next day, as Sylvia stepped off the streetcar at the bridge to return to the library, she noticed a little man sitting on a bench near the sidewalk. He was wearing a new-looking pale-blue shirt and a red tie that made his red face look even redder and exaggerated the rest of his rumpled, musty, cartoonish look, especially with the too-big City Works baseball hat held up by his oversized ears.

He was too little to be afraid of so she went right up to him. "Who was the man who jumped?"

He gave her a sleepy glance that told her he was drunk.

"My buddy, Caps."

"Why did he do it?" She meant several questions: Did he have a family, how did he end up homeless, what will happen to him? Will he have a pauper's funeral? What was his situation?

He pointed to the bridge. "If you sit here looking at it long enough it takes you up there. Once you're up there, it takes you down."

Sylvia looked up at the steel structure spanning the ravine, hundreds of feet high. Beneath it, where the jumper had landed, was nothing, no police tape, no forensics team taking photos, and sticking up little flags. Nothing but a patch of undisturbed grass and dirt, as though nothing had happened.

She asked, "Where did he live? In a shack they said. But aren't there shelters? Couldn't he have got help?"

The little man shrugged a "don't know."

"He's just a homeless man so no one cares?"

"The priest from The Daystar, Father Sutcliffe. He's having a little, you know, whatever you do when someone croaks. The priest can tell you. That's him over there, the one wearing the collar."

At least thirty men were standing around, including the big one with the beard. They all looked like they used to be someone somewhere. But now they looked like no one anywhere.

Then, from somewhere, the black-and-white dog appeared. It went to each of the homeless, sat for a handshake, then went to the big man with the beard who knelt beside it and gave it a hug.

My God, she thought. It's Amos.

But no. That was fifteen years ago. Not remotely possible.

The priest was wearing a clerical collar but his clothes amounted to a black shirt, blue jeans, and sandals. He glanced at Sylvia, probably wondering why she was there.

He started. "We are gathered here to honour the passing of our friend, Caps."

The priest looked at her again. She thought, he thinks I'm a relative. A daughter, maybe.

"Caps got his nickname from collecting beer caps. The walls of his tin and plywood shack in Silver City are lined with beer caps.

Before Caps moved from his modest bungalow in North York to Silver City, he worked in a hardware store. He met his wife at a square dance. They square danced for many years. But his wife was doing a little too much skirt work and she left him for one of the other square dancers. She took their kids with her. She'd found someone better."

Sylvia could not take her eyes off the priest. She guessed him to be in his late thirties. His hair was sandy blonde and longish. It was combed to the right side. He was slim, average height. A good-looking priest.

"Caps knew all about hardware but because of his failing eyesight, he had trouble with the computer. The hardware store owner found someone better. Home alone in an empty bungalow, Caps passed the time drinking and watching videos of himself and his wife square dancing to their favourite song: 'I'm Not Through Loving You Yet.' That is, until he ran out of money. Then the bank evicted him from his empty bungalow and sold it to someone better.

"Fallen to pieces and come undone, Caps ended up in the shack in the Silver City ravine. He didn't pass the time watching square dancing on television. He had no television. He didn't go square dancing. He had no wife. So Caps started a new dance, the hopeless dance of the alcoholic.

"Every night Caps lay in his shack reciting to himself the lyrics of his song: I'm not through loving you yet. Every morning he climbed down the bank of the Silver Ravine and walked through Silver Park and out onto the street to pan so he could buy enough glue to paste his broke and broken self together for that day. As you all know, Silver Park glue comes in three forms: one, Curveball, which is home-brewed wine; two, Majestic Diner, a home-brewed methanol–alcohol combination guaranteed to have you glued back together by nine o'clock in the morning, providing you get an early start; the third is Kawasaki, a high octane mixture made from dandelion leaves.

"One day a stray sheepdog came out of nowhere to look after Caps. He guided Caps to wherever he wanted to go. Like all sheepdogs, Whisper was trustworthy, loyal, and true, unlike Caps's wife. Whisper and Caps panned together, wandered the alleys and the streets together, came to The Daystar together. Whisper never let

Caps out of his sight, and Caps never went anywhere without Whisper. He stayed with Caps right to the end. Whisper didn't want anyone better."

After a pause, and a glance at Sylvia, he continued. "As many of you know, Caps was diabetic. Caps needed insulin shots twice a day: ten o'clock in the morning and four in the afternoon. I kept his insulin at The Daystar and twice a day I gave him his shots. Caps always knew when it was ten o'clock and had no trouble finding his way to The Daystar. But after all day drinking, Caps didn't always know when it was four o'clock. But Whisper knew. How would a dog know, you might ask? Maybe he heard a train somewhere that came by at the same time every day, or the Greyhound bus coming from somewhere and going down Sheldon Street every day at the same time, or maybe church bells that only Whisper could hear, tolling somewhere far off."

Father Sutcliffe paused in his delivery, struggling to control his tears.

"Bear with me," he continued. "There is much more to say about Caps."

Now it seemed to Sylvia that the priest had put his hand on her shoulder and was looking right at her as he continued:

"Some days Caps would be in worse shape than others. On these occasions, Whisper would start herding Caps to The Daystar earlier than usual to allow himself more time to get him there for four o'clock. If Caps was passed out stone cold from drinking too many bottles of bad memories, which he sometimes was, Whisper would come on his own to The Daystar. He would stand at the door and he would bark, something Whisper never did unless there was an emergency, and I would hear him and I would look at my watch and I would see that it was four o'clock and I would get the insulin bag and I would follow Whisper to wherever Caps was lying passed out stone cold, and I would give him his insulin.

"Caps's lifestyle made it difficult for the shots to keep him alive. Sometimes Whisper would come to The Daystar in the middle of the night and when I arrived at Caps's shack I could tell that Caps was going into a diabetic coma. 'How did Whisper know?' I wondered. I found an article in a medical journal about a family with a golden retriever. One of the kids was diabetic. When his blood sugar was off, the dog would pace back and forth and wouldn't settle down until the mother came and got the blood sugar corrected. How did the dog know before the mother? You might say probably through smell. I read that dogs can be trained to detect cancer cells in the body by smelling a person's breath. I think that might be the answer.

"Whisper was Caps's eyes, guiding him wherever he wanted to go. How did Whisper learn to do that, you might ask? Maybe he had been a seeing-eye dog before Caps found him. I don't know. One thing I do know: Caps did not find Whisper like someone would find a stray dog. Caps was too blind and too drunk to find anything. Whisper found Caps.

"The Out of the Cold program that doesn't allow pets told Caps he might be able to keep his dog for medical reasons. But first, he needed to stop drinking. So to keep his dog, for that one and only reason, Caps stopped drinking. He put the plug in the jug, as they say in Silver City. But then Whisper went missing. Caps and I spent two days looking for him, through the park, up and down the ravine, back and forth through the alleys. On the afternoon of the third day, I found Caps sitting on a bench. Blinking through the veil of tears that filled eyes that could not see, he told me what happened. Some Judas had phoned a 1-800 number. A Detective Roof had knocked on the door of his Silver City shack. Detective Roof had taken Caps to the station to ask questions about his missing wife. Detective Roof had phoned the Humane Society and told them to take the dog. Then the detective let Caps go.

"Alcohol did not kill Caps. Absence of hope killed Caps. The dog's name is Whisper. Caps's name for the dog was Hope. Hope does not disappear forever. Just because you can't find it today does not mean it's forever gone. I went to the dog pound. I learned that Jake had taken sick and his helper, Colin, had locked Hope in one of the cages on its way to the kill kennel in Montreal. The reason I didn't think of the Humane Society earlier was not just that this dog was not a dog that any person capable of kindness and empathy would put into a dog pound, just like no person capable of empathy and insight would put Caps in jail. But the other reason was that I thought Jake would be there to look after the dog supposing some Judas did betray Caps.

"I phoned Jake. He told me what to do. I bought a leash, I paid the fine, I took Whisper to the park. I let him go. I didn't know where Caps was, but I knew Whisper would know.

"You will be saying that Caps jumped off Silver Bridge on Tuesday of this week. That day, instead of drinking Curveball like he usually did, he'd been drinking Kawasaki and, as you know, as well as rotting your stomach, Kawasaki makes you do crazy things. My memory is filled with stories of the unpredictable consequences of drinking the most dangerous homebrew beverage of the Fringe Dwellers of Silver Park. Perhaps if he had not been drinking Kawasaki he would not have jumped. I don't know. But what I do know is that Caps did not jump off Silver Bridge last Tuesday. He jumped long ago and has been falling ever since.

"Alcohol turns the pages of the hopeless homeless story. The Tuesday Caps took the first drink in the morning to fix his broken self was the Tuesday he jumped, and all the other Tuesdays were a blur in his Silver City mind as he fell. They say he jumped last Tuesday. Last Tuesday was the day his fall ended.

"I paid the dog pound its fine of fifty dollars and I brought Whisper to the park. I undid his leash and I said, 'Find Caps.' Then, when I looked up, I saw Caps hanging off the bridge rail. Then, when I looked down, I saw a blur of black and white racing across the grass and up the bank of the ravine. At the exact moment Caps let go, Whisper grabbed his pant leg. Caps turned, trying to get hold of the rail and pull himself back. They say in a moment like this time slows down to fix in a picture you will never forget. It fixed for what seemed like ten minutes, Caps balanced there one foot on the concrete, one hand reaching for the dog, the other hand and foot falling forward midair. I was a long way off but I could hear the scrape of Whisper's claws scratching at the concrete and I could see the sparks from his nails flying up from the steel as he tried to save his friend.

"And Whisper would have. He is not a big dog and he is not a strong dog, but I know all that was needed to tip the balance was not the strength of that dog tugging at Caps's pant leg but the whisper of hope tugging at Caps's heart."

Father Sutcliffe paused and, like Sylvia, wiped a tear with the back of his hand before continuing.

"The whisper of hope is a mysterious thing, barely a sound, often not heard, maybe there and maybe not, maybe nothing, maybe a hint of…"

The priest was looking right at her.

"When two passers-by, wanting to save the dog, pried the pant leg free, Caps fell. But at that moment two things happened. Whisper, breaking loose, leaped from the pavement to the rail and launched himself into space like a dog jumping off a dock into the flat blue of the water to save his drowning friend. I stood there waiting for the dog to somehow catch up with Caps, somehow get hold of him, somehow make the landing gentle. I was so convinced that I would see this happen, I could not believe it when it did not.

"Then I saw my friend Salty reaching up to catch the man. I was so convinced that I would see Salty catch the man I could not believe it when he did not. I could not believe that a sighted man trying to catch a blind man could be blinded by the very sun that allowed a sighted man to see. This cruel irony that I saw with my own sighted eyes I will never forget.

"That is the story of Caps. Thank you for your patience. I know you're anxious to get back to your day's activities. The city is going to allow us to bury Caps in the wooden coffin Salty has offered to make for him. Burial will be in Mount Hope Cemetery. Our friend Mr. Bones has agreed to bring his banjo and sing Caps's favourite song, 'I'm Not Through Loving You Yet.'"

Sylvia turned away. When she glanced back, she saw that the men had gone. She continued across the park. But then she felt a pull, and when she looked back she saw that the dog was staring at her, watching her leave.

She did not want that man to be her father. She did not want him to be Dad. She wanted nothing to do with him. But that dog… When she looked back again, there he was, staring at her, worried about her, watching her leave the way he had every day watched her crossing the field from Eli Martin's gate to her own, making sure she got home safe.

Chapter Thirteen

Salty

Salty couldn't believe that Caps's dog had managed to track Caps from the hospital to the morgue to the funeral parlour, and now to the cemetery. But there he was, sniffing along the plain board coffin suspended across the grave paid for by the Coalition for the Fringe Dwellers. When Salty called, the dog came. He sat down and held out his paw for a handshake. As Salty crouched to scratch behind his ears and stroke along his head he noticed a girl who looked to be in her early twenties standing not far off from the grave. In the direct sun, even from this distance, Salty could see she had on heavy makeup, especially thick on one cheek. Because she was wearing sunglasses and a wide-brimmed hat, Salty couldn't see much else of her face. But she looked like the one who'd been at Caps's eulogy.

Salty could smell the girl's perfume. It wasn't the 80% Eau de Toilette that made you look down the street to see Juicy coming out of the alley with her shopping cart. It wasn't the stuff that Beets stole from Walmart to cover the blotch of wet Fuck me Jesus Christ looking down at the crotch smell coming from his bladder pants.

This was something not too strong, faint in fact, but familiar enough to elbow its way into Salty's memory and overpower the smell of Pavements who was standing next to him with a bag of ice on his jaw for the pain from the one molar on his right side, the others having rotted out and gone into the blue recycling bin in front of Soapy's.

It was something like the stuff Lee Ann used to spray on her wrist. He had smelled it the night she was bleeding out on the floor.

He hadn't smelled the blood, he'd smelled her perfume, and now he wasn't smelling Beets or Juicy or Pavements. He was smelling Lee Ann.

Pavements stumbled across the grass and stood staring at the coffin looking sad. Pavements usually didn't look like anything, only drunk. Next to Father Sutcliffe stood Mr. Bones. He must have run into something with his nose because he had stuffed one nostril with toilet paper which flapped and fluttered when he said his own version of may he rest in peace but the exact words were, "Now he's passed out permanent."

Father Sutcliffe asked, "Which end is the head of the coffin?"

Salty hadn't thought about that. The undertaker had put Caps in there. "Both ends are the same. What does it matter?"

"Tell me which end is the head and you'll see."

Salty pointed. "That end."

Where Salty pointed, Father Sutcliffe stood, looking at the coffin as though he was talking to Caps.

Father Sutcliffe said, "How did this happen, Caps, in case you're in there wondering? I can tell you. First, you took a drink and you felt good. So you had a second drink. Pretty soon you started to like feeling good."

Now Salty noticed the knot in that top board, which meant Father Sutcliffe was talking to Caps's feet. Salty went over. "I remember this knot. You're talking to his feet. He probably can't hear you."

Father Sutcliffe moved to the top end and Salty knelt in the grass at the bottom end.

"But then you woke up in the morning and felt like a gob of spit. You said no more, never again. But of course, never again meant until next time because you had discovered the magic of a drink in the morning to cure the magic of the drinks from the night before. You know the feeling of two or three in the morning when the magic gets triggered and you feel good again. But now you don't want to stop because you like feeling good."

Pavements sat down in the grass beside Salty.

"The trip to the bottom of every bottle is like the trip from the bottom of Silver Ravine and up the bank to Silver Bridge and back down. It takes years, one after another, each bottle a little deeper, each bridge a little higher, and so it goes for years and then..."

Beets sat down in the grass beside Pavements.

Father Sutcliffe paused, listening, looking over at Beets, as though Caps was telling him the smell coming off Beets was giving everyone a headache. Father Sutcliffe held up his arms, mumbled some more words, and that was it for the prayer for Caps, which probably would have lasted to lunchtime had it not been for the smell of Beets.

Salty was watching the dog. He'd wandered over for a handshake with the girl. She was giving Salty the feeling he had got when Madame Kratz had shuffled her cards and then listened to something far off and then said, "It must be that girl." Salty looked more closely. He remembered every detail of every stitch that had been sewed into Sylvia's cheek from nose to ear. This girl had no scar.

Everyone left except the girl who was patting the dog. Salty called for him to come but, fidgeting and fussing, the dog seemed not too sure who he should be with. He seemed to be waiting for someone to tell him. Salty called the dog again and he followed, but he was uncertain about it, glancing back at the girl.

Salty knew the girl was watching them go. He sensed her eyes following them across the grass. He could feel the movement of her legs walking with his. When he reached his park bench and sat down, it felt like, with her perfume hanging there in his nose, she was sitting with him.

Salty bent to pat the dog's head and scratch his ears. When Salty had finished patting and scratching, he got up and continued walking. As they turned into the lane that ran along the line of garages to the cement block workshop, the dog ran ahead. Reaching the door, he sat on the step, wagging his tail, waiting for Salty.

Salty looked back, still feeling that the girl was behind him. In that second the dog, as though he too had felt the girl was behind them, had disappeared. One minute there, next minute gone. He had not wandered away to sniff and poke along the alley. He'd just vanished along with that girl.

But no, for the next day, returning along the alley from Morning Scriptures and Hymn Sing with Big Breakfast Ham and Eggs at St.

Luke's, Salty noticed the dog eating a slice of bread out of the garbage behind Colonel Wong's. He called and snapped his thumb and finger. At first, the dog sulked away, not wanting to go with Salty. But when Salty whistled, the dog stopped. He seemed torn, like he was trying to figure out who he belonged to now. He'd probably been to the cemetery, been up the ravine to Caps's shack, been down to Caps's bench, been to the hospital, from one to the other looking for Caps.

Finally, he trotted to Salty. He licked Salty's hand as he stroked the dog's face and the fur of his neck. For the rest of that day, Salty and the dog searched the alleys and the lanes. Besides three slices of bread and one salami and cheese sandwich, they found one whole wiener and a piece of chicken, which Salty threw away. He wanted nothing to do with chicken. He sat down in the dirt and fed the dog the salami and the wiener. Then, satisfied that the dog had eaten enough, Salty picked him up and carried him to the shed. Salty, who had not felt anything for years, liked the warmth of the dog's body cradled in his arms. He set the dog down. He fed him a slice of bread. If he had had any money, he would've gone to McDonald's like he used to with Sylvia and bought the dog a hamburger without any ketchup and maybe got one of those little McDonald's hats for the dog to wear. But that was a long time ago. McDonald's probably didn't have them anymore.

He sat on the cement floor with the dog. He discovered that if he rubbed the dog's chest, back and forth over ribs that were now fur-covered bones, the dog would roll over and hold his front paws under his chin as though he were praying. Probably for Caps. When Salty stopped, the dog got up and climbed into Salty's lap. Salty sat rocking the dog. He thought of Eli's dog, Amos. "Dogs do not judge," Eli had said. "Their love and loyalty are unconditional. Like our Lord Jesus," added Eli.

During the night Salty let the dog out. He waited at the door but the dog did not return. Why did he leave, wondered Salty? He was at the funeral. He knows Caps is dead. But, after a moment's thought, Salty reminded himself that when the undertaker had cleaned Caps up, he'd probably pumped him full of formaldehyde, so that when the dog checked the coffin, sniffing along the edges, not able to smell Caps, he'd decided Caps was not in there.

Eli would say, "If one stray sheep under his watch has wandered away, the dog will look forever until one day he lies down somewhere in some alley and never gets up."

Salty sank down on his couch. Salty was big as a grizzly bear and tough as roofing nails but he could not stop the tears from forming in his heart.

Chapter Fourteen

Pavements

On the library computer, Pavements was looking through the RCMP Missing Links page and there she was, staring right at him, her name under the photograph: Lee Ann Saltzmanous. Case number 99-626-1090. Pavements studied her shoulders-up picture. She was sitting at a table, a cigarette in one hand, a glass of wine in the other. The background was a bare wall without pictures or shelves. But look there, oh boy, the locket around her neck, the same one that Salty carried around. All lockets looked the same, but look there, oh boy, that locket had bits of red around the edges, the same as Salty's.

Celia had one just like it. Inside was a picture of her fat cow offputting mother. He'd never seen anyone so fat. She couldn't come to visit because she was over the weight limit for crossing Silver Bridge. The day she died the ambulance guys laid her on the gurney lengthways on her side figuring she'd be narrow enough to go through the door. They'd even pointed her in the direction of her toes but she got stuck halfway through. Finally, they took her out the front bay window.

Strike me dead. In this picture, the writing on the door of the pickup says Saltzmanous Construction.

Pavements printed the pictures with the library copier and took them to his room in The Daystar. He pasted them on the wall next to his photocopied pictures from *The Missing Link* book. Pavements went to the 7-Eleven and bought a pack of Player's, his first cigarettes in years that weren't from the reserve, already spending the reward money he hadn't got yet.

***

Pavements sat down next to Mr. Bones, who was on The Daystar front step reading in the paper about the bedbug invasion. Pavements took out his bottle of Curveball and started his cardio warm-up: first ten thumb swings to the left, then ten thumb side-shuffles, then ten thumb circles, then, bottle in his right hand, he did ten full finger clenches with his left before twisting off the cap.

He said, "A regular physical fitness program will extend your life twenty years."

Mr. Bones said, "A bedbug can live about twenty years on one bite. That's it. Doesn't do nothing after that. I've got some living in my banjo. When I start to play that Merle Haggard, 'The Bottle Let Me Down,' I can see them jumping out. When I'm done, they jump back in again. A bedbug can jump thirty feet, it says here."

Pavements said, "Fuck me, here comes Celia." He tucked away his bottle.

"I've brought you the tie that goes better with that shirt."

Pavements stood and she fastened it around his neck.

She sat on the bottom step. "I'm pleased that you're taking an interest in reading. But if you're in the library you need to look decent, not like that man Beets. The library is hiring a security guard to stop the homeless at the door and tell them they have to be sober and clean to enter, so you better start keeping yourself clean and sober."

She asked, "Have you got enough money? I mean, are you still getting your disability?"

"It's only two hundred a month so I can scarcely get by and could use more."

Celia was looking at the tie, her head tilted. For Celia, ties had to match shirts.

"Well, I've been thinking. If you make a sincere effort to get yourself back together, maybe you and I can think about getting back together. The Bible says marriage is forever. I should not have given up on you. And get your teeth fixed."

Pavements was remembering how it had been with Celia. What drove him crazy was she had a little notepad. In the morning, she made a list of all the things about him he needed to work on that day, like not leaving the toilet seat up. She wouldn't say it right out. She'd go in after him and put it down. She kept a Kleenex in her purse that she'd hand him when he picked his nose.

But winter was coming, That was the thing, hanging out all day in the library with nothing to do because it was too cold to go outside and now they weren't going to let you in. Celia was starting to look pretty good. The weight she'd put on made her look homey and him feel horny. He imagined a comfortable chair and a bottle of Red Truck in front of the fireplace on a winter night.

Pavements said, "I'm coming into some money from a job I did. Enough to get a decent apartment across the bridge that we should get back together in."

Celia said, "Jehovah wants married people to obey their vows, for better or worse, whoever God has joined together let no man put asunder. But first, you have to stop looking like a street bum living in a homeless shelter. And you have to get a job with regular money coming in, not disability. And get your teeth fixed. You have to earn your way and wear clean clothes and look at those pants, they're a mess, and then we can think about it."

Celia left Pavements thinking about it. Mr. Bones went inside for a leak and, coming back, fell down the stairs. They went to the emergency where the nurse put him in a wheelchair and whoosh whooshed him through the swinging doors.

After a while, the doctor came out. "Mr. Bones has a sprained ankle, nothing serious. Other than the fact that if he doesn't stop drinking, he will soon be dead from liver failure."

***

It was raining the next day, so Mr. Bones did a gig under the awning at the pawnshop. Salty had made a sign with two pieces of plywood on hinges with the words "Willie Nelson Live" painted in red from a can he'd found in the garbage. He'd done the same for movie night at the church. A couple of weeks ago Salty had shingled Caps's roof. One time before that he'd found a window in the alley and installed it in

Caps's shack. Now that window and that roof and those signs were saying to Pavements, "Salty's Construction."

With his City Works baseball hat upside down on the sidewalk for the money, Pavements sat against the wall out of the rain. Everyone who came by asked Mr. Bones to sing their favourite Willie Nelson with Salty as backup. Everyone said Salty looked like the singer in the Crazy Heart movie. So now Mr. Bones called Salty Crazy Heart like he had called Caps Jeff Healy.

Because the rain was coming down hard, a crowd had gathered under the awning. Mr. Bones was doing a George Jones that someone had asked for when the minister from the Presbyterian church stopped to listen. He gave Mr. Bones ten dollars.

Mr. Bones played three sets straight. Pavements's upside-down City Works baseball hat was soon filled to the brim. At three o'clock in the afternoon, as they were wrapping up to head for Dixie's Donut Shoppe to buy two bottles of Majestic Diner, the minister came back. He said, "My name is Reverend Schofield. You'd easily make a hundred dollars singing hymns in front of my church Sunday morning. We can split it, fifty-fifty; provided you're sober."

Mr. Bones put his banjo aside. "Will my singing hymns help get Caps into heaven?"

"I'm sure it will."

Pavements asked, "If I bought him some flowers and laid them on his bench, would that help?"

"Indeed it would."

The rain stopped and the sun came out, drying off the park benches while they passed the Majestic Diner back and forth.

Mr. Bones said, "It ain't right sitting here without Caps."

Pavements said, "Caps was dying anyway."

That was the way Pavements was looking at it. Caps's wife probably deserved whatever she got. She was probably a no-good slut, sleeping around and spending his money. The other way, it was Colin's fault for taking the dog. He should have known Caps would jump.

***

Supper time at The Daystar. Two chairs over was Salty. His beard and long hair reminded Pavements of monkeys becoming people. Salty's ancestors must have been the King Kong type. On the other side of the table sat one of the Cape Croker Indians living at the Outreach. His hair was combed back like Elvis. Indian Elvis, they called him. His sister was the homebrew dealer, Dixie. Next to him sat Kemosabe, Indian Elvis's brother, but not his sister's brother, and next to him sat Mr. Bones, and next to him sat Beets, who drooled while he was eating.

Donkey Man came in. His real name was Domiscki but Father Sutcliffe had nicknamed him after the wild donkey man in the Bible. His eyes were small and black and glinting like the snakes he had tattooed on each arm. Donkey Man's hair was long and black and he kept a comb in his back pocket and ten times a day he combed his hair. He had a key which he said was to the Playboy Mansion, but Pavements knew it was to a condemned house on Seaton where the last owner had left boxes of Playboy magazines going back to 1960. The house was waiting to be torn down and replaced by city mixed housing.

Donkey Man elbowed his way into a seat at the table next to Indian Elvis, across from Salty. He pretended to pull a hair out of his head and pick off the lice and drop them into Indian Elvis's soup. Indian Elvis got up and left, leaving his unfinished soup on the table. Donkey Man shifted into the space and spread out his elbows and helped himself from the pile of sandwiches. Donkey Man was bigger than Pavements but not by much, only six or seven inches. Donkey Man liked to make himself bigger by picking on anyone bigger than him.

A knock sounded on the front door, and when Pavements turned to look he saw Jake, the dog catcher. He said to Salty, "I saw Whisper out behind the Chinese restaurant. I think he's dead."

Salty led the way, walking so fast that Jake and Pavements had trouble keeping up.

Jake said, "I was on my way to the office so I was coming along the street and I looked up the alley and there he was."

Salty crouched by the dog. It had enough strength to lick Salty's hand. But that was all. Pavements thought he saw tears fill Salty's eyes as he picked up the dog and, with Pavements and Jake following, carried him from the alley to a park bench.

Jake asked, "Do we need to take him to the vet?"

Salty was busy with the dog, looking for anything broken.

Jake said, "Yes, he needs to go to the vet."

Pavements could see there was no life left in the dog. The skin was hung over his boney frame in folds and his eyes were clouded from starvation. Pavements said, "The last time we saw him was at the funeral, two weeks ago. He probably hasn't ate anything since. He's going to kill himself looking for Caps."

"I think he needs to go to the vet," said Jake.

Salty said, "They'll put him down."

He held the dog in his arms and left, walking slowly, head bowed.

Jake said to Pavements, "Let Salty deal with it."

Salty disappeared around the corner.

Jake asked, "How's things going, Pavements?"

"Celia brought me this new shirt and tie. We're thinking about getting back together."

Jake said, "With a decent pair of pants you'd look pretty good. First a shower, though."

"How much does a pair of pants cost from a real store?"

"I don't know for sure but my guess you'll need about forty dollars. That would be a start. Decent clothes and a shower and you might be able to get a job and your own apartment."

Pavements said, "Caps jumping off the bridge has got me thinking about getting my own place. That's what happens when someone dies. You think about yourself dying and about getting on with whatever shit you want to get started at, like, for me, getting back with Celia."

Chapter Fifteen

Salty

Salty undid the tangles under the dog's belly and cleaned the dirt off the rest of him. He brought scraps from The Daystar's kitchen. The dog especially liked Father Sutcliffe's meatloaf. Each day Salty picked him up to test the weight gain to make sure he didn't have worms. Salty marked on a calendar he had found on the sidewalk how much the dog ate each day. He marked down the number of strokes for each day's brushing, each day adding one more until a gloss returned to the dog's coat. On the fourteenth day, when Salty ran his hand along the dog's back, the fur snapped with electricity.

Salty held the dog's head in his hands and talked to him. He said, "I knew a dog once called Amos. You are so much like Amos that I am afraid to call you Amos."

He said, "I liked to look out the kitchen window and watch Amos with the sheep. I used to wonder if he knew how to count. Then I'd wonder how could he keep track of the counting when they all looked the same."

When Salty stopped talking, the dog took one hand in his mouth and held it and wouldn't let go until Salty continued the conversation. "Every morning we had to do a handshake as though him and me together were on a contract to look after Sylvia. If you were Amos, I would apologize for not keeping my end of the bargain."

But then, but then, Salty couldn't help it. One day when Salty stared into the dog's soft brown eyes, they seemed to lose focus and Salty seemed to be looking into two pools big enough to climb into and sink down into someplace better than the alcoholic emptiness of what Salty had become and he said, "I am so sorry, Amos."

That night, after Salty had climbed under his blanket, the dog stretched out on his front paws beside him, his head lying so close to Salty's that he could hear the soft in and out of his breathing. Salty said again to the dog, "Amos, I am so sorry."

Salty knew the dog could not be Amos. But he knew that Madame Kratz would say he would feel better if he apologized as though the dog was the spirt of Amos. Salty thought, it must be because all these years I have slept with one ear listening for the sound of boots on the gravel as the policemen stepped up to my door. But now the dog is doing the listening for me. I can wake up in the middle of the night and open one eye and I can see that the dog is watching for the slightest movement and listening for the faintest sound.

During the day, as Salty went about his business, the dog stayed at his side. He didn't wander the way he did with Caps. He's afraid of losing me, thought Salty. But the moment he thought that, he realized it was him that was afraid of losing the dog. Salty worried that the dog would only stay long enough to gather strength before heading off, looking for Caps, like in that war movie at St Luke's, the dog who'd been shot about ten times took shelter in some cottage in the hills and got nursed back to health by the old hermit. Then he left to carry on with his search for the soldier.

Salty went to see Madame Kratz. "I want to know about a dog I knew once called Amos. Years ago. He lived on the farm next one over from me."

She shuffled the cards. "I don't like what they're saying."

Every time her hands turned her cards over made him think she had a crystal ball set up in her bedroom like a flatscreen and she could watch his future in it like an evening movie. Salty had the feeling that, if he turned around and looked, he would see the spirit of Amos sitting there all this time in her candle-lit reading room waiting for Madame Kratz to turn up the card with 2020 written on it.

But she said, "Something about the triangular three: fate, future, destiny."

When she said that, the candles and the purple curtain fluttered, and all her bracelets clattered like clanking ankle chains on convicts.

She excused herself, hurried away in fact, and in a few minutes came back with tea and biscuits, the tea leaves floating around in the already-poured cup. She laid it out like the queen in her palace, the cup to his right hand and to his left a plate with a biscuit, and then directly in front of him a little silver tray with the cream and the sugar.

She said, "It has to be triangular. You take the cream and then the sugar and then you stir. You can't take one and not the other because they all go together in threes. You can't say you don't want that biscuit. You have to have the tea and you have to add the cream and sugar and you have to eat the biscuit."

She waited while he did it. When he had finished his tea, she looked into his teacup like into the crystal ball flatscreen. But it wasn't just a look. She seemed to be watching his tea leaves squirming around in there like maggots in a dumpster, writing his future in their squiggles.

She said, "As I look into your tea leaves, somewhere in the back of my brain wise counsel is poking about in the uncertain vagaries of your existence and stirring up bad thoughts about the dog."

She seemed to be listening. "Do you hear that?"

"Hear what?"

"It must be the dog next door."

"What does that mean?"

She gathered her cards and tucked them away in her drawer. She gathered her tea set and disappeared through the purple curtain, like being in one of those little rooms with the doctor, prescription given, he disappears through the door, leaving you there to find your own way back into the street with your sickness.

Salty got up and left, back into the street with no prescription for his sickness.

Chapter Sixteen

Pavements

Lunchtime at The Daystar, Father Sutcliffe announced that the older kids from Rosemount Pentecostal were going to hold a car wash on Saturday to raise money for The Daystar.

Father Sutcliffe said, "They want to see what their money is being used for."

Pavements said, "To see what we look like, check us out, like going to the zoo." Pavements removed his baseball hat to scratch a bedbug bite above his right ear. "Roger over at the Outreach tried the same thing with that queer preacher from St. John the Apostle. The queer went around giving out sandwiches and shaking hands with the Outreachers who were standing around picking their noses. Can you imagine how much dried snot ended up in those sandwiches?"

Mr. Bones said, "How many of those sandwiches did you eat?"

"The queer said the sandwiches were blessed by Jesus and so was the snot."

"So, did you eat one of those snot sandwiches?"

"Beets ate about six. I wasn't hungry right then because I'd just finished Morning Scriptures and Hymn Sing with Big Breakfast Ham and Eggs at St. Luke's. Then I went to Market Mission for the free coffee and donuts, and then back here for when the mailman delivers my two hundred and five dollars monthly homeless cheque plus fifty dollars special diet allowance signed by Dr. Singh. You know Dr. Singh? He doesn't speak English so he doesn't know what he's signing."

The Rosemount Pentecostal kids arrived with picnic coolers packed with juice and sandwiches. The minister introduced them, three girls and two boys. They were wearing "Help the Fringe Dwellers" T-shirts that said on the back, "The meek shall inherit the Earth."

Pavements thought, I don't want the Earth. I want that five thousand dollar in cash that should have got hand-delivered in a plain brown envelope by one of the detectives.

The minister said, "These young people made the sandwiches themselves from donated bread and peanut butter." Then he added, "One loaf and one bottle of juice to feed the five men at The Daystar."

They sat at the dining room table. Pavements counted: Beets, Mr. Bones, himself, and two from the Outreach. While the kids went around serving the glasses of juice and peanut butter sandwiches, Pavements tried to figure it out: one loaf would have, say, twenty slices, two for each sandwich. Each man at the table had taken two but there were still lots left over waiting to be passed around. And the juice. The minister said they'd bought one bottle, but there were three jugs on the table, plus everyone had a full glass.

After Pavements ate his sandwiches, he took the minister aside. "How can one loaf and one container of juice feed five men?"

"Yes, that is a good question. Our Lord Jesus fed the multitudes with one loaf and one fish. He prayed and asked his heavenly Father for enough to feed the multitudes. Very simple."

"My wife Celia divorced me, but now she says Jesus wants us back together. Do you think if I prayed the Lord Jesus would help me?"

"I'm sure he would."

"First, I want to set myself up in a decent apartment with decent furniture and then I invite her so I can show her the apartment and say, 'Let's move back in together right away, and start fresh.'"

"It sounds like you need start-up money. So first you'll need a job. So first, pray to Jesus to find you a job."

"Find a job? I was thinking about going to college."

"Well, maybe. But Our Lord Jesus wants us to have basic working jobs. Landscaping. Construction. That sort of thing. Sweat on our brow, callouses on our hands."

"Is that why he gave us thumbs?"

"Exactly. Yes. Praise be to Jesus."

Pavements left when the food and juice were gone. It had started to rain. Pavements settled down in the soft chairs by the library magazine rack. He picked up an *Apartment Living* magazine. He leafed through it, imagining how he would arrange the furniture. Celia liked to cook, so she would need a nice kitchen. He remembered the kitchen knives he'd found, left there by Jesus, for sure, the same as this Kitchen and Bath magazine, left here by Jesus for me, Pavements, to look through, like that Missing Link book, left there by Jesus for me, Pavements, to look through and be rewarded for finding missing links.

Pavements put the magazines back into the rack and picked up the newspaper and licked his thumb to turn the page to see what Jesus might direct his eyes to next. There it was:

The Commissioner of Police and the Mayor of the city have announced that the Fringe Dwellers are upsetting the women and children who ought to be able to enjoy the facilities in Silver Park undisturbed. Effective immediately, the park will be patrolled by three more bicycle unit police officers.

The librarian came over. "My goodness, Pavements, look at you in your nice new matching shirt and tie. Pretty spiffy."

Pavements looked at himself. Usually, he would be sitting in an off-putting manner with an odiferous smell and his legs stretched out and his City Works boots on the magazine table. But he didn't do that no more. If Celia came by, she would see him sitting up straight, feet on the floor, reading in *Better Homes and Gardens* about planting flowers.

When the rain stopped and the sun came out, Pavements walked the five blocks to the cemetery. He returned with some flowers, donated by Mrs. Elizabeth Mae Schmidt (1946-2018), who wasn't using them anymore. He arranged them in the slats of Caps's bench. After a while, Salty came along with Whisper and an almost-full bottle of Majestic Diner, which they passed back and forth.

The first one to notice the bicycle crossing from the far side of the park was Whisper, who was poking around in the grass. First, his head came up and then he sniffed the breeze and then he looked around, and then the policeman came along, riding a bicycle and wearing policeman sunglasses. As he pulled up, Salty slipped the bottle into the inside pocket of his coat.

"My name is Officer Cobbs."

He was looking at Salty.

"Why is this bench covered with flowers?"

No one answered.

"Where did the roses come from?"

Pavements said, "I picked them in the woods."

"Did these 'woods' have a cemetery in them?"

"Not that I noticed."

Looking directly at Whisper, who was standing next to Salty, Officer Cobbs said, "We have orders that all dogs must have a tag and be on a leash. Do you have a leash and a tag for your dog, sir?"

Pavements had never heard anyone in Silver Park being called "sir". But the officer was looking at Salty sitting in the roses looking more like Hulk Hogan at the Better Homes and Garden Flower Show than anyone called "sir."

"No, I don't have a leash and a tag for my dog," said Salty. "How do I get one?"

"Go to City Hall, fill out the form, giving your name and address. It will cost twenty dollars. In the meantime, I'll phone for the Humane Society and we'll look after your dog in the pound."

He took out his pad and pencil "What is your name, sir?"

"Salty."

"Your real name."

Strike me dead, thought Pavements. Now the truth comes out. If Salty says Harold Saltzmanous, there goes out the window up in smoke down the drain five thousand reward dollars.

"Everyone calls me Salty."

Pavements held his breath, imagining *The Missing Link* reward money that was going to buy Celia back disappear along with Salty into a cell at 54 Division.

"What's your last name?"

"Bacon."

"Salty Bacon. What's your dog's name?"

"Dog."

"How long have you been living down here, Mr. Salty Bacon?"

Salty pulled back the sleeve of his left arm. "Hard to know without a watch."

"How'd you get all those scars on your arm, Mr. Salty Bacon?"

Salty pulled down his sleeve.

Officer Cobbs took out his cell phone.

Salty said, "No need to phone for the dog truck. I've got some money put away. I'll buy him a tag."

Officer Cobbs snorted a chuckle. "Yeah, right. You're loaded with money. The truck will be along in a few minutes. Best you give up your dog without a fuss."

Officer Cobbs rode his bike to the street and waited for the cube van. Salty did not move. Whisper continued his wandering. The truck must have been parked around the corner because it pulled up to the curb right away. Pavements heard the dog pound truck's side door open. He recognized the driver was not Jake but Colin. Oh, oh. He looked over at Whisper, who was sniffing the breeze coming from the truck. What was that smell telling him? Dogs in cages? Tranquilizer guns? Dead dogs loaded up and hauled away? In a blur of black and white, Whisper crossed the park and disappeared.

Officer Cobbs came over, sunglasses off, waiting for the dog to come back. Colin stood next to him, waiting. No dog. The policemen straightened his back, squared his shoulders, and returned his cell phone and his sunglasses.

Pavements said, "Strike me dead. Vanished into thin air."

Pavements watched Officer Cobbs mount his bike. "Next time I come by I want those flowers gone. The bench belongs to the public. And the dog belongs in the pound."

Salty said, "Funny thing about that dog. Who knows where he went? First, he comes and there he is and then he's gone. He may never be back. He'll probably turn up somewhere else. I doubt that you'll ever see that dog again."

As the policeman set off on his bike, Salty said, "See you next round."

Pavements closed his eyes and imagined the five thousand dollars creep under his hat and back into his head.

Chapter Seventeen

Salty

Father Sutcliffe came by. "Is it okay if I join you and Whisper and Pavements on Caps's bench?"

Salty took the dog up on his knee to make room. Pavements sat in the grass.

Father Sutcliffe was staring up at the sky. "Sitting on his bench with the flowers makes me think that if I look up I will see Caps floating above the bridge, looking down."

Pavements looked up, his City Works hat tilted on one ear.

Father Sutcliffe said, "I need to have a word in private with Salty."

Salty looked up. Caps was up there, probably from the clouds watching coming down the road the fate and destiny Father Sutcliffe was here to deliver.

Pavements left.

Father Sutcliffe said, "Two detectives came by asking me if I knew anyone with scars on his arms. I said I don't know anyone with scars. Is there anything about scars, Salty, that you'd like to tell me? Remember, this park is my church. This bench is my altar. What you say to me will be held in confidence."

Salty was tempted. He was thinking, scars, too many scars, scars from all those years and all this time rolled up in the carpet I am right now kneeling on in front of that square iron box with "2020" wrote on it.

Father Sutcliffe said. "My brother drank a bottle a day until the doctor told him his liver was shot and he'd die if he didn't quit. So he did. He got himself together and solved his problems, which he had always thought unsolvable, and then he went back to the doctor and said, 'I quit and now everything's good and I feel fine.'"

Father Sutcliffe crossed one leg over the other. He reached over to scratch behind the dog's ears.

"The next week my brother died. I wrote his obituary for the newspaper, his life story summed up in one column two inches wide and four inches long. But he should have been writing it, not me. Our most important choice in life is to write our own story."

The dog stepped down off the bench and wandered off. Salty watched him sniff his way from shrub to tree to bush, reading the news of the day. He didn't need a newspaper to tell him what was going on. The events of today and yesterday and the day before came to him, carried by the currents from the past and the present and the future at each sniff.

"Helen dropped by yesterday. She said to tell you those two detectives are looking for Sylvia."

Salty was keeping an eye on the dog, making sure he didn't wander too far off.

"Sylvia is connected to one of those cold case files they're talking about. Every day another cold case file, going back years."

Father Sutcliffe was nodding his head, in agreement with himself it seemed. "Cast your bread upon the water. It will come back after many a day."

He got up to leave. "Jake asked me to talk to you about getting a tag and keeping Whisper on a leash. Jake said for him to take Whisper would be like taking somebody's kid. But if Jake doesn't take your dog, they'll fire him and Colin will and Whisper's life ends in the gas chamber."

Father Sutcliffe walked away a few steps, then he turned and said, "And these flowers. They're past their prime. Why not throw them away? I'll get you some daisies from the supermarket."

Salty looked at the roses. Daisies would suit Caps better.

***

Salty paid the money and went into Madame Kratz's little room with the door covered by the purple curtain. Salty realized for the first time that she looked the same now as she had at the Teeswater Fair. Even the chair for sitting in was the same, as though after all these years, no time had passed. Frank had been afraid of her then and would probably be afraid of her now. Salty had said, "So she dresses weird. Don't be a suck." A small word then, a big word now.

Except for one thing different, Salty noticed. Now, instead of the candle, when she sat behind her little table a hidden switch lit her up with fluorescent light as she shuffled and laid out and studied.

"You are at the cosmic axis of past and future."

She shuffled from a different deck with different pictures.

She shuffled again.

"The three forces are at this minute planning your now."

She tidied away the cards.

"Do you hear that, Salty?"

Salty listened but could hear nothing.

"It's the girl next door crying. I better go over."

Salty did not need to ask her what that meant. It wasn't the girl next door she could hear crying.

***

Father Sutcliffe came by with the daisies. He said, "Whisper is still running loose. Officer Cobbs is a man of rules, and rules can't be broken; laws must be written down and followed. This is the square dance that Officer Cobbs steps to. He wants Whisper in the pound. If the rules allowed it, he would shoot Whisper on the spot with his service revolver, or give him an on-the-spot lethal injection. Stray dogs and homeless people are the same thing for Cobbs — he wants them out of the park."

Father Sutcliffe said, "In that World War Two movie we saw, remember the Nazi captain said to the private who didn't like his boxcar job? 'The weak and the defective must go to the wall and because they are weak and defective they need help to get there.' That's who you're dealing with, Salty. He doesn't care how big you are."

Chapter Eighteen

Roof

As Detective Roof pulled up to the curb he saw Father Sutcliffe kneeling on the floor of The Daystar porch helping Beets untangle his foot from the wrong leg of his trousers.

Father Sutcliffe finished with the trousers and stood for a handshake. "Good morning Detective Roof. Good morning Detective Dickie. How can I help you today?"

Roof was not interested in pleasantries. "The man called Salty. We understand he's one of your flock. What can you tell us about Salty?"

"I am a priest. Anything one of my flock tells me is told in confidence."

"Yes I know, and this is your church." Roof stepped back, off the porch, on to the front walk for a look at the property. "It doesn't look like a church to me. It looks like a house."

"A church is a building, bricks and mortar, same as this."

"And the only time the men talk to you is in confession?"

"You might say that."

"What can you tell us about Harold Saltzmanous?"

"There is no one here that goes by that name."

"Do you know that withholding information will make you an accomplice?"

"Accomplice to what?"

"What looks like a homicide."

"What is the nature of this homicide?"

"The disappearance of Lee Ann Saltzmanous under suspicious circumstances."

Detective Dickie was rubbing his jaw, saying nothing.

Roof said, "Could we talk to some of your parishioners, Father?"

"They're all doing activities off the property. Besides, the last time you talked to one of my parishioners, he jumped off the bridge."

"Activities like drinking bootleg liquor?"

"I don't know what they do while they are not here."

Dickie continued to rub his jaw.

"Have you got a sore jaw, Officer?"

Roof answered for Dickie, "54 Division had a charity baseball game to raise funds for the homeless here in Silver Park. Dickie got hit with a line drive."

"Nice try, Detective."

Roof said, "We understand they all go by nicknames. A good way of losing their identity. Hiding, in other words."

"Protecting their identity, yes."

"And that's what you're doing?"

"I don't ask their names. The name they give is the name I use."

"I heard that the Fringe Dweller advocates — Fringe Dwellers is now the politically correct term — have a plan to house the homeless in boxcars in Silver Ravine."

"Yes, I heard that. Your friend Officer Cobbs would say they should park the boxcars at the vacant chemical factory lot at Cherry Beach."

"And what do you say, Father?"

"I am reading a book called *The Lost Sheep*. Its premise is that in human behaviour the obvious patterns explain the hidden mysteries. The mystery is why the individual is following the patterns he is following. All patterns will make sense when you solve the mystery of why that pattern. My job is to offer help in managing the patterns. Sometimes, I can give them help with the mysteries causing the patterns."

Dickie said, "I get it, Father. My friend Roof buys a new Dodge Ram pickup every year. That's a pattern that makes no sense if you live in the city and don't need a pickup the size of a boxcar for buying your sixpack. So, if you checked back, I bet you'd discover he has some mysterious cock-extension inadequacies left over from grade nine."

Father Sutcliffe smiled. "So tell me, Detective Roof, are you finding that the Dodge Ram is helping you with your problem?"

"You don't worry about my problem. You should be worrying about your problem."

As Roof turned to leave, Dickie following, Father Sutcliffe said, "Have a nice day, Detectives Roof and Dickie."

Chapter Nineteen

Salty

Salty noticed the girl crossing the open space between the two lines of lilacs and the board fence along Bridge Street. Then he noticed the Donkey Man crossing the grass towards her, the snakes tattooed on each arm swinging in time with his long, black ponytail.

The girl put her head down and hurried on. But as she attempted to walk around him, Donkey Man blocked her path. He must have said "Give me all your money," because she went through her purse and gave him what she had. Then she took off her watch and gave it to him. When she couldn't get the ring off her finger, he put it into his mouth, wetted it with spit, and yanked it off. He put the watch, the ring, and the money into his pocket and continued across the park.

***

Lunchtime at The Daystar. Salty took his seat with the rest of them: Beets next to Salty, Pavements across from Mr. Bones, Father Sutcliffe at the end with two spaces open for visitors. Indian Elvis wandered in first, followed by Donkey Man. They passed the sandwiches. They ate, nobody talking, everybody busy slurping up their soup called Cream of Notsurewhat that Father Sutcliffe made in an old-fashioned pot every morning.

Donkey Man gave Indian Elvis a poke in the ribs. "Indian sign language. Means move over, you fat pig, and give me room."

Indian Elvis shifted over and Donkey Man spread his elbows and slurped up his soup. He said, "So how's Caps's dog doing, Salty? Do sheepdogs eat sheep, Salty? Ever watch Caps with his coffee? He put in so much sugar he had to crank his spoon with two hands and when he let it go, it stood up by itself."

Donkey Man slurped up his soup. "I had a dog once. I trained it to catch dew worms for when I went fishing, the nightcrawlers, you know, big as snakes." He pointed to his bare arms, his T-shirt rolled up to show his snakes. "The dog could smell them. Elvis here knows about fishing. That's what Indians do, sell blankets and go fishing."

Donkey Man finished his soup and pushed back his chair and pulled his comb from his back pocket. He unfastened his ponytail and let his hair fall to his shoulders. He reached out and dipped his comb into Indian Elvis's water glass. He combed three strokes and then, looking Salty straight in the eye, reached out to Salty's water glass. He dipped in the comb.

Salty watched the drips of water trail across the tabletop as the comb traveled from the glass to the hair. The comb combed two or three times and then came back and dipped into the glass and then combed again, the beads of water in Donkey Man's black hair glistening in the overhead light like silver glints on a black fishing line.

Salty pushed back his chair and stood. Pavements, Mr. Bones, and Beets put down their soup spoons and shifted away.

Donkey Man returned his comb to his back pocket. "I met a nice girl in the park this morning. She told me she liked my hair. Girls like guys with nice hair. You ought to get yourself a comb and fix your hair, Salty. You ought to put on some decent clothes and clean yourself up. Look at Pavements, how nice he dresses now. He's trying to get back with his fat cow wife so he can get some pussy. Clean yourself up and you and me might be able to get some pussy. If you don't use your grapes, they wither on the vine."

Salty moved his chair aside. Father Sutcliffe came from the kitchen.

Donkey Man said, "What do you say, Salty? You get yourself cleaned up and maybe I'll have a word with that girl in the park. Maybe she likes big guys with beards. That way you wouldn't have to flog your poodle every night."

Salty knew better than to get sucked into a fight with Donkey Man, but the words came out anyway. "Give me her ring and her watch."

"I'll tell you what. If you forget about the ring and the watch, I'll forget about your dog running loose. That dog I was telling you about? He had this bad habit of humping everyone's knee. I'd invite a girl to my place and the first thing he'd do when she sat down was hump her knee. Finally, I got tired of pulling him off people's knees. So on garbage day, I put the dog in one of those big garbage cans. You can get rid of almost anything now with those big garbage cans because the driver don't need to get out of his truck. Dead dogs even, no one knows the difference. So, if you forget about the ring and the watch, I won't put your dog into a garbage can."

Father Sutcliffe held up his cell phone. "Your choice, Donkey Man. Shut the front door or I phone 911."

Donkey Man turned and left. Salty left by the back door where the dog was waiting. The dog following along at his heels, Salty went up the alley to the street where Pavements was waiting. Pavements followed Salty across the street to sit on Caps's bench. Salty saw that Pavements had fixed the daisies all around.

A city worker on a ride-around John Deere was cutting back and forth at the far end of the park. Pavements said, "I know him. His name's Merv. I could go over and ask him, if Salty and me held Donkey Man down, would he run over his legs with his lawnmower."

Salty remembered that Eli had had a John Deere tractor that he'd kept in the same field as the sheep.

Pavements said, "It wouldn't need to be a special trip. We could carry Donkey Man over to where Merv is cutting and lay him down with his legs in its path. It's got a thirty-six-inch blade that would take his legs off up to the knees."

Salty looked around and saw the girl coming across the park on her way to the library. It was like looking out a big picture window at a little girl walking across a green field.

Pavements said, "I was planning to go over anyway to ask Merv if we could nail Caps's name in beer caps along the top board of this bench."

The dog saw her. His head went up and his ears went up and Salty knew his nose was reading in the wind the little girl coming across the green field. The girl saw the dog and knelt down. The dog trotted forward and sat for a handshake. The girl stroked him and hugged him. When she got up, he followed her as far as the sidewalk.

Pavements said, "Father Sutcliffe might give us the money to buy the beer."

Salty watched two women come out of Soapy Suds Laundry carrying garbage bags which looked like they were full of clothes. The other day Pavements had done his laundry in Soapy Suds, sitting there all cleaned up reading the Bible he'd stolen from the library. Salty had felt more comfortable sitting next to the old Pavements, who used to smell like he lived in the same dumpster Salty had put Lee Ann in. It made him feel secure, knowing from the smell that she was still in there. Now Pavements's smell, like that stuff Lee Ann used for cleaning the bathtub, was making Salty nervous, like she had got out of the dumpster and come back to life to do a clean-up. And his shirt was the same colour as that blue stuff she put in the toilet before asking, would it kill you to put the toilet seat back down, Harold?

Pavements said, "I've been thinking about borrowing a shovel and digging up the dirt around the bench and planting some daisies. Then they'd come up year after year for Caps to look at, up there above the bridge, floating around in the warm sunny summer sky. How are things up there, Caps? Not too bad, Pavements. Lots of time to ponder."

The girl was standing on the sidewalk, waiting for a break in the traffic so she could cross. The dog was looking both ways; stop, look, and listen, like he was guiding her across the street the way he did for Caps. The dog crossed halfway with her and waited to make sure she reached the other side.

Chapter Twenty

Sylvia

Now all Sylvia could think about was this homeless man called Salty who had tried to catch the jumper but who had not tried to prevent her from being robbed. The crazy thing was, none of this would have happened if she hadn't been using the library on Bridge Street to research a summer school paper on Hemingway. Even crazier was that Salty looked like Ernest Hemingway. It was like some subliminal message had come from some dark corner of her brain into her mind and directed her to choose an online course on Hemingway. Some subliminal message in the library had directed her hand to a book containing photos of Hemingway, many of him standing beside the fish he'd caught. Then this subliminal messenger had directed her hand to a book with Hemingway's boxing photographs. These triggered memories of her father's flattish nose and she remembered his line, "See you next round." Sylvia did not want to see her father next round. So whether or not Salty was her father did not matter.

But when she saw Salty and the dog sitting side by side on a bench covered with daisies, a strange thing happened: she changed her mind. It was not changing her mind after thinking about it. It was a spur of the moment, no-good-reason change of direction.

She expected to see homeless men gathered around the front door of The Daystar, some passed out on the sidewalk, others leering at her from behind a tree. But there was no one outside. She knocked on the front door.

Father Sutcliffe was wearing jeans and a "Staff" T-shirt. In his right hand, he had a paperback book. He said, "Why, hello. The girl from Caps's funeral. Is that proper terminology? 'Girl?' 'Young woman' might be better."

"I think 'girl' is fine."

He led her inside. The living room, dining room, and kitchen looked neat and clean, almost homey. But there were no pictures on the walls, no end tables or plants or decorations of any sort. The floors were bare wood, no carpets or scatter rugs. His office had no plaques or bookcases or filing cabinets. The only way anyone would know it was an office was the desk with the black leather swivel chair behind it, and a plain wooden one in front. There was no way of knowing he was a priest other than his manner, which reminded her of Eli, the Mennonite farmer. In fact, everything about The Daystar reminded her of the austerity of her childhood Mennonite neighbours. With a gesture of his right hand, he invited her to sit. He pulled up the swivel chair and they faced one another.

She said, "Some long-haired homeless character with snakes covering his arms robbed me of my money, my watch, and my ring. Does he live here?"

"I know who you mean. No, he doesn't live here."

"The one they call Salty was sitting on a bench covered with flowers. He did nothing."

"It's the law of the street: avoid trouble."

"Does Salty live here?"

"He's not one of mine. I have four permanents that have managed to survive my rules, so with six bedrooms I usually have one or two available for transients. But no, Salty is not one of mine."

"What is the name of the man who robbed me?"

"One of my rules is I don't give out names. I respect everyone's right to privacy."

"The one they call Salty. He saw it happen. He might know his name."

"He might, but he won't say."

The priest leaned back in his chair and crossed one leg over the other. He asked, "Did you know Caps?"

"No. Not at all. But I was there when he jumped. It got me thinking about, you know, life, the homeless, about reaching an unhappy end."

She felt comfortable with this priest. She wanted to tell him she had this crazy idea that Salty might be her unwanted father. She said, "What can you tell me about Salty?"

Father Sutcliffe shrugged, "He comes and he goes. He stays out of trouble, minds his own business, bothers no one."

"And now he has Caps's dog."

The priest swiveled the chair half a turn from the desk, tilted himself back, and stared at the opposite wall. He said, "I watched Caps fall. Salty had his arms out for him. Caps was a skinny little guy. Salty could have caught him easily. I know the newspaper said he was blinded by the sun. But what it looked like to me, somehow in mid-flight, the dog and the man either intentionally traded places, or their places were intentionally traded, and the one to land in Salty's arms was the dog."

Sylvia thought, here comes the religion, the hand of God stuff.

She said, "He is big enough and strong enough to catch a man, but not big enough or strong enough to prevent that snake character from robbing me. He just sat there and watched."

Father Sutcliffe swiveled into a leaned forward position and placed his elbows on his desk. "If you tell me what your interest in Salty is, I might be able to help."

"I was five years old when my father abandoned me. I had no contact with him until three weeks ago. I got a message saying he was living with the homeless in Silver Park. Then, when I saw Salty, I had this feeling that it was him."

"But you think you could be mistaken."

"Yes. I probably am."

"What if you're not?"

"I don't want a homeless man for a father."

"What if he needs your help?"

"The same answer. I don't want a homeless man for a father."

Father Sutcliffe was staring at her, reminding her of the Mennonite messenger who had said, "How can you not care about your father?"

Father Sutcliffe said, "You see the wall behind me? It's blank. Look around, up and down. All the walls are blank. What answer is written on a blank wall?"

Sylvia shrugged. "I guess no answer."

"No questions. No answers."

"So you're saying that's how I should leave this father question? Blank?"

"They leave family and friends for one of two reasons: they don't want to go back, or they can't go back. Blank walls mean no judgmental slogans in this church. In this church, you are accepted for what you are, not for what someone else is suggesting you should be."

"I'm not saying he should be some other way. I'm saying I don't want him to be my father. Especially if he sat there and watched me get robbed."

"You were at Caps's funeral. Did you wonder if Caps was your father?"

"Of course not."

"But you think Salty might be. Our thoughts become our reality. Now that you've asked the question, you won't be able to let it go until you find the answer. What we ask determines what we do."

"Not always, no. I've made up my mind."

"I have noticed, twice now, that your left hand reaches up to rub along your cheek. Why is that?"

She dropped the hand. "Under the makeup is a scar. But now that you mention it, I think I just started doing it. It's from a childhood thing, memories coming back to me."

"Tell me about your childhood. Your mother, for example."

This was a question easily answered. "She died when I was five."

"Then what?"

Sylvia thought, then what? This is where this conversation should end. But, crazy thing, now that he'd gotten her started, she did not want to stop. "When I was little, the Mennonite farmer next door had a dog the same as Caps's, now Salty's. Amos, his name was, after the prophet in the Bible. Every day, I would go to the field to pet him and tell him stories — about myself, of course. I look at Salty's dog, and the way it looks back at me, I don't know, it feels like it's asking me to finish my story. I keep picturing it, me with Amos, so clearly. It feels like I've come back to that field to finish my story."

"They call him Whisper. Are your feelings coming to you like in whispers?"

"Sort of, yes. At first. But now in recollections, like Salty sits on that bench with the flowers carving with his pocket knife. A fish, I think. And I saw him one other day. He was looking at a letter and, I think, a locket."

"So you've been watching him."

"Not really. I cut across the park to the library."

"So you've been watching him."

"Well, okay, yeah. But not watching. It's more like looking at a photograph of yourself when you were little, like you're there, but not really. I know if I went up to him and looked closely, I would see through the bushy beard and the long hair and the ragged clothes that this man is a complete stranger."

"But your father is a stranger."

She nodded. "Yes, more a stranger than a father, that's for sure. My first foster father wasn't religious, but he thought I should get religious instruction, so he sent me to Sunday school. Protestant, not Catholic. It was closer. The Sunday school teacher gave every kid in the class a bedtime prayer and said that when we prayed, our guardian angel would fly up to heaven and tell God what we wanted. I believed him. I didn't have a real mother or a real father, so my guardian angel was like a mother looking after me. So every night I prayed for my father to come back. And that always made me feel better. For a while, anyway."

His eyes, full of understanding, were drawing out her story she couldn't help but finish.

"I was abandoned when I was five years old. I don't remember much, but the few things I do remember are that I wore print dresses, and my father worked in construction, and next door lived Amos the sheepdog. Every single day, I went across the field and patted Amos, and then I asked Amos if I could pat the lambs and he would bring me one.

"But my father. For a long time, the only thing I remembered about him was that he read me a story and played his guitar and he sang me this song: 'Everything's going to be alright, rock-a-bye, rock-a-bye.' He would put me on his knee and we would sing the song together with me plunking the chords: 'Everything's going to be alright rock-a-bye, rock-a-bye.'

"I got my face cut when I was five." Sylvia traced it with her finger. "I cover it with makeup so it's hard to see. My first foster parents adopted me and gave me their last name, Evans, and then they split. So, I went back into foster care. After that, no one wanted me because of the scar. It seemed to get bigger as I got older.

"I lived for a while with new foster parents. The foster mother was nice, she meant well, but was sort of phony, like the way she dressed, dyed her hair. But all their furniture was cheap and junky and I had to wear cheap, junky clothes from Walmart because she spent all the money the CA gave her on clothes for herself. That's how foster care works. They do it for the money.

"Then I lived with a lady who pretended she was my aunt. I had to call her Aunt Katie. She didn't want her neighbours to know she took in foster kids. She took me to the movies every Saturday. That was the good part. The bad part was that the apartment was on a long street of low-rise government apartment buildings, you know, like they want to build here in the Thorn. They were all dirty inside and there was garbage all over the place. There was one superintendent for every three buildings, and he didn't do anything. The little kids peed in the halls and people left their garbage all over, so there were cockroaches all over the place. That was the worst place I ever lived.

"One day, I was about nine, I think, someone told me my father lived in a little place called Cedron, so I took the bus to find him. I just sort of hung around, hoping I'd see him. There wasn't much there, just a church and one restaurant and a bowling alley. I didn't know what he would be doing there. He worked in construction. I stayed there for quite a while, wandering around, but he wasn't there so I went back home.

"Lately, I'm remembering all kinds of things. My father had a scar on his forehead. He had this way of walking, like a boxer. He'd say, 'I'll see you next round.' And he had spare change in his pocket, that's what I remember."

The words rushing out were draining her. She shifted from a slump and sat up straight. She drew one leg up underneath her. "When I climbed up on his knee, the change rattled in his pocket. He was good with his hands and liked to carve fish. 'They're always swimming upstream, like myself,' he'd say.

"I remember his strength. I remember him being big and strong, with big hands. But I was little, so that doesn't count. But mostly, I remember his eyes were soft, and... I don't know, they just were. The reason I remembered that was that they were like the eyes of the farmer next door. Eli his name was. Kids remember strange things. I guess that's why I couldn't believe he left me. There had to be a bigger reason, like caring for someone else besides me. That is what I used to tell myself. Then when I got older this changed to anger at him for never coming back."

"And that's where you are now."

With her left hand, she traced the scar.

He said, "The scar, you're reading and rereading it like Braille."

She dropped the hand. She said, "It's like I'm unzipping it, one stitch at a time, like a coat needing to be taken off and thrown away."

He said, "Or donated to a homeless man."

He said, "Or mended and put back on."

He said, "Sylvia. Why don't you just go up to him and ask him?"

"I've already thought of that. I'm a foster kid. I know how it is when an abandoned kid turns up in your life. That is when the big lies start. I know all about the little lies. I watched parents lie to social workers, and social workers lie to one another, and parents lie to each other, and all this time the child is standing there wanting nothing more than to be wanted by someone who doesn't tell lies. The little lies were bad enough. I'm not interested in getting into the big lies."

"But what if he is your father?"

"A homeless alcoholic? I know all about alcoholics. My third foster father was an alcoholic. Have a drink after a hard day. I deserve it. Have a cold beer for a hot afternoon. Have a hot toddy to take the chill off the cold night. My wife is unfaithful and my life is empty so I have a drink to take it all away. I'll have one now but not another until five-thirty. I'll take sips rather than gulps so the drink will last longer.

And so it goes, hot for the cold and cold for the hot and full for the empty, the covert agenda of the alcoholic mind. A homeless alcoholic? No thanks. I don't want to be lied to. I don't want excuses. I don't want to pretend. I don't want games."

He said, "I think, Sylvia, that the games have already started."

"No. It takes two to play. If you want to play catch, both players have to throw the ball."

She got up to leave. "I never intended to have this conversation. But thank you for listening."

He stood and offered a handshake. "You know where I live. Come back when you need me."

Sylvia did not cross through the park. She took the bridge. She did not want to see Salty.

But crossing the bridge, looking down, Sylvia noticed him sitting in the middle of the flowers, the dog lying at his feet, its head resting on front paws. For ten minutes she stood at the rail. The day was warm, the grass was green, the sun was shining, and there, like in one of those crazy Dali paintings, in this bed of flowers sat this bearded vagrant dressed in shaggy clothing being watched over by his sheepdog. Or, she thought, put a staff in his hand and add some sheep in the background and you've got something out of the King James Illustrated Bible. At the far side of the park, a man with a shopping cart was pawing in the trash bin, like a raccoon, for bottles and cans. Dali would add a sign to this painting: Please don't put your cans into your bottles.

She retraced her steps and crossed the grass and hid behind the park's only tree. She waited. A middle-aged woman in a waitress uniform crossed from Colonel Wong's Southern Fried Chinese Chicken. She stopped to pet the dog, then, without talking to Salty, continued. A middle-aged man coming from the same direction stopped and leaned over to pat the dog. He continued to the next bench. He opened a paper bag and began to throw popcorn to the squirrels.

Sylvia stepped away from the tree, intending to go back to the bridge and continue with her business. But when the dog noticed her, he took a few steps forward. His soft brown eyes searched her face and his tail wagged a friendly wag. He advanced a few feet, ears forward, waiting to be invited over. In the sun, slanting in a wide bar across the grass and settling on the dog, she could see the flecks of white in the black hair around the dog's muzzle: the dog was old. As he got closer, she saw that his eyes were brown. Her gaze met the gaze of the dog and she saw his eyes deepen. Sylvia saw that his eyes had shades of brown expanding in circles from the black of the iris. And, as in the circle of each she saw her reflection, she felt a chill up her spine. The dog lowered his head and approached. Sylvia knelt in the grass. The dog sat down and held up the paw for a handshake. They shook hands. She patted the dog. The dog rested his head on Sylvia's knee and, when the petting stopped, he looked up with eyes like two deep pools, filled with happiness for having found her at last.

No, she thought, getting up. This cannot be.

He nudged her hand. Then, he walked off a few deliberate steps closer to Salty and turned, waiting for her. She approached Salty, who was ignoring them. She took her time finding her money, glancing up from her purse to look closely at the weathered face. She had noticed that he had not lowered his eyes as the two previous visitors approached to pat the dog. They were lowered now.

The other two had not given him money. And she had never seen him standing with outstretched hand on any corner. But too late to turn around, she gave him a five. Not looking at her, he took the money. He was close enough for her to touch him, close enough to ask the question that was on the tip of her tongue. She knew when she asked it, he would look up, and she would be able to read hidden in the lines across his forehead the scar that would give her the answer. But afraid that the question would force him to lie, she did not ask it.

He sat staring down at the five-dollar bill that he held in his lap. So, too embarrassed to say anything, not even some judgmental "Hope this helps out," she turned away and left, afraid to glance back until she reached the street.

She looked back, hoping to see that he was watching her go, wondering about her. But what she saw was him folding the bill, tucking it into his shirt pocket. What she saw was the dog standing by the bench, watching her leave, ears cocked, eyes wide and expectant, tail wagging gently, like the ghost of Amos standing in a field of daisies pleading her to please come back.

Chapter Twenty-One

Salty

Salty was sitting on Caps's bench of daisies, waiting for Pavements to finish his cardio workout and open the bottle of Curveball. The dog was checking out the sunbeams along the sidewalk. When Father Sutcliffe arrived, the dog came over to give him a handshake before settling down on the grass and laying his chin on Salty's boot.

Father Sutcliffe said to Pavements, "I think the last step before twisting off the cap should be to spit on your hands and rub them together."

Pavements spit on his hands, rubbed them together, flexed his fingers, and twisted. He hoisted the bottle to glug-glug the first drink before handing it to Salty.

Pavements took out a cigarette and sailed the empty Smoke Cignals filter sidearm at the garbage bin. It bounced off the top and skipped across the grass. Father Sutcliffe got up and went over and picked it up and dropped it in. He came back. He said, "I am about to break my own rule. I am about to interfere with what is happening and give advice."

Salty passed the bottle to Pavements.

Father Sutcliffe said, "Winter is coming, Salty. Ice and snow and freezing cold. You should think about getting into that new East End Housing Program instead of living in that back-alley garage. The city is discontinuing the ID rule. If Salty is your name, then Salty is your name."

Pavements said, "By the way, I was wondering, what is your real name? All this time we've been hanging out and I don't even know your real name. Like my real name is Nelson. Last name Hynes."

Father Sutcliffe said, "You tell yourself that the back-alley garage suits you fine. It's warm enough in the winter. The window lets in the sun. The door keeps out the ice and snow. You like living where you are. But where you are living is in the shadows of the past, lost in the psychic fog of your lostness. But here's the thing, Salty: the stones in your heart that pull you down into your state of lostness are not heavier for you than for anyone else. Tim Silver, for example. He crossed the bridge. He didn't blame anyone else for his condition. He blamed himself. He said blaming your condition on anything outside yourself is like blaming your hair for being too long."

Salty said, "The East End don't allow dogs."

Father Sutcliffe said, "I'll keep Whisper at The Daystar. I'll feed him good food and keep him on a leash. Which reminds me: if you don't, you're going to lose him."

Pavements said, "Maybe Officer Cobbs should find something better to do with his time."

"Put him on a leash, Salty. What's wrong with that? Everyone's on a leash. I know what you're thinking: 'Here comes the Parable of the Leash. The Sermon from the Bench.' But you're on the shortest leash of all, Salty. The leash of your thoughts. What seems like a physical battle with your body, keeping warm in the winter, is a psychic battle with the babble in your mind, which is spending its days doing penance for what is long gone."

"What's he doing penance for?" Pavements glug glugged the Curveball.

"Tim Silver wrote the book on it. There are two bridges. There is the bridge we're looking at, and there is the bridge we've created in our mind. We're looking at both as we sit here on this bench. Our mind creates our thoughts. Thoughts become beliefs. Beliefs become facts. Victims become victims because they start believing they are victims. A self-created leash, Salty, preventing you from crossing both bridges."

"What's he doing penance for?"

"Penance, yes. I quote Tim Silver: 'From the shelters and the streets, we hear the muffled wails of hidden remorse in a penance we will never understand.' You are not a victim, Salty. That is a concept created by groupthink. If everyone is thinking alike, no one is thinking. You are free to have different beliefs and think different thoughts and make different choices. Hopelessness is a choice the same as which side of the bridge you live on is a choice."

"What's he doing penance for?"

"I quote from Tim Silver: 'We are what we think. All that we are arises from our thoughts. With our thoughts, we make our world. We are making our reality, moment by moment. We, moment by moment, are creating our own heaven and hell.'"

"I treated Celia bad and when she left me I crossed the bridge. So now I'm trying to cross the bridge back to her. What about you, Salty? What made you cross the bridge?"

Father Sutcliffe said, "A warm place to stay for the coldest months, showers, meals, TV. That would be a start."

"Just like back home with the wife in the kitchen baking the biscuits. By the way, where are you from, Salty? I mean before you crossed the bridge?"

"And real dog food for Whisper. Purina dog chow. This isn't just about you, Salty. This is about Whisper."

Pavements said, "By the way, Salty. I mean what did you do to make you cross the bridge? I've been wondering about that, like Caps. What made him cross the bridge, like the real bridge that he jumped off of? Like the first bridge, not the one in his mind, the real bridge, the one we're looking at, sitting here near the bottom of it this tastes like goat piss when you get near the bottom."

He handed Salty the bottle to finish off the goat piss.

"So, I asked Celia, 'Instead of jumping off Silver Bridge, what do I have to do to cross it and come back to you?' The way I said it was, 'What do I have to do, Celia,' as though I was on my knees. So, Salty, you could get on your knees and ask your wife the same question. 'What do I have to do...' what's your wife's name so I can say it the way you should say it."

Father Sutcliffe said, "You can't un-jump a jump. But you can un-choose a choice. First, this girl with the scar appears in the park, and then she comes over to The Daystar to see me, and now it's time for you to make a choice."

As he finished the bottle, Salty was realizing that the reason Dixie called it Curveball was the way the high-octane sediment at the bottom hit you without you seeing it coming. Sometimes it made your head spin. Sometimes it made you feel like an egg being boiled. Otherwise, Salty would not have said, out loud out of the blue, the words coming to him like a curveball and hitting him unexpected in a complete surprise splat that took him off down memory lane to Rhoda on that stump.

He said, "I killed a chicken once. Her name was Rhoda. There was blood all over the place. Halfway through the swing of the axe, I changed my mind. That was a choice. But I chose too late. Down came the head of the axe and off came the head of the chicken. The chicken got up off the ground and ran off, squawking and flapping."

"Into the house?" asked Pavements.

"That's right, Salty. Just like it was too late to stop the axe, it was too late to save the chicken. You can't un-time time and you can't un-chop a chop."

"Blood all over the place," said Salty.

"In the house?" asked Pavements.

"That's why I never eat ketchup."

"Tim Silver has a chapter on memories. Not past and not long gone but here and present, that's how we're tied to our memories. Memories are like those black squirrels." Father Sutcliffe pointed. "Memories hunt for what's buried in your mind like squirrels hunt for what's buried in the grass."

Pavements said, "Celia says she got squirrels in her attic. She lives on the top floor of this house and she can hear them up there all night long. They're giving her nightmares."

Father Sutcliffe said, "Once they get into your attic, namely your mind, you can't get rid of them. They gnaw holes into your heart, dig up old wounds, carry them from one bad branch to the next, busy and black, creating your Silver City nightmare."

"I said to her, 'That's why we should get back together, so I can look after you. My wife's name is Celia. What was your wife's name, Salty?"

Father Sutcliffe stood. He said to Pavements, "Sometimes, Pavements, you don't know when to shut the front door."

"Yeah, Father. I know. Shut the fuck up."

Pavements got up and headed at a tilt in the direction of Dixie's Donut Shoppe.

The dog was watching the squirrels coming down from the tree to search busy and black in the grass. Salty liked to watch the dog chase them away from Caps's daisies. The dog would sink down on his belly a few feet from the bench, chin resting on front paws, and wait. It was like he had put up an imaginary fence around the bench, and if a squirrel crossed the line, the dog's head would come up. The squirrel would stop, one eye on the daisies, the other on the dog. They would eye one another. If the squirrel crossed the line, the dog would get up and the squirrel would go back to the tree.

Sometimes, lying awake in the dark of night, Salty could hear the dog whine, and Salty would look and he would see that the dog's legs were twitching in his sleep. Salty figured that if your dog was a pointer its dreams would be about pointing, and if it was a retriever its dreams would be about retrieving. So, he knew the dog was dreaming about guarding the sheep, chasing those thin white legs, dodging between hammering hooves as he herded them home for the night.

Eli had told Salty how sheepdogs hypnotize the sheep. The dog senses when one is going to wander and the dog lowers its head and fixes its eyes on that one sheep and locks it in a stare so it will not wander into danger. So this dog, who must be Amos but can't be Amos, when he arrived at Silver Park, had seen how Caps's eyes were clouding over, and had locked Caps in his stare so he would not wander into danger. And after Caps, this dog who must be Amos but can't be Amos, had seen that Salty's eyes seemed to be clouding over and had locked Salty into his stare so, as he wandered through the park and up the streets and along the alleys, he would not fall into danger.

Salty had seventeen fish on his shelf, seventeen apologies to Frank. But the one chance he had got to carve an apology to Sylvia, his eyes had clouded over, not so much that he couldn't see her crossing the park grass from the field grass. He had watched her dig through her purse for her five-dollar admission into his life. She had paid her money and gotten her ticket and he should have let her come through his door and let her take a seat in his heart, if that was what she wanted.

But he knew he could not let that happen. He could not let her in, for there she would be, like one of those black squirrels having gnawed her way into his skull to dig up long-buried memories and lay them in front of him to look at while she stared at him through the upside-down eye of that chicken.

It's a long way down, said Caps, rising from the daisies to take a seat next to Salty. It takes a long time. The three-second drop from the bridge to the dirt is like months if you're a chicken, years if you're a person. It's been a long run and it's taken a long time for the number 2020 to come up, but now it's here.

Chapter Twenty-Two

Pavements

Pavements was sitting on Caps's bench, enjoying the afternoon sunshine and the smell of the fresh-laid daisies, which were covering the smell, worse than goat piss, of his almost-empty bottle of Kawasaki hidden under his shirt.

Celia came by. She handed him a notepad. "This will fit into the same pocket you carry your cigarettes in."

He slipped it into the same pocket as his cigarettes.

She said, "You've been dressing better and smelling better. But if you're serious about getting back together, I have to see you're making the effort. I want you to write down in your notebook the places you've applied for work. And not with any paving company."

"Aren't you going to ask me what I've been reading in the Bible?"

"Take out the pad and write on the top of the cover page: 'Jobs.'"

He did it.

"You put the date at the top of the next page and print the heading: 'Jobs.' This is your application list. Write it up every morning and then stroke it off when you've done it. And then show me."

"Aren't you going to ask me what I've been reading in the Bible?"

"I can't imagine anyone stealing a Bible." She hurried away. She turned and came back. "I will apologize to the library for you. No normal, intelligent person would steal a Bible."

That was true. He'd never read in the paper or seen on the news about anyone stealing a Bible.

As soon as Celia was out of sight, Pavements finished off the Kawasaki and got up and crossed the street to Dixie's Donut Shoppe. He came back and made space for himself among the daisies. He took a long pull from his new bottle.

Pavements had figured from what he read in the Bible that a guy who killed his wife would not be up there. He'd be down there. Sure enough, when he looked, Caps was staring up at him like he hadn't died yet. Well, his eyes looked like he was brain-dead but that was like always.

"How you doing down there, Caps?"

Pavements figured these words would get carried through the roots of the grass to Caps like words got carried on the 1-800 telephone wires to Richard in Malaysia.

Feeling the tickle in his ear, Caps would answer, "Cosy."

"I'm feeling a little bad, Caps. I didn't mean for you to jump. All I did was, you know, tell them your name, but I figured they'd feel sorry for you because you're blind. They don't put blind people in jail. At least, I never heard of a blind person being put in jail."

Caps said, "I was planning to die anyway."

"I wish you hadn't. Especially now, since I started reading the Bible. I don't know. But I guess if I get the reward money it will be worth it. In the Bible, it says you deserve what you get if you kill your wife. So, I guess I deserve the reward money I get for you killing your wife. What good's it going to do you? By the way, is there anyone down there you could ask if Lee Ann is Salty's wife, since she's dead too?"

"I'll ask around. By the way, what's the matter with your foot?"

Pavements's eyes blinked open. He blinked again and into focus standing in front of him were two bicycle riders. Pavements did not recognize the first. The other one, Officer Cobbs, was standing with one boot on Pavements's foot.

Officer Cobbs said, "This is Officer Hill, Pavements."

Officer Hill said, "Those are nice new shoes you're wearing. Almost as shiny as Officer Cobbs's."

Pavements sat straight. He picked up his hat from the grass and said, "My wife Celia picked them up for me. The cargos too, they got good pockets for me to carry my notebook in. I write down the names of where I've applied for work. Sometimes I write down stuff I read in my Bible so I can read it back to myself."

Officer Cobbs said, "Like what?"

"It's always stuff about wilful idleness and lack of self-discipline and the lump of clay I need to get my fingers into, start shaping my new self. Get my hands into myself, into the dough, and start framing the man hiding in the sticky, stodgy mud of sloth and get saved by Jesus Hallelujah."

Officer Cobbs said, "Praise the Lord."

Officer Hill said, "That notepad is leather. Mine is almost the same." Officer Hill took it out and Pavements compared the two.

"My wife Celia gave it to me. We're planning to get back together so I can go to college."

"What college would that be?"

"That's what I've been pondering. First, we get an apartment. I'm writing up a list of new furniture. Where Celia lives now is a dump. It's got squirrels in the attic."

Officer Cobbs said, "You figure if you make up some kind of bullshit story you won't have to go into a shelter. Is that it?"

Officer Hill said, "How do you like our nice new balloon-tire bikes, Pavements?"

Pavements got up for a closer look. "My sister had one like this."

Officer Hill said, "They're mountain bikes, good for riding in parks."

Pavements said, "My sister's was a CCM with whitewall tires like in those old Coke commercials."

"How would you like me to help you fill out the homeless shelter application?"

"Thank you for the offer but, in fact, I haven't told anyone yet, I've got my application in for fall admission at the college of my choice to further my studies. I think UCLA, but keep it a secret for now."

Officer Cobbs said, "Time is running out, Pavements. The Outreachers from the Light for the Lost are being moved over to East Jesus as we speak. The Daystar is next on the list. So, save your bullshit for your bottle-baby friends. One of the East Jesus shelters is where you're going."

Officer Hill said, "There are lots of different programs over there. You'll qualify for one of them. You could probably get your own balloon-tire bike."

"My sister's was a three-speed. This sucker you're driving is a ten-speed. See how the links go from here to here, flipping back and forth? You change the gears with these two things. My sister couldn't get the hang of it and she had only one shifter."

Officer Hill said, "I'm wondering, Pavements, out of curiosity, a lot of the Silver City residents don't want to move to shelters. Why is that?"

Pavements slanted his City Works hat a little lower against the sun. "I studied the problem of shelters in my UCLA Advanced Thinking program last semester. Examining relationship networks among the Outreacher subspecies of the Homo sapiens populations when rehoused. I'm having it published in my own registered words."

Officer Cobbs said, "You're not allowed to call the homeless a subspecies. You call them 'Fringe Dwellers' now."

Pavements said, "Here is what my study found: There are too many rules, and too many people living all in one place. You have to get in the supper line to eat and get in the toilet line to piss and get in the bed line to sleep on a mattress that's been farted into fifty times every night. And every room is filled with snot and coughing and the last time I stayed there someone stole my shoes."

Officer Hill said, "That is valuable information, Pavements. I think you might be a reliable source of information to help me better understand the men I will be working with."

"Which reminds me," Pavements glanced around to make sure no one else was nearby. He stepped a little closer to Officer Cobbs who, bending down, turned his ear to catch every detail. "Talking about information. I'm the one who gave you guys the information leading to... You know. When do I get my money?"

"For what?"

"For Caps."

"What about Caps?"

"It says in the book. Five thousand dollars reward."

"What book?"

"The book on missing links, about suspected murderers who disappeared."

"What suspected murderers?"

"Like Caps. I'm the one."

"The one what?"

Pavements raised his voice a notch. "Fuck me, Officer Corncob. Can't you read? At the back of the book, it says there's a reward for any information leading to an arrest of any missing link and to the solving of the crime."

"What crime?"

"Fuuuck me."

Officer Hill said, "He means *The Missing Link* book. I was glancing through that book the other day. So, who else in Silver City is a missing murderer?"

Officer Hill took out his notebook and pencil, ready to copy down Pavements's information. This was like working undercover. They should be in an alley or behind a pillar in the underground parking. Pavements took a quick look around to make sure there was no one passing by. He took out his notebook and pencil, printed a name, and handed it to Officer Hill.

Pavements said, "Her name is Lee Ann Saltzmanous. It shows pictures of blood on the wall. Here is some new information — are you ready for this? The blood in the house is chicken blood. If they're thinking murder, on account of the blood, that is chicken blood."

"How long ago was this murder?" asked Officer Cobbs.

"Fuuuck me. How long ago was the murder? You can DNA stuff from a hundred years ago, Billy the Kid's DNA off his toothbrush from the hotel he stayed at in 1870."

Officer Hill was writing it down. "Who told you it's chicken blood?"

"I've got sources. I know more than you think. Her husband is the missing link. There's blood but no body. What they don't know is that the blood belonged to a chicken. But back then DNA testing was not as good as now. So, all the facts about the case they put together back then are wrong. That is why it went cold."

Officer Hill was writing it down. "What else can you tell us?"

"Nothing, until I get my reward money."

Officer Cobbs said, "What reward?"

"Fuuuck me." Pavements glanced at Officer Hill. "Who is this motherfucker you got working for you? If he's going to work with me down here in Silver Park, he needs to get rid of the cool and put in the smarts." To Officer Cobbs he said, "In the back of the book, Moron."

Officer Hill said, "Pavements is right. I've read the book. There's reward money for information on any of the cases in *The Missing Link*. Yes. I remember the name, Lee Ann Saltzmanous. She is one of them. Well done. We'll look into it, Pavements."

Pavements watched them pedal away. They drove up to the street and across the bridge, on their way to the station to look up cold case files and then contact the RCMP and tell them about the chicken blood. Oh boy. The first five thousand is almost here. The second five thousand on its way.

Pavements finished his bottle of Kawasaki. He was feeling pleased with himself. Pavements got up and crossed the street for another one. He drank half of it in the alley. He returned to the bench. He stared at the bridge, floating up there. It was like sitting in a pew in an empty church with nothing else to look at, except — not Jesus hanging on the cross, that was for sure — but Caps hanging off the handrail. He was so sure it was Caps that he got up and walked up the ravine to the middle of the bridge. Then, when he looked down, he saw that Caps was lying on the ground in a patch of daisies. So then, he had to go back down to check it out, but there were no daisies. Instead, there was a door there where Caps had landed.

Pavements got down on his knees. "Knock, knock. Are you down there, Caps?"

Caps opened the door. "How you doing, Pavements? What can I do for you?"

"What's it like down there, Caps?"

Caps opened the door wider.

Strike me dead, thought Pavements, as he toppled over into the dirt and passed out.

Chapter Twenty-Three

Salty

Tuesday. Lunchtime at The Daystar. Salty was sitting across the table from Pavements, Mr. Bones and Beets. Father Sutcliffe was sitting at the end where he always sat. The Donkey Man elbowed his way in between Mr. Bones and Pavements, almost knocking Beets off his chair.

"How come they don't have glass Ketchup bottles?" The Donkey Man poured the ketchup over his fries and his meat patty and then reached across the table to pour ketchup over Pavements's fries and meat patty. He ran his finger around the rim of the plastic bottle and licked the ketchup off his finger.

Father Sutcliffe explained it the same as the last time the Donkey Man had asked: "The seven commandments of The Daystar. No alcoholic beverages, no weapons, no fighting, no stealing, no shouting, no mirrors, and no glass bottles."

"Why no mirrors?" asked Donkey Man. "What if I want to fix my hair?"

"Fix your hair some other place."

"What's the matter with glass ketchup bottles?"

"Too many fights ended up with broken ketchup bottles as weapons."

"I like my ketchup in a real bottle. How come you never eat ketchup, Salty? Everyone eats ketchup, so why don't you?"

The Donkey Man hunched over his plate and shoveled in the fries. Salty watched the Donkey Man's long hair swing forward into the ketchup.

The Donkey Man said, "Some of these nose-pickers, that's all they eat is ketchup."

Something about the ketchup spread out over the Donkey Man's plate reminded Salty of blood on that stump. Or was it that the meat patty under the ketchup reminded him of Lee Ann serving those same kinds of frozen meat patties that she covered with ketchup? Or was it something about the ring and the watch the Donkey Man stole off that girl? That must have been the one that got him started. "Your hair is in the ketchup."

The Donkey Man unfolded his paper napkin.

"If you wear your hair like a girl, you got to eat like a girl."

The Donkey Man wiped off the ketchup.

"Girls sit up straight so their hair doesn't hang into the ketchup," said Salty.

The Donkey Man stopped wiping at his hair. He picked up the ketchup and poured it over Salty's fries. Then he stood and reached over and pulled a hair from Salty's head and shook it over Pavements's plate. He added some ketchup. "Ketchup goes good with head lice." He dropped the hair onto Pavements's fries and ketchup and sat down.

Salty looked at Pavements's plate. It was round like a tree stump, patterned around the edges with little markings, now partly covered with ketchup. A line of red drops trailed from the cuff of Salty's shirt across the plastic tablecloth away from the stump and across the yard and up the lane. He'd scrubbed the stump and cleaned up the mess so Sylvia didn't get into it. He'd made sure she was in the house so she would not see him doing it.

Salty slid his chair away from the table. He wiped the ketchup off his shirt and then rolled his sleeve up. He had begun to roll up the other sleeve when he noticed that ketchup was smeared over the crisscrossed scars along the inside of his arm. He stopped rolling, and minutes passed as he remembered the scars.

The Mennonite farmer, Eli, had owned a Standardbred. Its mane was long and straight and shone in the sunlight of the lane. Its eyes, round and soft, had followed Salty's flat-palmed hand as he'd brought up one of the pieces of carrot that Sylvia had taken from the refrigerator but was too afraid to come close and give to the horse.

Salty had stroked the neck of the horse, smooth and soft as velvet. When it had turned its head and nudged Salty's chest, he'd run his hand along the soft neck to the shoulders of the horse. Salty had looked over at the girl sitting on the porch step watching him, waiting to see if he would let her feed the carrot to the horse. Salty had taken Sylvia's hand and led her close to the horse. He'd placed the carrot in the palm of her hand, which wasn't much bigger than the piece of carrot. The horse had lowered its head to the hand and, with lips gentle so as not to scare the little girl, had taken the carrot.

Salty stood. He saw Pavements and Mr. Bones slide their chairs back and move out of the way. He saw Father Sutcliffe watching from the kitchen doorway. He saw Caps's dried up bones stand up in his coffin and shift his chair back from the table and take his place, tall and straight, next to Mr. Bones. Salty saw five-year-old Sylvia sitting on the porch step waiting for her father, big as a grizzly bear, who, with one swing of his grizzly bear paw, would destroy the Donkey Man who had stolen her ring and watch.

Salty saw that they were all lined up along the wall waiting for the force that was Salty to step around the table and hoist the Donkey Man overhead and throw him off the bridge, like in the King Kong movie they'd watched the day before in the St. Luke's basement.

Salty said, "I think you should give back her ring and her watch and her money, with interest."

Salty watched Donkey Man's scowl trying to follow his memory backwards to what he might have spent that money on.

Salty said, "I can see by the look on your face that you don't remember what you spent that money on."

The Donkey Man said, "I can see by the look on your face that if you don't want the sheepdog to end up in the dumpster you should mind your own business."

Salty was looking over at the unscarred girl, Sylvia, watching him, waiting to see what he would do next. Then Father Sutcliffe stepped up. "Either shut the front door, Donkey Man, or I'll phone 911."

Donkey Man left. Salty turned away. He left the room and went out onto The Daystar porch and sat on the step.

Father Sutcliffe came out and sat with Salty.

Salty said, "I took my daughter to McDonald's and got her one of those cardboard Ronald McDonald hats. She liked to put ketchup on her McDonald's."

"Do you want to talk about your daughter?"

"I'm not much of a talker."

"I'm not much of a listener. But I might make an exception. Just this one time."

Salty said, "I'm not much of an advice taker. But I might make an exception just this one time."

Chapter Twenty-Four

Pavements

Pavements was sitting on his bench with his bottle of Curveball. He was at that spot between not-too-sober and not-too-drunk that he got after the bottle was one-third gone, just before the goat piss near the bottom. He was feeling good about himself and about how things were working out. He was wearing his blue cargos and a dinner jacket that Celia had gotten for him with a big inside pocket and leather patches on the elbows. Celia had picked it up at the Second Hand, the same day she got the red shirt with a matching blue tie. Pavements figured that with his City Works hat slanted across one eye he must look like an undercover RCMPCIA agent.

He was thinking, *The Missing Link* says the source of the information, that would be me, Pavements, would never be revealed. Come forward, it said, give your information, and collect your money.

But there was still no money.

Pavements had seen how Salty backed away from the Donkey Man, who wasn't much bigger than Pavements. Standing there, twice as big as the Donkey Man, Salty looked like that big kid in grade six who was afraid of everyone, even Pavements. But it wasn't the Donkey Man Salty was afraid of. It was the cops.

Pavements found Officer Cobbs by the bridge questioning Mr. Bones about where the bootleg homebrew was coming from: "...and don't say the Coca-Cola Reserve. There's no such place." Pavements motioned for Officer Cobbs to step aside, out of earshot, behind the tree, for a private conversation.

"I got you a hair from Salty."

"A hair? What for?"

"Didn't you tell them about the chicken blood?"

"What chicken blood?"

"In the kitchen."

"What kitchen?"

"Remember? We were talking about DNA testing? I got you a hair from Salty." Pavements held it up. It was a good one, about 6 inches long.

Officer Cobbs frowned.

"To see if he's the missing link."

"Right. A missing link." Officer Cobbs extended his hand, palm up.

But when Pavements dropped in the hair, Officer Cobbs looked like he'd been given one of those slimy white bugs that lived squirming under a rock.

He said, "It's all slimy and sticky. What're you giving me?"

Pavements was losing patience. "It's evidence. Do I have to do your job for you? Put it in one of them sealed bags."

Officer Cobbs placed it on a leaf he found in the grass.

"So now I want the reward money for this hot tip, plus witness protection: a new identity, and relocation to Florida. Haha, just kidding. But not about the reward money. I want it in cash delivered undercover to my suite at The Daystar."

Officer Cobbs was staring at the hair like a girl holding a dead worm.

"Remember, the back of the book says five thousand dollars for information."

"Right. Five thousand dollars."

"And witness protection, new identity, relocation to Florida. Haha, just kidding."

"Good as done." Officer Cobbs tucked the leaf away in his pocket and rode off.

***

Pavements had settled himself on Caps's bench when the girl came up to him and said outright, "Does Salty live in Silver City?"

Pavements moved some daisies and shifted himself to give her room to sit. She shook her head. He said, "Only the Outreachers live in Silver City now. The Fringe Dwellers got moved."

"Which ones are they?"

"In the paper, they call them all Fringe Dwellers. But they're two different species. The raggedy ones you see hanging around and going through the garbage are throwbacks from the cave days. They have opposable thumbs like the Fringe Dwellers, but bigger jawbones which is why they eat out of the garbage. They used to eat roadkill but that caused traffic jams."

He took a long pull from his Curveball.

"Why aren't they in shelters?"

"They can't be house-trained. They have to live free-range."

"Anyone can be house-trained."

"They can't tell time on a clock. That's why the church people put in the sundial." He pointed to it, three benches over. "Like in the Cave Days."

"Anyone can be house-trained and anyone can tell time."

"That's people you're talking about. I'm a university graduate of Caveman Studies. The Outreachers are like a subspecies. Their ancestors were the ones that ate nothing but meat so they were slower to become people. Our ancestors ate vegetables so we became people."

When the girl gave a bit of a smile, Pavements saw that one cheek didn't match the other cheek. It looked like she had a scar there on one side. He remembered reading in *The Missing Link* something about the daughter of Lee Ann Saltzmanous having had a cut cheek. He was going to ask her about it when she said, "Do you eat your vegetables?"

"I do."

"Does Salty?"

"Salty, yeah, he looks like Captain Caveman, like he was frozen for a million years and then unthawed. But he eats his vegetables."

Her smile disappeared and the scar disappeared. "What's his real name?"

"That's what I'm trying to figure out." Pavements looked around to make sure they were private. "I'm working with the RCMPCIA, infiltrating the homeless camps as an undercover agent." He showed her his notebook. "Mostly now I go around observing and making notes in this RCMPCIA notebook in my own registered words."

She moved the daisies and sat down beside him. "So what have you found out about Salty?"

"That's all written up in my confidential police reports in my own registered words. But it's confidential."

"I understand. But I was wondering, what is Salty's real name? I think I remember him from somewhere."

"That is confidential. We're doing DNA testing. I should know in a few days. I will be writing it up in my registered report in my own registered words, but since it's an ongoing..."

"I know. Investigation of the homeless."

"That's the thing. They're not all homeless. Some are Fringe Dwellers, but doesn't matter, they all have families who might have useful information."

The girl said, "I guess. But how they live now, in groups, the group must be their family."

Pavements nodded. "Exactly. That is how they survived in the cave days. Like herd animals that live in groups, or ducks that live in flocks."

"I know. Living in nomadic groups looking out for one another."

"Exactly. Nomadic. The city moved most of the benches to the other side of the park so they'd stay in one spot and not wander so much. That idea didn't work because they still came over to this side because there's better garbage here. The other day I tripped over one sleeping next to that garbage can over there. He'd been lying there so long the squirrels were taking shortcuts across him to the other side."

"Well, he was having a long nap."

Pavements liked this girl. She seemed interested in his investigation. "The Outreachers, most of them got no teeth, that's how you tell an Outreacher. They hang out behind Soapy Suds and sit there in the bare dirt drinking Curveball and picking fights to see who's boss. That's a top dog in the doghouse thing, like all herd animals."

Sylvia was nodding her agreement. "I think some of these men are hiding out from the law. Fugitives from justice. Is Salty one of those?"

"I can't say, names are being withheld so the press don't get hold of it and give out an important clue. For example, and you might find this off-putting, some of them got toe fungus from never washing their feet. That might be an important clue. You test a sock for DNA and you find the toe that was in that sock had toe fungus and then…"

"I know, swab the toe for DNA fungus and then look up and see whose toe it belongs to."

"But first you have to ask around to see who has toe fungus."

"Wow, yeah, that would be written in your registered report. Change of topic. Do you know the name of the younger one with the long hair? He doesn't look like he's homeless."

"He goes by the name Donkey Man. I think that's his last name. Donkeyman, like Hoofman, Postman. But everyone calls him the Donkey Man."

When she showed a bit of a smile, that one side of her face twisted up in a half-moon curve.

She said, "Thank you. It's been nice talking with you."

***

Celia came by. "What have you got on your tie? It looks like ketchup."

Pavements held up the tie. He rubbed at the stain, but this smeared it into a blotch.

"You can't go looking for work wearing a tie with ketchup on it. And there's ketchup stains on your new pants."

This ketchup had hardened enough that she could pick it off.

He said, "I've got a line on a job. Not laying pavement. Building condos. They need guys who can work long hours. I said, 'I'm your man!' I used to lay pavement. I know all about long hours."

Celia closed her eyes, which she sometimes did when she was asking Jehovah for patience. Like counting to ten.

"When do you start?"

"Any day now you'll come by and I will have a mitt full of cash and we can go together to find a place that don't have squirrels in the attic and buy some decent furniture, like, I've been looking through *Better Homes and Gardens*, like that."

Celia sighed. "Good for you, Nelson. At least you're trying."

Chapter Twenty-Five

Pavements

Pavements was sitting with Father Sutcliffe and his buddy, Roger, in The Daystar laundry room. Father Sutcliffe had poured the coffee. Roger, who used to work at the Sally and then at the Outreach and then at East Jesus and now at the rehab in the Rose, leaned his elbows on the table and rested his chin on his hands. Roger had a bald head and some reddish-brown chin hair hanging down like the frayed end of a rope, long enough that he could pull on it as he was getting ready to say something. First, his head would tilt back and his half-shut eyes would start to flutter, and then his right hand would come up to give the pull on the rope that would lean him back in his chair and make him say, "I've been thinking."

His T-shirt spreading out wide at the bottom to cover his belly that bulged out when he leaned back in his chair, he said, "I've been thinking. My friend Pavements is trying to cross the bridge. He's got Celia working with him. But she says he's got to get a job."

Father Sutcliffe stirred his coffee, not saying anything.

Roger leaned further back in his chair. "I've been thinking. The men down here, they sit in the park and look up and see the bridge hanging across the sky. Everyone down here has burned their bridges. That is their last one."

Roger stretched out his legs.

"But not Pavements. He's determined to cross the bridge. I've been talking with Pavements about it. I told him there is only one bridge that will never be burned. That bridge is Jesus."

Roger folded his arms over his belly. "One day, years ago, a drunk Roger fell down the stairs. This fall resulted in a scar on his lower lip."

Roger pulled back his lips for everyone to see. "I had tried Catholicism, Protestantism, Nothingism, and finally Alcoholism. It was while I was lying, head down, at the bottom of the stairs that I met Jesus. From that day on, nothing has weighed on my mind except how to save people like my friend Pavements."

Roger pulled at the frays of his rope. "I've been thinking. Did I tell you, I've taken the job in the Rose? Why? This area is going to be taken over by the Silver Park cleanup. They've already turned off the power to Light for the Lost."

"There must be a message in there somewhere," said Father Sutcliffe.

Pavements said, "My wife Celia is a Jehovah's Witness. She was telling me that this park cleanup is the beginning of God's final cleanup before Jesus comes back."

Roger said, "That is true. I'll tell you why. The drunks in the Rose aren't any different than over here in the Thorn. The Rose drunks have wheels and gadgets and coloured trinkets and everyone is a prince or a princess in a fairy-tale life with a thousand things to amuse themselves with, like a thousand chickens chasing a thousand mechanical bugs. A drunk is a drunk no matter what side of the bridge he lives on. The drunks in the Rose smell better though. Like Pavements. What is that you're wearing, Pavements?"

"Celia got it for me."

Father Sutcliffe said, "We should get some for Beets. He's been barred from the library."

"Anyway, I didn't come here to tell you about drunks in the Rose. A girl named Sylvia came into my new office and asked if I knew Salty. She was wearing nice perfume. Not strong, mind you. But I liked the fragrance. She wasn't wearing makeup other than a sort of cheek blush. I wouldn't have thought about it except for the perfume. I looked again and I saw the blush stuff was covering a scar, which made me think of my scar which made me think of that fall down the stairs. I said, 'Yes, I know Salty.' She said, 'No, I mean his real name.'"

Pavements said, "The same girl's been asking me. I'm sitting in the park and she comes up to me and says, 'Do you know Salty,' and I says, 'Yeah,' and she says, 'What's his real name?'"

Father Sutcliffe asked, "What is his real name?"

Roger said, "I had a summer job doing the Strongman Hammer. In September and October, we'd do the fall fairs around Dundalk, Markdale, that area. We'd say, 'Oh, oh, close down for lunch. Here comes Harold Saltzmanous.'"

"Are you certain they said Harold Saltzmanous?"

"I think they said 'Harold.' I'm not a hundred percent certain."

"But that doesn't mean Salty is Harold Saltzmanous."

"No, it doesn't. But the booth next door was the fortune teller, Madame Kratz. Harold and his little brother liked to visit her, not to get their fortunes read but because she showed them magic tricks. She called him Salty."

Pavements was out the door and on his way to call *The Missing Link* 1-800 number on the library telephone.

Chapter Twenty-Six

Salty

The dog had found the lost sheep Salty, and then the dog had found the lost lamb, Sylvia. He had brought her to him, and now Salty, sitting on Caps's bench staring at the bridge running between what had happened and what would happen, unable to go back and unable to go forward, saw no direction at all.

The dog climbed into his lap. Salty hugged the dog's warmth against himself. He stroked his head and scratched behind his ears. When the dog rolled over, Salty gave him his daily chest rub, the dog lying upside down, staring up at him. In the dog's eyes, Salty could see the same design of circles he saw on that stump as he tried to scrub it clean. He could see Madame Kratz in the centre of the circles saying, "One night, Salty, you will wake up and you will hear the crunch of the policeman's boots in the gravel outside your window, and then you will hear the knock of the policeman's fist on your door. One then two, next comes three, in that order, Salty, each pointless day dragging you closer to dumpster 2020."

Salty was not surprised when he heard the crunch of boots in the gravel outside his shed and he was not surprised when he glanced out the window and saw two policemen on bicycles and he was not surprised when he heard the knock of the policeman's fist on the door. But he was surprised to see Jake.

Salty said, "How's it going, Jake?"

Officer Cobbs said, "Jake is going to find your dog a good home."

Salty glanced at Jake, who had walked right in and sat on the couch and was patting the dog. Officer Hill was looking out the window. Those two didn't seem interested in taking the dog.

Officer Cobbs pointed. "That dog's got to go to the pound. I told you that before."

Salty stood next to the door. When Officer Cobbs reached down to take the dog, it slipped under the workbench. When Salty opened the door and called the dog, Officer Cobbs stuck his foot in the way, almost hitting the dog with his boot.

"If I was you," said Salty, "I'd be careful what I was doing with that boot."

This time, when Officer Cobbs reached for the dog, Salty shoved the policeman away, almost knocking him over.

Officer Cobbs got his balance and squared his shoulders. "Assaulting an officer, Salty. I can take you in for that. But I won't if you give up the dog. No more trouble."

Salty was bigger than both of the policemen. He was not afraid of Cobbs's billy, which he had unfasted from his belt. Then Jake stepped forward. "Me and Officer Hill have been talking about this dog. I told him this used to be Caps's dog. I've been saying, maybe we can make an exception for this dog the way they do for dogs in nursing homes. They're called comfort dogs."

"I've been saying," said Officer Cobbs, "a dog is a dog and this one belongs in the pound."

Officer Hill sat on his heels and studied the dog. "I took my daughter to the sheepdog trials once. These are amazingly smart dogs." He removed his hat. "The law is the law, I know that. But from what Jake tells me, this is an unusual dog. And from what Father Sutcliffe has been telling me, he would qualify as a comfort dog. I think maybe with this dog we can make an exception, not because it's a seeing-eye dog or a comfort dog, but because it's an unusual dog."

Cobbs said, "The law doesn't make exceptions; the rules are the rules. Where would human progress be without rules? They're made for a reason. Otherwise, we'd all behave like animals. No exceptions, Salty. Give up the dog."

Jake said, "To tell you the truth, I don't want to take the dog. Taking someone's dog is like taking someone's kid. I've got a leash in the truck. Promise me you'll keep him on a leash, Salty, and you'll be alright. If you don't, I've got no choice. I've got to take him away. It's the law. If I don't follow the law, I lose my job. Maybe I've lost it already."

He glanced at Officer Cobbs.

Jake left and returned in a few minutes with the leash.

Officer Hill said, "But you've got to go down to city hall and register the dog, name, address, whatever they want. Use the The Daystar address. But don't give them a phony name, because they'll check."

Jake left. Salty heard the whirring of the motor as his van drove away. Officer Hill went around to the driver's side of his bicycle and climbed on and pedaled away. Having no choice, Officer Cobbs followed.

Salty stretched out on his cot. He felt like he was teetering on his 2020 tightrope like Caps on the bridge railing. Many things weigh on your mind, Father Sutcliffe would say. You have a choice to let them weigh you down or let them float away. Imagine the weight of an iron ship, yet it floats on water.

Salty thought, imagine the weight of Dr. Reed's rowboat, yet here it is floating on the water in my brain. Imagine the weight of an iron dumpster 2020, yet here it is floating on the waters in my mind.

Salty got up and started off down the alley, leaving the dog behind. The Outreachers were being routed out of Silver City so now they were hanging out at the end of the alley, and there was no telling what they would do to the dog. But Salty wanted to find a bigger box for the dog to sleep in. After weeks of easy living, he had gained a little weight. Along the alley which ran behind the stores and down the lanes to Bridge Street, Salty searched. Late that afternoon he found a cardboard box, almost big enough for a doghouse. He dragged it to the shed and cut a hole in one side for a door. Several times he put the dog inside but each time he jumped out again. Maybe he liked the other box better.

***

Salty was sitting on Caps's bench, listening to the hum of the back-and-forth traffic on the bridge, reminding him of what's coming down the road. Father Sutcliffe had brought fresh daisies but had said no to Pavements's idea of putting a fence around the bench and planting a daisy garden. Salty noticed what looked like two Jehovah's Witnesses coming towards him from the street. But they were not carrying black briefcases. They introduced themselves as Detective Roof and Detective Dickie. Roof, the bigger one, sat on the bench beside Salty. He asked, "What is the meaning of the flowers, Salty?"

Salty said, "This is a memorial bench."

Dickie commented, "I see them on the roadside sometimes, not benches, I mean a cross, an altar sort of. This altar is for one of the men living here in the park, I take it."

Salty nodded. "Caps. Now he's pushing daisies."

Roof said, "There's more people than Caps pushing daisies. We're tracking down a missing person who we think has been pushing daisies for fifteen years."

Dickie corrected, "Maybe not pushing daisies. Maybe just missing. That is why we're here."

"Lee Ann Saltzmanous. Married to Harold Saltzmanous, with a daughter Sylvia. Harold was never reported missing, so he's around somewhere. Sylvia was bounced around in foster care. We can't find her. But she's around somewhere."

"Never heard of him," said Salty.

"Never heard of who?"

"The one you mentioned."

"I mentioned three. Harold and Sylvia are around here somewhere, maybe sitting on benches close by. Lee Ann's around here somewhere, pushing daisies, maybe close by."

"Sorry. Can't help you."

Roof said, "You seem to like daisies. In forensics, they say the body tells the story. With you, maybe it's the daisies that will tell the story."

"All I know about pushing daisies is Caps who jumped off the bridge."

"Caps was a missing person case, solved by DNA."

Dickie moved some daisies and sat. "We had one other missing person case, a hoarder who got buried and smothered to death under his own junk. At first, we thought the neighbour did it. But Forensics worked through all the clues and decided it was an accident. The guy had buried himself in his own junk. Sometimes what looks like homicide is an accident."

Roof said, "What does the name Salty stand for?"

"I like salty bacon."

Dickie continued. "Remember the missing doctor? We thought his wife did him in. But it turned out his girlfriend lived in a farmhouse with a big stone chimney. He'd climbed down the chimney to break into her house and catch her with her lover. That's where we found the doctor, stuck in the chimney. His wife was innocent."

He added, "Because it was an accident. In a farmhouse."

Roof said, "Smith becomes Smitty. Jones becomes Jonesy."

"Sometimes missing bodies get found by sniffer dogs in the landfill," said Dickie. "That's where the saying 'into thin air' comes from. The methane gas from all the cold case bodies makes the air thin."

"Black becomes Blackie, Roberts becomes Robbie."

"We had a detective who was adopted as a baby. He was investigating a missing kid. It turned out the missing kid he was looking for was himself, solved by DNA testing."

"Saltzmanous becomes Salty."

"Missing people get found eventually," said Dickie.

"You are absolutely right on correct. Men come down here to the Homeless Hub to disappear, but they get found eventually."

"But sometimes they end up down here because of some misfortune caused by an unfortunate accident, like the one in that farmhouse."

"Misfortune. Right. We were talking to Madame Kratz about reading tarot cards to predict your misfortune."

With those words, Salty saw his candle-flame future flicker and blink out.

"We told her we wouldn't close down her illegal operation if she told us what we wanted to know."

Dickie said, "My daughter's got a dog like yours. Those are farm dogs. You were a farm boy, I understand?"

"Me? Never been on a farm in my life."

"So how long have you been here?"

Salty pulled his arm from the sleeve of his plaid shirt. "Without a watch, it's hard to tell."

Salty knew the second he'd pulled his arm from his sleeve that he'd turned over another one of Madame Kratz's cards. He could see Madame Kratz leaning over to squint at it as Roof leaned over, squinting down at the arm.

"How'd you get all those scars?"

"Street fights."

"So Salty is a fighter, like Marvelous Marvin or Sugar Ray. What is your real name, Salty?"

"Salty. It's Polish."

"That's your first name?"

"Zalty. With a Z."

"What is your last name?"

"Bacon."

"Well, Zalty Bacon, back in the nineties, DNA technology was not advanced enough to do a single hair, which we now have. Now we have a fortune-teller who remembers you from when you were a lad, growing up in an area near Mt. Forest. Outside of Mt. Forest is a farmhouse being renovated; at least, it was until the contractor found blood below a sub-floor. So, in the meantime, as they say in the movies, don't leave Dodge City."

They left, walking side by side, like two Jehovah's Witnesses.

Chapter Twenty-Seven

Sylvia

The words of that Mennonite farmer that had started Sylvia thinking about her father had taken over her mind. Stupid, she thought, because she still did not want to have anything to do with him. But she couldn't walk away. She felt the same as when you leave your apartment and you can't remember if you've locked the door and the question won't let you go until you check, even though you know you locked the door.

She had told herself she was on her way to the library, but there she was sitting on a bench across from the daisies, far enough away that it would not look like she was waiting for him. In her mind, she was calling Salty "him," not "Dad" or "Father," fooling herself into thinking she was not going back there.

She waited for half an hour. Just as she was getting ready to leave, Pavements appeared, the dog trailing along behind. Pavements was stumbling, obviously a little drunk. He collapsed on the daisy bench and began to throw a red tennis ball for the dog to fetch. Sometimes he threw overhand, sometimes sidearm. Sometimes the best he could manage was to roll it across the grass. Each time, the dog raced for it, brought it back, and dropped it into Pavements's hand. Sometimes in the handover, it fell to the ground so that the dog had to pick it up and give it to Pavements to try again. This continued for about ten minutes until the dog, getting tired of it, lay down in the grass.

Then, noticing Sylvia, the dog picked up the ball, trotted over, and dropped it at her feet. Sylvia told herself, do not pick up the ball, because if you do, you will have started to play the game and she did not want to go back there.

When she did not pick up the ball, the dog carried it off a few feet, dropped it, then brought it back and waited. He looked up at her. He looked down at the ball. He nudged her knee. He waited. He'll wait there forever, she thought. We will be frozen here forever, him staring up at me, waiting for me to throw that stupid ball.

Pavements came over and picked up the ball. He said, "Here's how to do it." He threw it underhand. It arched through the air, into the tree, bounced off a branch, and dropped. The dog leaped and turned and caught it mid-air and trotted proudly back to drop it at her feet. Pavements threw the ball and the dog raced away and leaped and twisted and brought it back and dropped it at her feet. This could not be Amos. Amos would be too old to race and leap and twist and fetch.

Pavements blinked at her with a glassy-eyed scowl. He turned his baseball hat sideways. He said, "Whisper won't play fetch with anyone he don't know. He knows you. So now he's decided to play fetch with you. All you got to do is throw the ball."

He handed it to her.

She took the ball and she threw it. The dog raced across the grass, caught the ball mid-air, and brought it back.

"Now you have to pat him."

She patted the dog.

"Me and my wife Celia used to play catch down here in this exact spot. We're separated now but I'm trying to put it back together. Maybe you've seen her. She carries this big shoulder bag with Watchtower magazines in it."

"I see her giving out the Watchtower. She gave me one. She seems like a good person."

"Maybe you could, like, have a word with her, saying something like, 'Pavements is really trying. He's not drinking no more, he's put the plug in the jug, and is spending all day long looking for work.'"

He was a pathetic little man wearing a sideways baseball hat, dressed in a stained shirt and tie and a jacket with one pocket ripped. A beanie propeller on the hat to match the red ball would have completed this picture. He would have been the kid they picked on in the schoolyard. He would have been the one not chosen for the team. He would have been the one that didn't get a date for the dance.

Pavements took back the ball. He teetered his way across the grass to the last bench before the sidewalk. Hanging onto the wooden slats of the backrest, he steadied himself before setting off again. The dog caught up with Pavements and trotted along at his heels. When Pavements stepped off the curb to cross against a red light, the dog moved in front of him, blocking his way. The dog stayed there until the light turned green and then stepped aside. They crossed the street. On the other side, when Pavements did not seem to know where he should go, the dog grabbed his pant leg and tugged him to the right, leading the way along the sidewalk to the entrance of the first alley, where again the dog seized Pavements's pant leg and pulled him to the left, towards The Daystar, tilted and stumbling, the dog herding the drunk sheep home.

Sylvia wondered, why am I calling the dog 'the dog' when I know his name is Whisper? Her brain was telling her, this is Whisper, but her heart was telling her, this is Amos, but her mind was telling her, this is not Amos while her emotions were telling her, don't go back there.

Father Sutcliffe was coming across the grass, as usual wearing jeans and a T-shirt that said "Staff," not looking like anyone who would give communion or baptize babies. He sat with her on the bench.

"Pavements has a book. More accurately, he stole a book from the library. It's about cold case missing links. The name in one of the cold cases, written in bold print, is Lee Ann Saltzmanous, married to Harold Saltzmanous. I tried to convince Pavements to take back the book and forget about Harold Saltzmanous, but he wants the reward money."

"Is Salty Harold Saltzmanous?"

"According to Pavements, yes. And he's told the police that."

"I have contradictory feelings about what I should do but, since so far I have no proof either way, I'll let the police figure it out."

"When that happens, what will you do?"

"What I will do is wait and see. When I go into a store and can't decide whether to buy this or that, I say to myself, 'Wait and see', which for me is walking out the door."

Father Sutcliffe asked, "Did Harold Saltzmanous murder his wife?"

"No, he did not. I am the witness that he didn't. It was an accident."

"Do you want me to tell Salty that?"

"Maybe Salty isn't Harold Saltzmanous."

"Maybe he is. Then what?"

"I don't want Salty to be my father. I don't want my father to be a homeless vagrant. That is not how I remember him. Besides, even if he is, he will be too ashamed to admit it. Besides, if he is Harold Saltzmanous, the reason he's here is that he's in hiding. So he can't or won't admit it to me even if he is. So, first I have to know for sure, without a doubt, that he is my father so that when I do ask him, if I do, I can't be put off with denials."

"You're dodging the question. 'Wait and see' is almost here."

"I'm a foster kid. I know how it is. When an abandoned child turns up, it's like opening a closet door that the parent wants to keep closed. Is the mother you've never met going to confess, 'Guess what. I used to be a prostitute. Your father was a John I picked up on the corner.' If she can get away with denying, she can't be held accountable. For some people, denial is how they solve all their problems. I would want my father to want me back for me, not because I can keep him out of jail."

Chapter Twenty-Eight

Salty

The goldfish that Beets kept in a bowl for company in his Silver City shack always ended up floating sideways in the dead water that Beets never changed.

Beets would say, "It smells like dead fish in here."

So, Salty would throw the fish and the water into the ravine. But the next day Beets would buy a new goldfish in a bag full of fresh water to keep him company until the fresh water ran out. So, now Salty was sitting with Caps on his bench, carving Beets a goldfish that would not end up floating sideways.

The dog was sniffing along the edge of the sidewalk, reading the day's doggy news, his leash dragging along behind. He stopped to greet Juicy, who was pushing her shopping cart full of her stuff across the park on her way to the garbage behind Colonel Wong's, and from there to the dumpster behind Colonel Wing's.

Pavements came from the alley with a new bottle of Majestic Diner. The dog came over and sat next to Salty and Pavements. The sun was glancing off Pavements's new black loafers that Celia had bought for him to apply for a job in. She'd also bought him a new blue shirt and red tie to match his repaired suit jacket. She'd even got him an appointment at the dental clinic. Pavements took off his baseball hat to show Salty the haircut Celia had given the fringe that grew like a horseshoe from one ear to the other. His bald head that never saw daylight was whitish-grey, like the underside of those little frogs Salty had used for bass fishing.

Father Sutcliffe crossed the grass and moved some daisies aside to make space to sit. "Is that your idea of keeping Whisper on a leash?"

Pavements did his cardio warm-up with his thumb and then hacked up a gob of spit the size of a snowball into his palm and rubbed it into his hands. He twisted open the bottle and got started. "Celia told me if I want to get a job I should pray to God. So I said, 'Hello, God, my name is Pavements and I need a job.'"

Pavements took a long pull on the bottle and passed it to Salty, who said no.

"But Celia told me you don't ask God like that, not in words, but sort of in a vision because that is how you communion with God up there in heaven, not like down here in grunts like with the Outreachers."

Father Sutcliffe said, "I don't think Celia said it quite like that."

Salty was watching Juicy going through the garbage next to Soapy Suds. Sometimes it had pretty good clothes in there. He was remembering Lee Ann pushing the baby carriage and Sylvia in a pink bonnet and booties fast asleep as they walked along in the shopping mall. This felt like Madame Kratz had laid down two baby carriage cards side by side for him to look at.

"Celia told me you have to ask it like in the Bible, like 'In Thy wisdom, if Thou willest, find me a job.' So I've been doing that; well, I change it around. I say 'If thou willest send me a few thousand so I can tell Celia I got a job without really having to get a job."

Pavements closed his eyes. "Hello God. Pavements here. No good thing should be withheld from those who deserve it. If thou willest it, send me five thousand dollars."

Pavements took another drink.

Father Sutcliffe said, "Hello Pavements. God speaking. It won't take Celia long to catch on that you don't have a job. My advice is to get a job."

"Hello God. Pavements here. Five thousand isn't much to ask for, not like what you give the Pope, millions of dollars and his own airplane."

Pavements got up off the bench, the bottle hanging down from his right hand pointing his way across the street to have a leak behind Soapy Suds.

Now that there was more room, Father Sutcliffe settled himself on the bench. "For Pavements, the goal in life is about reaching Soapy Suds on the other side of the street before he wets his pants, like Beets. For you, Salty, it's about reaching the girl sitting on the bench over there on the other side of the park. Her name is Sylvia."

The dog saw her and went over.

"Do you see her over there patting Whisper, Salty? Her name is Sylvia. I shouldn't be telling you this but she is your witness; it was an accident. She wants to find her father and clear his name so he can come out of hiding and cross the bridge. What advice do you want me to give this girl?"

Salty squinted against the sun, trying to bring into focus the bridge stretching across the ravine between now and fifteen years past.

Pavements came back from having a leak.

Father Sutcliffe asked, "So, Salty. What is your advice?"

The dog had settled at her feet, his head resting on front paws, eyes closed, lost maybe in his memories of green grass and hillsides and sheep on a hot summer day on a Mennonite farm.

"So Salty. What is your advice?"

"Free smoothies," said Pavements. "On hot summer days, like today, The Daystar should give away free smoothies."

"I'm serious, Salty. What advice can you give me regarding this girl?"

"Advice," said Pavements. "You know how you've been wanting to get the Outreachers to move into the shelters? Hang pictures of naked women on the walls."

Father Sutcliffe said, "Shut the front door, Pavements. Let Salty and me have this conversation."

Father Sutcliffe waited. He rearranged himself among the daisies. Finally, he said, "Here is the truth of it, Salty. One too many drinks at the wrong time and you're on the run forever. The stories never end. No sooner does one hit the dirt than another takes his place. I'm pointing to you now, Salty. I want you to stand up and go over and tell Sylvia your story because when you tell it, it's over, gone to wherever told stories go."

The dog was stretched out on his back, the girl giving him a belly rub. Salty imagined her in a print dress like a Mennonite girl, rubbing the belly of Amos. As Salty studied this picture, the weight of it on his mind seemed to double his vision so that he saw two girls, one younger, the other older, together blurred double, switching back and forth and changing places, one little, one big, but both giving Amos his belly rub.

Father Sutcliffe put his hand on Salty's arm. "You can't unring a bell any more than you can unchop a chop, but you can stop her ringing the doorbell she's been ringing. Open the door and let her in."

"I don't know anyone named Sylvia."

Pavements said, "She's that girl over there. She asked me what your real name is."

Father Sutcliffe removed his hand. "One of the classic rules of AA counseling: never try to use reason or logic with a client who isn't sober. Well, you are sober. Almost, anyway; sober enough to understand the chainsaw logic of the consequences you will soon be facing. I offer you a chance to get your life back and you turn it down."

Pavements said, "There used to be a TV show called 'What's My Line.' You had to guess the person's real name. Like me, my real name is Nelson. Let me take a guess. Maybe it's something like Harold. Am I close?"

"Shut the front door, Pavements."

Salty said, "I don't know anyone named Sylvia. All I know about that girl over there is I see her in the park. Maybe she's married to one of those lawyers at the other end of the bridge. It looks like she's done all right for herself. For a girl, married happily ever after, may God love being with her, amen."

"She doesn't live in any big house. She lives in a small room at the university and is doing her best to support herself. How do I know this? I have talked to this girl many times. Now it's your turn. If someone has their hand outstretched, and if you take that hand, then the two hands together can work both ways, the same as a bridge goes both ways. Light at the end of the bridge, Salty."

The dog was eyeing Beets, who was now crossing the park towards the bench Sylvia was sitting on. The dog was on his feet, his head low, positioned in front of Sylvia. Beets's legs collapsed and folded together and he flopped down and began to snore. The dog did not move; he stayed with the girl, his eyes on the intruder.

"Notice, Salty, that Whisper is there at her feet. He is waiting, watching over her. And look now, he is standing up, glancing over at you, Salty, wondering why you aren't there with her, standing ready, watching over her."

Out of his farmhouse's kitchen window, Salty could watch Eli's sheep grazing peacefully. He could see how they would look up and see that Amos was there and then the sheep would go back to grazing, knowing they were safe.

"How does this happen, Salty? I've seen it many times but I still don't understand. The breaking into pieces and falling apart of a good man, that part is easy to understand. I used to be in the navy. We called it looking for the wrong Captain Morgan. Instead of looking for the Captain in the sky, you're looking for the Captain in the bottle. But not putting the pieces back together, not turning hopelessness into hope, that is the part I don't understand. If this were nighttime and I had my finger pointing upward and you couldn't see for sure what I was pointing to, you would say, 'Father Sutcliffe is pointing at the bridge.' But you would be wrong. I would be pointing to what is beyond the bridge. Look at her, Salty; your chance to make everything right, and you're turning it down. What do I have to say? What do I have to do? Get down on my knees? I will. I will get down and crawl on my hands and knees. Your chance to go back across the bridge and make everything right. Don't turn it down."

Pavements said, "Celia would say, look at the knees of those new pants. What have you been doing, crawling around on your hands and knees?"

"I wrote the cheque to pay Whisper's fine with these fingers, Salty, crooked lines on white paper. Every single word I put down, letter by letter, felt like I was writing a page, page after page, because that is how long I've been trying to point with these fingers your way to that girl. Observe, Salty. Look at where my finger is pointing."

Salty turned his head the other way.

Father Sutcliffe got to his feet. "I give up. But my guess is the two detectives won't. They were around again the other day. People disappear daily, I said. It happens all the time. Maybe Lee Ann Salzmanous fell off a cruise ship. That's all I told them."

Pavements said, "I read in a book I found in the library — true stuff, with proof — that people are abducted by aliens in a spaceship that comes down to Earth to take them back for slave labour. It showed real pictures. Like those real pictures in *The Missing Link*."

Salty was waiting for Father Sutcliffe to say, "Shut the front door, Pavements." But when he didn't, Salty knew Father Sutcliffe had no choice but to leave it open. The horse is already out of the barn, Eli would say. There's nothing to be learned from the second kick from the mule, Eli would say.

Chapter Twenty-Nine

Sylvia

Man and dog, like two long-time friends, side by side among the daisies in the shade from the bridge, Salty dressed in his usual plaid shirt, work pants and work boots, his dog sleeping beside him. Salty seemed to be looking at something shiny, holding it up, staring at it in the palm of his hand, feeling along its surface, turning it over and over. A gold locket, Sylvia realized. He wiped and polished it clean with a small piece of white cloth. He put it into his pocket. She remembered now a clear-as-day picture of her father kneeling over to take a locket off her mother's neck. Then he had rolled her up in the carpet and carried her out and placed her in the back of his pickup. Sylvia had started to shiver then. She had thought it was from the cold, even though it was a warm evening, so she went back upstairs, and climbed under the blankets and, groggy from the pain killers, went back to sleep.

She crossed the grass and crouched out of sight behind the one big tree. When Salty got up, she followed. He did not seem to notice. Or maybe Salty knew but was pretending not to. The dog knew. He kept glancing back; encouraging her, it seemed, inviting her to come along. When Salty reached the bench nearest the sidewalk, he sat down, leaned back, and had a rest. He looked up at the clouds drifting overhead. He watched the people passing by. He took out the locket and flipped it open and held it between his thumb and forefinger and stared at it. Finally, rest over, he got up. He waited for a break in the traffic and crossed the street, the dog following. Salty seemed different from the last time she had seen him, his back a little stooped, his movement a little slower, his demeanor a little sadder.

He started up Sheldon Street, the dog as usual trailing behind. At the lane which ran between the line of garages near Colonel Wong's Chinese Chicken, he turned. He stopped at the door of a cement block shed, took a key from under the mat, and opened the door. He returned the key to its hiding place and went inside.

To discover that Salty lived somewhere surprised her. She had assumed he lived on the street and slept in the alley. By crouching at the side wall and hanging onto the window ledge, Sylvia could peek in. In one corner stood a wooden table with one wooden chair. Next to it was a workbench covered with fish carvings; some completed, some half-finished, some barely started. She remembered that her father had carved fish. I'm always swimming against the currents, he had said. Above the bench hung an assortment of tools. Next to the bench, on a small metal stand, sat a kettle and microwave. In one corner sat a guitar.

As she watched, he removed his plaid shirt and hung it in the closet. He went to the washroom to fill his kettle. While he waited for the water to boil, he sat on a worn-looking couch with armrests, way too big for the small space. He took off his boots and put his feet up on a little wooden bench. The dog, meanwhile, had climbed into a cardboard box in the corner, lowered his head, circled twice, and laid down. As soon as the water began to steam, Salty took a package of tea bags from the shelf above the table. He made the tea and sat back to drink it.

As Sylvia dropped down from the window and started up the laneway, heading for home, she noted that the lane of garages ran behind the narrow lots and tiny backyards of the houses on either side: Shuter Street on the left and Sumach on the right. For most of the houses, a board fence, or what was left of one, separated each yard from each garage. When she glanced back at Salty's shed, which was a converted garage, she noted that the fence behind it was in good repair, probably the work of Salty. So, whoever owns the house must know Salty. She counted the garages from Salty's to the last one before the street. Five. She turned left on Sheldon and passed three storefronts and turned left again before stopping in front of the fifth house: an old Victorian brick structure with a sign in the front window for Madame Kratz: Fortune Telling. She could not see behind the house to know if this one matched the shed but, according to her count, it did. A knock on the door produced Madame Kratz, a middle-aged woman dressed in a red, low-cut gown. From her neck, ears, and wrists loops of garish plastic and glass dangled. A boldly-printed sign on the entrance wall stated her mission: "To discover the hidden secrets of your future before they happen." The sign on the door into her reading room said, "Open the door and unlock your destiny."

Sylvia stepped into a small, dark room with one wooden table painted purple and, on either end, two chairs painted blue. Classical music was playing in the background. Light from somewhere under the table produced an eerie glow upward, creating shadows on Madame Kratz's face and neck as she took her place in the blue chair nearest a purple curtain that Sylvia assumed covered a door. All that was lacking, thought Sylvia, taking her seat, was a dry ice machine steaming in the fog.

"I'm not here for a reading. I'm looking for someone. I want to know the name of the man who lives in the shed behind this house. I think he's my father."

Madame Kratz gestured to a "donations" box on one corner of the table. "Fifty dollars."

"I don't want a reading."

"Fifty dollars."

Deciding it was too late to change her mind, Sylvia put the money into the box.

Madame Kratz began shuffling her cards.

"I don't want a reading. I'm wondering about the man who lives in the shed."

Madame Kratz was laying out the cards. "In these cards is your fortune and you've paid me to give it to you."

Sylvia leaned over for a closer look. "Those are just nonsense pictures. They don't mean anything."

"There is a dark cloud hanging over you."

Sylvia studied the card. "I don't see any dark clouds."

"Be patient and see what develops."

"That's not an answer."

Madame Kratz turned another card and studied the picture. "You will get a sign very soon."

"That is not telling me anything. Is that shed yours? If so, who is living in it?"

She turned over another card. "I see a dog with your future in its hands."

"A dog doesn't have hands."

"You are having trouble saying the name of this dog because you are afraid of what it might reveal."

This was getting spooky. "How do you know that?"

Madame Kratz gathered up the cards and reshuffled. "My information comes from various divine spheres of influences which, young lady, your doubts are blocking. It is not what I say. It is how you interpret what I say. Your destiny is already fixed. The manner in which it will be fulfilled is up to you, but it *will* be fulfilled."

"What are these various spheres of influence?"

Madame Kratz's eyes swept the surroundings. "Drifting through the ether of this room is the music of Beethoven. You can't see Beethoven and you can't see the force that allowed him to create the music. But you can hear and feel what that force has created. Divine in result must be divine in cause. The essence of what's absent is the substance of what's not seen."

"Those cards are nonsense."

Sylvia set off for home.

Chapter Thirty

Roof

Roof and Dickie found a drunk Mr. Bones, described by Officer Cobbs as "Willie Nelson, only better dressed," on the street corner.

Roof said, "We're friends of Pavements. Where can we find him?"

"Pavements doesn't have any friends."

"And why is that?"

"If you were friends, you'd know why."

Dickie said, "I've got one for you, Mr. Bones. What is forty feet long and has eight teeth?"

"No idea."

"The front row of a Willie Nelson concert."

Mr. Bones was busy with his banjo.

Dickie asked, "For how long, for how many years, has that banjo been buying you your homebrew? And how can your fingers work those strings in the winter?"

Roof said, "So we're not friends. But we'd like to talk to him."

"I think he's on holiday in the Alps."

Roof handed Mr. Bones ten dollars. "Try again. We'd like to talk to Pavements. Where can we find him?"

But there was no need for bribery. They spotted Pavements on the park bench next to the lilac bushes. They crossed the street, Mr. Bones trailing after them. Bottle in his right hand, Pavements was slouched over, snoring.

Roof gave his leg a poke with his shoe. Pavements sat up. He swatted at a fly that had come out from under his City Works hat and was crawling across one cheek. He rubbed his eyes. He blinked them into focus. He turned his hat sideways.

Roof took his bottle and smelled the contents. "What is this?"

Mr. Bones said, "Give me a drink and I'll tell you."

Roof handed over the bottle.

"Mine now." Mr. Bones hurried away. But his long legs were not able to keep up with themselves and he knocked himself over. He sat muttering and mumbling about having to move to East Jesus.

Roof turned back to Pavements, hunched over snoring again. Roof considered the reliability of this runty derelict and the likelihood of him knowing anything about anything. But he'd been right about Caps.

Roof gave him a poke. "Pavements, wake up. We're going to take you home."

As they helped Pavements to his feet, Dickie said, "What would these people do if they didn't have the church looking after them? What would you do, Pavements, if you didn't have the church looking after you?"

Roof added, "And the air-conditioned library to hang out in."

"That's where I discovered the book," muttered Pavements. "As my wife Celia would say, the Lord chose me to discover that book."

"Free housing, free meals, free clothes. But not free books. The head librarian phoned 54 Division and said, 'After all they've done for Pavements, he stole our only copy of *The Chain Reference Bible.*'"

"Not a path I would have chosen," said Pavements. "But the Lord Jesus put that book in my hand. My wife Celia told me. Seek and ye shall find, take and it will be given unto you."

Roof said, "That is not how the library works."

While they waited for a break in the traffic, Pavements lit a cigarette.

Roof commented, "Those cigarettes smell funny."

"Budget cigarettes from the Coca-Cola Reserve. They taste like donkey piss."

"They smell like donkey piss." Roof waved away the smoke.

"My wife Celia says 'If you don't like budget cigarettes, get a job.' But I can't even get part-time work as a cart boy at Loblaws."

"Maybe you should join AA."

"No one knows how hard I tried. Morning till night, one rejection after another."

They followed Pavements through the entrance of The Daystar and straight ahead up the stairs that Pavements was with difficulty climbing, stumbling at every step, catching the railing, hoisting himself, step by step, one foot after the other, continuing to mutter about no one knowing how hard he tried.

The upper hall was well lit, freshly painted, and, apart from the subhuman wheezings coming from the room next door to Pavements, all was quiet. His room was tidy with a single bed and chair, a dresser with two mismatched socks laid out on top, a closet and, on a small table, a notepad. Roof was about to comment on the tidy part when he noticed two pictures above the table. Roof looked more closely to make certain he was not mistaken: Photocopies of Lee Ann Saltzmanous.

"This is the book I was meant to discover." Pavements extracted it from under his mattress and gave *The Missing Link* to Dickie, who turned the pages to the Lee Ann Saltzmanous case.

Pavements bent over to take off his shoes. He said, "I gave Officer Cobbs one of Salty's hairs for DNA. And I told him, that's blood on the wall. But you won't get a match for Lee Ann because it's chicken blood."

"Chickens in the house?" asked Dickie. "How do you know that, Pavements?"

"Salty told me."

"So you showed Salty this picture and he told you it's chicken blood."

"Something like that."

Roof said, "Don't you wash your feet, Pavements?" He opened the window.

"My wife Celia is bringing me new ones. Socks, I mean."

"Did she get you that dinner jacket? It looks almost new. But look here at the rip along the seam."

Pavements looked.

"Tell us about Salty looking at that picture and saying it's chicken blood."

"The book says a reward for information leading to. First, I want the reward money upfront. I haven't got my last reward money yet."

"We've got your money. That's why we're here. But you've got to be sober enough to sign for it."

Pavements slumped on the edge of the bed, head in his hands, eyes closed, and, in a few seconds, began to snore. Roof had not thought that possible. He'd thought you had to be lying down to snore.

Dickie picked up *The Missing Link* and studied the pictures. "Forensics says there is no match with that hair."

"Maybe he's making it all up. Just because his information on Caps was good doesn't mean this is. Maybe he thinks made-up information will get him another reward."

Roof shook Pavements awake.

"Wake up, Pavements. Listen to what I'm going to tell you. Lying to the police is a criminal offense, worth up to five years in prison."

Pavements's eyes opened.

"It's considered a crime of dishonesty, Pavements."

Dickie said, "We had a guy like you down in Chinatown. Chang Liu his name was. He saw a picture that looked like his neighbour. He phoned Crime Stoppers for the reward. We took Chang Liu away in handcuffs. We call that 'cash motives,' people looking for easy money."

Roof knew this story wasn't true but he went along with it. "Is that what you're up to, Pavements? Easy money?"

"I pray to Jesus but he doesn't help me."

Roof stared down at Pavements, now flopped over on his back.

Dickie said, "How does this get started? Like you, Roof? A six-pack after work? No one at home but the cat?"

"I don't have a cat."

Dickie picked up Pavements's feet and laid them on the bed. "He's too drunk to sign for his money. Even if he could sign, he probably wouldn't remember getting it. But we can't just leave five thousand dollars cash sitting here."

"So we try again some other day."

From the bedroom door, Roof glanced back at Pavements, lying there snoring like a snowblower.

Chapter Thirty-One

Sylvia

Sylvia wanted nothing to do with this man, Salty, yet here she was sneaking along the laneway, glancing up and down, approaching the shed door that she discovered was open. She crept closer and glanced inside. If Salty was in there, she was going to say she was lost and needed directions to Bridge Street. Then they would be face to face. But she would not say, "I'm Sylvia, your daughter." She would comment on the weather, tell him she was new to the area, anything to allow her time to study his forehead to see if she could find that scar.

She tap-tapped on the door frame. Receiving no answer, she took a step forward. The dim light from the window fell on the couch and table, but the corners were too shadowed to see much. Salty could be standing there, watching her, and she wouldn't know it.

Waiting for her eyes to adjust to the gloom, she heard a faint sound coming from somewhere. As her vision cleared, she saw not Salty but Pavements lying on the floor, flat on his back, fast asleep. When she stepped back, intending to leave, her hand knocked a metal box off the table.

Pavements sat up. He rubbed his eyes, but, unable to blink them into focus, he did not notice her in the shadows of the corner by the door. He got up and went to the window. He was wearing an expensive-looking herringbone Eddie Bauer dinner jacket with leather patches on each elbow, the kind worn by English gentlemen in the drawing-room smoking pipes. When Pavements reached up to adjust his baseball hat, Sylvia saw that the seam above the pocket on his right side was ripped open, showing bare skin underneath.

He gave himself a shake and then he left. Through the window she watched him, head down, stumbling up the lane, baseball hat tilting him to one side.

She tried to open the metal box, but it was locked. A quick search produced no key. A further search produced no papers or pictures or mail, nothing that might give her a clue to Salty's identity. She peeked out the door. Then, on the lookout for any sudden movement on either side, she hurried away, past the line of garages to Sheldon Street.

Pavements stood at the corner, waiting for a break in traffic. He dodged his way across the street and turned up the alley which ran behind the stores. She followed him to a second alley which ended at a lane which led to a third which, she reasoned, ran parallel to and behind the stores along Bridge Street. Walking quickly now, he reached in a few seconds a high, wooden fence with two boards missing. He slipped between the two crossbeams and knocked on the back door of the donut shop. It was answered by a squat woman with long, black hair.

From where Sylvia stood by the window, she could see into what seemed to be a living room with odd pieces of torn and broken furniture. A short, fat Indigenous man with straight black hair and a ripped sweater sat reading a letter in an old easy chair minus its legs, while a girl of about ten, skinny and pale, crouched on hands and knees on the bare floor, counting change. She stacked the money in front of her. When she had completed the piles, she began to count the stacks: five of loonies, three of toonies, and four of quarters. Then she sat up, shoved the money into her pocket, and disappeared into another room.

Sylvia left that window and crept to the next, which was a kitchen. Pavements was counting out his change. He gave it to the woman and took the two full bottles, which were clear and without labels. Pavements headed up the alley and disappeared around a corner.

She wondered, what is this stuff they're drinking? Made how, and from what? She had heard that moonshiners used old car radiators as stills, which meant the liquor could contain lead. If the distiller wasn't careful, it could contain methanol. How much of this stuff does Salty drink? In fact, maybe that is why he doesn't recognize me. The homebrew has damaged his brain.

Now she had a new question. What shape was he in mentally? To say nothing of the damage to the liver, pancreas, and stomach. Did she want to end up looking after an invalid? Sylvia couldn't get home fast enough. She had a shower. She turned on the TV. She watched the news and went to bed.

She was no further ahead with her questions when she awoke the next day. She waited until the early morning rain had thinned to a drizzle before setting off. Side-stepping the puddles, she crept along the side of the shed. She stole a cautious peek through the window. The light inside was dim, with too much gloom to see anything clearly. But finally, after cupping her hands and putting her nose up against the glass, she decided no one was there. She tried the door, but it was locked. She had seen him put the key under the mat, but she would not have the courage to use it even if it was there.

She would come back later. But then what? When will it end? Feeling aimless, she followed the lane to Sheldon Street and stood opposite the park, wondering what to do next. She turned to her right, passed the 7-Eleven and Colonel Wong's and then started across the bridge. She stood at the rail, searching the park. No Salty; only Pavements, who got up from the daisy bench and teetered across the grass to the sidewalk. Salty's dog appeared. He trotted along behind Pavements. So, what has happened to Salty that Pavements now sleeps in his shed and has his dog?

Pavements stood at the corner, rocking heel to toe as though blown by a wind, either trying to figure out where he was, or waiting for the light to change. When it did, too intoxicated to notice, he remained standing until the dog, tugging at his pant leg, got him moving. At the next light, the dog blocked Pavements's path until, when the signal turned green, the dog tugged at his legs to get him in gear. Having crossed the street, he stopped. He seemed to have no idea where he was going, or why he was standing there. Finally, after stumbling a few steps forward, Pavements propped himself up in the doorway of Colonel Wong's. The dog again took over, pant leg in his teeth, pulling backward, tugging and jerking along the sidewalk, past Dixie's Donut Shoppe and onto a little patch of grass under a tree in front of St. Michael's Church. Pavements collapsed in the grass and lay without moving, head resting on one arm, fast asleep, the dog standing guard beside him.

Sylvia sat on the front step of the church to wait for him to get up, or for Salty to appear. The morning sun was now high enough to shine on Pavements's face. His size made him look young, but Sylvia saw from the lines and the wrinkles in his face that he was probably in his late forties.

No one passing paid him any attention except an old woman entering the front door of the church. She gave him a stony glance as she hurried by, shaking her head and clucking her tongue. No one could be more in need of salvation than this lost and helpless little man with his filthy shirt and dirty pants and ripped dinner jacket and the too-big baseball hat.

Pavements lay where he had fallen. The dog wandered off and disappeared. What seemed like ten minutes passed before Pavements's eyes blinked open, perhaps awakened by the sun that was now directly above him. For a while he lay there, staring at the passersby who were careful not to stare at him. Then, raising his head, he looked directly at Sylvia. But she could tell by the daze in his eyes that he did not recognize her. Maybe he did not even see her, for he seemed unaware that she was watching him. And, she realized, even if she had the courage to go over and ask him what had happened to Salty, he was probably too drunk to know.

Pavements began to cough, so harshly that his flushed face drained white. When this subsided, he struggled up on one elbow only to begin again, hacking until, after spitting up a large gluey gob like grey slush into the grass, he sat upright. He must have lung cancer, from the smoking. He must have burnt-out brain cells from the drinking. He must have hepatitis from eating garbage.

The coughing and spitting seemed to wake him enough to climb up on his hands and knees. He got to his feet. He removed his baseball hat to mop the sweat from his face with his sleeve. His bald head was a startling contradiction for a skinny little man not much bigger than a boy.

The dog must have heard the coughing, for he returned. When Pavements started off, Sylvia following, to wherever he thought he was going, the dog guided him safely across another traffic light and up an alley where he collapsed in the dirt and leaned his back against the wall. From the pocket of his dinner jacket, he brought out a bottle. He raised it to his mouth, tilted his head, took a long swallow, smacked his lips, raised it again, and drank more.

He sat drinking from his bottle. He patted the dog. He lit a cigarette and smoked and drank from the bottle. After a while the dog wandered off again, sniffing along and up and down and here and there, finally disappearing around the corner. Sylvia followed, along one alley to the left and one to the right. The dog knew she was following, for every few steps he glanced back. He probably knew she'd been there all along. Now he was leading her to Salty's shed. The dog sat down on the step. It seemed to be waiting for her to open the door and step in.

She crept to the opposite side and approached the window from the back. There Salty was, sitting at his little table drinking from a teacup. Yes, it was tea, for she could see the teapot on the workbench. He got up, cup in hand, and opened the door for the dog. Leaving the door ajar, he sat at the table and picked up his guitar. He strummed a few chords. He drank the last swallow and set the cup down. He took off his boots and flopped over on his back on the couch. The dog curled up on the floor beside him.

All they do is drink and sleep, drink and sleep. A few minutes ago it was Pavements she was looking at, fast asleep. Now it was Salty she was looking at, fast asleep. The difference was that Salty had been drinking tea.

Sylvia waited and watched, uncertain what to do next. The dog knew she was out there because from time to time he lifted his head to glance at the window. Finally, he got up, went to the door, and nosed it wide open. The dog returned to Salty and sat down. He seemed to be waiting for her to come in.

Sylvia listened at the door. The heaviness of Salty's breathing told her he was deep in sleep. Bars of sunlight slanted through the shed window to light up the inner shadows. But she was afraid to step out of the daylight. She would have turned around and gone home except that she could now hear the swish of the dog's tail on the floor, welcoming her in.

First, she hid behind the open door. Then, gathering courage, she crept to the centre of the floor where, afraid to get any closer, she stopped. She sat on her heels, not knowing what to do. She listened to the soft rasping of Salty's breathing as his lungs heaved in and out. She moved forward, on hands and knees now, close enough to see that the dog was waiting for her, coaxing her nearer. She folded her legs underneath herself and sat on the floor beside Salty. Because of the poor light she could not see his face, but she could see the pattern of his shirt, frayed at the neck, the top two buttons undone, a grey T-shirt underneath.

How could anyone accept this shabby vagrant as a father? If Pavements had a daughter, what would she do when she found him passed out in a churchyard? She would go home and never look back.

But when Sylvia stood, ready to leave, forever as far as she was concerned, the dog came forward. Then, as she put her hand on his head and stroked along the fur of his neck, abruptly her sight grew better. Now she could see Salty clearly, lying with one arm thrown back, the other hanging down. Unexpectedly becoming braver, she leaned forward, close enough that she could touch one arm. She nudged him a little. The even breathing did not stop. She nudged his shoulder. Maybe because his breathing had deepened, or maybe because she was standing looking down at him, or probably because the dog was beside her, she felt strong enough to slip her fingers into his shirt pocket. She drew her hand away and with her other hand she felt his pants pocket. She wanted the key to that metal box. She wanted to see the picture in the locket.

Both pockets were empty.

The dog backed a few steps away, ears cocked, watching intently, giving her room.

To get at Salty's other pockets, wedged between his body and the back of the couch, she had to move him a little forward. When she did this, he mumbled but did not wake. Inside the first, she found a key.

Now, although she was close enough and there was enough light, she could not find a scar in the creases in his forehead. And she could see nothing in that face that she could recognize. Staring down, she thought, maybe it is him, but she quickly doubted herself, thinking, no, it's not him.

She thought, if I touched the face and felt along the lines and the creases with my fingers, I would be able to read what they said, and I would know. But to do this she would need to bend over him and come close and touch his skin, and she could not do that. She slipped the key back into his pocket. She did not want to know.

As she straightened up, ready to leave, the dog nudged her hand. She knelt to him and held him. She buried her face in the soft fur along his neck and hugged him. She sat down on the floor and pulled him into her lap and rocked him. He licked her face and then he licked Salty's hand which was hanging down beside them. As the dog continued to lick the hand, starting at the fingers and working his way up to the wrist, Sylvia noticed the scars. She reached out and pulled up one sleeve and traced her fingers up and down the jagged barbed wire lines crisscrossing from the heel of his hand to his elbow. She reached up and felt along the scar of her cheek, one single straight line with a jog at the end near her mouth, as though someone had jarred the hand as it cut.

Whatever doubts she had about Salty being her father vanished as the memories of these scars came flooding back. She took the key from his pocket and put it into her own. She tucked the metal box under her arm. She knelt beside the dog for a final pat. She went to the door. He followed her, looking up at her, his eyes asking her to stay.

She sat behind the open door, the dog in her lap. After a while, it started to rain. It began to drum on the shed roof. Salty sat up, pulled on his boots, and climbed to his feet to look out the window. In the light coming through the dusty glass, she saw his face clearly, not because her vision was better but because her memory seemed clearer, so that the lines in his forehead were easier to read. Without any difficulty, she was able to find the scar above his right eye. And, she realized, his slightly-flattened nose like a boxer's, how could she not have recognized it sooner? See you next round, he used to say.

He flipped the wall switch to turn on the overhead light. He slipped one hand into his pocket. He got down on one knee to search underneath the couch. He's looking for the key, she realized. Unable to find it under the couch, he began on hands and knees to search along the floor, the dog searching with him, sniffing from one spot to the next. Finally, giving up, Salty climbed to his feet to search through his pockets, but all he found was a matchbox with three matches left. Light flared up as he scratched one across the striker. For a moment, he held it up like a torch to look for his key under the couch. As it flickered out, he sat down.

For a while he sat there, rubbing the tips of his fingers along the scars on his wrist. Sylvia remembered him sitting at the kitchen table smoking, listening to his radio, rubbing the tips of his fingers along the scar on his forehead. When he stood, she would hear the muffled rattle of change in his pocket. He didn't smoke now, she realized, and he had been drinking tea, not liquor. Maybe he's quit. Maybe he's going to get cleaned up and come to her and say, "It's me, Dad," the same as the dog had come to her and said, "It's me, Amos."

Well, now she knew the Dad part was true. The Amos part was wishful thinking.

Salty got back down on his hands and knees and again searched across the floor. She did not like to see him crawling on the concrete. He was big and he was strong and he was proud and she wanted to go over to him and take his hand and stand him up straight. She remembered that hand: Pattycake, pattycake, baker's man. Sitting on the floor with him, turning his scarless arms in circles, making the dough.

He crawled towards her. All he had to do was close the door. But before he reached her hiding place, he gave up the search. He turned off the light and left the shed, closing the door behind him. With the dog at his heels, they disappeared up the alley.

She inserted the key. Inside, she found the locket with the picture: a five-year-old girl sitting on the top step of a farmhouse porch. Behind her, the radio was playing. The lunch bucket was on the kitchen table, open, but not yet packed. In the corner stood his guitar. On the mat were his boots, enormous boots that clumped across the front porch in the middle of the night, returning from work. They would probably have been unsteady from drinking, but for her, they weren't unsteady. They were rock solid.

She held the locket up to the light. Across from her, behind the camera, the long black strands of the barbed wire fence ran parallel to the gravel lane. Beyond the fence was the field where Amos guarded the sheep and then, beyond that, the Mennonite farmer's house with the three little girls. Your mother has left, Salty had said. You stay here with Mrs. Martin until Uncle Frank comes for you. Her cheek was too sore to talk and too sore to cry, but the tears came down anyway and laid a stinging line of salt along the sutures. Mrs. Martin had found some paper towels to stop the tears before they reached the cut and Sylvia had held that under her eye. She had watched her father's boots walk across the field until he was gone.

There was nothing else in the metal box except a letter, worn out as if from too many readings:

Dear Harold,

Me and Frank have decided it's time to stop playing games.

Sylvia starts school this September. She needs a permanent address that does not get moved from town to town, trailer to trailer, as you shift from job to job. Frank hasn't told his wife yet but he will. One thing at a time. You first. So we need to get together and talk.

Lee Ann

***

The black car was parked in front of Sylvia's dorm. Two men were seated in the front waiting for her. She saw that they were watching her approach in the side-view mirror. They climbed out and showed their badges. "I'm Roof. He's Dickie. You're Sylvia."

He opened a plain brown envelope and showed her a photograph of Salty, sitting on his bench with the daisies.

"We've been wondering, who is this girl? Where does she come from, and, more importantly, why is she interested in this daisy man? Why is she following him around and peeking into the window of his shed?"

Dickie said, "That's where it gets interesting. You are no doubt aware that the police are tracking some of these Silver City men. We've already talked to a man called Pavements."

Sylvia was surprised that her heart wasn't pounding. They might have been asking directions to the library. In truth, she felt relief. It was over. Let the police figure out what to do with him.

She said, "I'm a student. I use the Thorn library. I come and go through the park. I've developed an interest in the homeless. I was wondering myself; who is the daisy man? Perhaps you can tell me."

"If we knew, we wouldn't be asking you. If you have any information on Salty, we would like you to tell us."

"I don't know anything about the daisy man other than that his name is Salty."

"When was the last you saw your mother and father?"

"I'm a foster kid. They disappeared when I was five years old."

"From a farmhouse near Mt. Forest."

"Something like that."

"Sylvia. No matter what your feelings are for your father, he is going to jail. For what, we don't know yet. If not for murder, for involuntary manslaughter; if not that, evading justice, and whatever else we can charge him with."

She said, "Thank you for the information. But there is one problem: the Salty in the park is not my father. His name is Salty, yes, but my father Salty was way taller and had way bigger hands."

She thought, it's not really a lie, since that is how I remember him.

Sylvia went into her dorm room and flopped down on her bed. Although she was calm when she talked to the police, now she felt like that red ball being knocked back and forth. The police knew she was the daughter of a man called Salty who had committed a crime. But they did not know if that Salty was this Salty. The whole business was way too complicated. She wanted nothing more to do with it.

Chapter Thirty-Two

Roof

Roof and Dickie were standing at the front door of The Daystar. No one answered the bell, so they tried the door, which was unlocked. They called, "Hello," but when no answer came, they climbed the stairs. They found Pavements asleep on his bed.

Dickie said, "We can't give him the money until he's sober enough to sign."

"That's going to be a long wait. He's never sober."

"If we give it to him when he's drunk, he'll lose it and then say he never got it."

Roof took out the plain, sealed envelope addressed to Nelson Hynes. "I'm tired of carrying it around. This is our third time here and every time he's the same."

"Wake him up, then. Maybe we can help him sign."

Roof shook Pavements upright. "Sign here, Pavements. I'm leaving it on the desk."

Dickie said, "If you leave it out in the open someone will steal it. That's a suit jacket he's wearing. It's going to have deep inside pockets. Put it in there."

"Tucked away, Pavements. Here it is. Touch it. When you wake up, put it in the bank."

"He won't have a bank."

"Not our problem. If he signs for it, it's his problem. Sign here, Pavements."

They propped him up. He signed and flopped back down on the bed.

Dickie looked like he was feeling sorry for him. Roof said, "Don't give me your social worker stuff, Dickie. Our job here is finished. Let's go."

"What's the difference between you and him? You got a job and drive a Dodge Ram cock extension with those big cock extension wheels but say something goes wrong, you lose your job and you up the six-pack to a twelve-pack and so it gets started."

"Fuck off."

Dickie picked up Pavements's feet and laid them on the bed. They left him there, snoring like a snowblower.

Chapter Thirty-Three

Salty

Salty, Pavements, and the dog were relaxing on Caps's bench in the afternoon sun. Beets was asleep in the grass, drooling from one corner of his mouth. Officer Cobbs appeared and pedaled along the path towards them. He stopped and, without getting off his bike, gave Beets a prod with his boot hard enough to blink his eyes open.

Pavements said, "That's a nice bike you're driving. Like I said, my sister's was a three-speed CCM. Her cousin who was twelve, a year older, she saved up from her paper route and got a ten-speed the exact same as yours."

Salty was watching the unfolding of Pavements getting up from the bench, his baseball hat slanted, sauntering over to Officer Cobbs and fastening one small hand on the handlebars. Pavements had been drinking Kawasaki and that always made him a little crazy. By the look of things, the craziness now taking shape in Pavements's brain had something to do with the prod of that boot.

"Mind if I take Beets for a ride on your cousin's bicycle, Officer Corncobs?"

In his uniform with billy and gun and shiny belts and straps, Officer Cobbs looked like an SS officer from that movie they had seen at St. Luke's. In a suit jacket and trousers that looked like Pavements had been living in them since Celia had put them on him two weeks ago, Pavements looked like a concentration camp survivor, still wearing the clothes he'd had on when they put him in the boxcar.

Officer Cobbs swung his leg over the seat. He lifted the bike and pulled but Pavements did not let go.

"For one thing, Pavements, my name is Officer Cobbs."

"Mind if I take Beets for a ride on your cousin's bicycle, Officer Corncobs?"

Cobbs shifted his billy to his right hand and tapped Pavements's arm with the blunt end. "For another thing, Pavements, take your hand off my bike."

Beets, awake now, sitting up and excited by the idea of a bike ride, was slobbering drool into the collar of his shirt. Watching the tug-of-war, Salty did not notice the Humane Society truck pull up to the curb. Colin had tightened the catchpole around the dog's neck and dragged him across the park to the truck before Salty could get up off the bench.

Pavements said, "Strike me dead."

Cobbs pulled his bike loose and pedaled away, giving Salty the finger, leaving him standing in the park minus the dog.

"What do I do now?" Salty asked Father Sutcliffe.

"Am I hearing correctly? Salty wants Father Sutcliffe to tell him what to do about the dog. How many times have I told you? Now thanks to you, Whisper, who would not hurt a fly, is locked up in a cage on death row like Hannibal Lecter in that movie at St. Luke's. How many times have you been warned to get him on a leash? Instead, you let him wander about because Salty the mountain man can't walk around with his dog on a leash like those sissies across the bridge in the Rose. But I'll tell you what. I'll go down to City Hall, say the dog is mine, get a tag and pay the bail and get him out of the pound and keep him at The Daystar until you get yourself sorted out. I'll do that to save your dog on one condition. Walk yourself over to the address I'm going to write out for you and make things right with Sylvia. Don't pretend you don't know what I'm talking about. That's the deal."

Chapter Thirty-Four

Pavements

Pavements saw that Beets was not doing too well on the Bridge Street corner with a made-up sign saying, "War Veteran. Please Help me."

Pavements asked, "What war?"

"The second one."

"That would make you about a hundred years old. Why not write up a sign saying 'Need $ for nose job.' People coming by will think, look at that poor bugger's nose. And then when they get up close they'll say, whoa. Get a whiff. No wonder he's got that nose. You got to make a sign that gets people's attention, like stepping in dog shit. Whoa. Who stepped in dog shit?"

So, Pavements had gone to the library and got a beet-coloured crayon and wrote it up on a piece of cardboard he'd found behind Colonel Wong's. As soon as Beets had collected ten dollars in Pavements's City Works hat, they went for a bottle each of Kawasaki at Dixie's Donut Shoppe.

Because Beets smelled like dog shit, Pavements wanted to drink his bottle undisturbed in his Daystar room. But, turning the corner, he saw that there in the front yard was Indian Elvis, passed out sitting up in the grass like the fat Buddha picture in the library, his chin sunk into his chest and his hairy belly busting out of his shirt. Sitting on the top step was Mr. Bones, showing Father Sutcliffe a new pair of cowboy boots. He was saying, "I keep a close eye on the bridge for jumpers so I can go up and ask, 'Can I have your stuff?' Then I make them sign a note I keep in my pocket at all times saying, 'Last will and testament: all my stuff goes to Mr. Bones.'"

Nobody had jumped off the bridge in the last few days that Pavements knew about, but he'd been drunk for six days, the last three he'd missed completely.

Mr. Bones took off the boots to show Father Sutcliffe that the soles weren't worn and there were hardly any scuff marks. "He didn't give them to me right away because he was going to use them to walk over to the jump-off. He'd tied his shopping cart full of his clothes and shit to the guard rail. I says, 'How come you Outreachers always get the ones with four good wheels?' He said, 'Fuck you.' His last words. 'Fuck you.' I liked that. Then he'd dialed the 1-800-SUICIDE line to report the jump to Richard in Malaysia. He'd signed the last will and testament saying everything in his shopping cart goes to Mr. Bones. So I said, 'What about them boots you still got on your feet?'"

Rather than share with Mr. Bones and Indian Elvis, Pavements decided to slip up the lane and sneak in the back door and hope Father Sutcliffe didn't catch him. He set off, only to slow down and stop. Strike me dead. Sitting on the back stoop, three Outreachers were passing around their paper bag. In the back yard next door were three more. They'd been on the list for resettlement counseling and habitat relocation and had been taken by a cube van to their new place, but here they were, back again. It was like trying to relocate black bears in Kenora, where Pavements grew up. They'd move them away from the dump in pickups, but the bears would be back almost the next day.

Pavements tucked his bottle into his dinner jacket and headed for the house further along with the demolition sign on the front door. He had almost gone past the corner when Mr. Bones called him.

Mr. Bones said, "The city came with a bulldozer to flatten the Silver City. When they got to Caps's shack, some church people lay down in front so the city workers had to quit and go home. But they left the bulldozer."

"So?"

"Where's Salty? We can't find him. We got the idea to cover the bulldozer with daisies and drive it to city hall and leave it there in the square by the fountain. So we want Salty to drive the bulldozer. I'm going to sing some songs. You can make a sign like the one you made for Beets."

"Saying what?"

"About 'Fringe Dwellers have rights,' like 'save the whales.' Write up some shit like that."

Pavements crossed the street and hurried past the house with the demolition sign. The next house in the row was boarded up. He sat behind a tree on the front lawn out of sight of the street so he could drink and smoke in peace.

***

Pavements's eyes blinked open. His City Works hat was in the dirt at his feet. His bottle, which had been almost one-third full, was now empty. He hadn't drunk the whole bottle on the way from Dixie's Donut Shoppe to this tree. He knew that. He bent over and put on his hat. He heard a racket that sounded like black bears and looked up. He saw three Outreachers across the street. Strike me dead. They stole my bottle and gave it back empty, those fuckers.

Pavements didn't like begging. It felt like when he had worked door to door selling storm windows in Kenora. When the person answered the doorbell he'd look at Pavements like he was dog shit. Pavements was thinking about this when he saw, coming along the street, two men in nice suits. The lady trying to keep up with them was wearing sunglasses and a wide-brimmed hat. She was carrying a carton of Colonel Wong's Chinese Fried Chicken takeout. When Pavements saw that all three of them were carrying Bibles he said, oh boy, oh boy. Jehovah's Witnesses. They'll be good for a toonie each at least, maybe more. And maybe the lady will give me her Chinese chicken.

Pavements could smell it. He could almost taste the little squares of chicken. He could see those chicken squares staring down google-eyed from the carton at the lady's bare legs that were too short to keep up with the two men who were looking up and over and away, in any direction other than at the Outreachers' outstretched hands, straight ahead. Pavements could almost hear the jingle-jangle of change in their pockets. Pavements could almost see that change disappearing into the Outreachers' pockets.

Then the Jehovah's Witnesses stopped. The Outreachers were standing square in the centre of the sidewalk, blocking their path. Pavements could see in the faces of the two men that they were asking Jehovah what to do next. Then Pavements saw the answer coming to them in a vision of a silver-forked path laying in the road, glinting in the sunshine: Detour away from these lepers who look like none of them have washed since grade two, cross the black asphalt, hang a left, and follow a safer path to the deserving one, namely Pavements.

Oh boy. The vision of toonies in his brain, Pavements reached out his hand. The two men emptied their pockets and filled his open palm. They stepped aside so the lady could step up.

"Oh my goodness, Nelson. Is that you?"

Pavements looked up. His hands fell to his side.

"Nelson! I've been looking all over for you. Your dinner jacket is ripped. And your trousers are filthy. What happened, Nelson? You look terrible. How many days have you been drunk for?"

"I've been on construction. I've been saving my paycheques..."

"Nelson! You're drunk as a skunk. Look at you."

He lowered his head.

"And look what you've done to your nice dinner jacket."

Pavements looked down at his unbuttoned jacket. "I've been going to work in my good clothes. I didn't want to spend the money I was making on work clothes."

He managed a glance up at Celia.

She sighed. "What's the use."

One of the Jehovah's Witnesses said to Celia, "A group of us are talking to the men in Silver Park. It's our mission of the week, over there by the bridge. Maybe he should join us."

Celia sighed. "What's the use."

The man said, "We could pray for Nelson right here then, on the street."

"What's the use of that?"

"We're going to pray for you, Nelson. But you have to pray for yourself. Our Lord will help you if you ask."

Pavements stared at his feet.

"Join us in prayer, Nelson. Right here, all four of us together."

One of the men put his arm around Pavements's shoulder and the other the same. They bowed their heads. "Dear God. Save Nelson from the drinking fever and restore him to health. Amen."

The two Jehovah's Witnesses dropped their arms and quickly stepped away.

Pavements said, "What about our plans to get an apartment and get back together. Can we pray for that?"

She sighed.

One of the men said, "Alright, Nelson. Bow your head."

They all bowed their heads.

"Please, dear God, help Nelson get a decent job so he can earn the money he needs so he and Celia can get back together."

Celia had turned to go, waiting for the other two, when she said, "This is your last chance, Nelson. No more chances. Here. You can have my chicken."

Pavements took the chicken and watched them leave. He was feeling embarrassed about Celia, but he was feeling good about the money in his pocket. The two Jehovah's Witnesses had looked like they were feeling good about how it had worked out. If they had taken the other fork, instead of the one that had brought them to Pavements, and passed by the Outreachers and not given them any money, well, they wouldn't feel right about that.

Pavements checked his pants pocket. He had two toonies, a loonie, and some quarters. Enough for another bottle of Kawasaki. He looked into the box of chicken, almost all there except the feathers. It even had a little fork in there. "Hello, Chicken, it's me, Pavements. I'm sorry to say the farmer probably promised you a life of happy days of pecking for grubs in a farmyard. Instead, you got life in a cage followed by a bumpy ride down life's bumpy road to hang head-down from a chain in the slaughterhouse and then lay down headless on a conveyor then ending in square pieces in a box and here we are, Mr. Chicken, Dixie's Donut Shoppe. On the seventh day the Lord created the homeless, Mr. Chicken, and on the eighth day the Lord created Jehovah's Witnesses and on the ninth, He created spare change and on the tenth He spake to me. I could feel His very words in my heart, as if said in a command from a mountaintop, and He said, here is the straight of it, Pavements, and here is how it works, so learn how to work it. Take up the change from your pocket and give it to Indian Elvis's sister, she's called Dixie. Dixie, this is Mr. Chicken."

"How much money have you got there, Pavements?"

The gates of Dixie's Donut Shoppe opened and he followed Dixie into her homebrew kitchen.

"This is a high-octane brew, Pavements. Be careful."

She always put the bottles in paper bags. Better for the environment, she said. He continued up the street to a fenced-off alley that ran behind the pool hall. Usually, he would settle down against the board fence at the end, next to the wall of Soapy Suds Laundry, the one place he could relax for a quiet drink. But two Outreachers were there busy with spray bombs, adding to the caveman art on the brick wall of Colonel Wong's. When they saw Pavements, they threw away their spray bombs and left.

Strike me dead, said Pavements to his chicken. Dixie has given me Kawasaki. Makes you do crazy stuff, like jumping off the bridge. Put Kawasaki in a spoon and strike a match and poof.

Pavements settled down behind Soapy Suds for a drink.

The little man who owned it came along. He'd had a throat operation, so when he spoke, out of a little funnel thing under his chin came a gurgly voice: "Did you do these drawings, Pavements?"

"Those drawings are from the caveman days. Do I look like a Cave Man?"

"They aren't from Cave Man. Did you do them or didn't you?"

His words when they came out sounded like when the laundry water was draining. Celia would say, rinse and spin, Nelson. Rinse and spin. To wash your clothes is not a sin.

"See the footprints left there in the mud? If you follow them you'll find the Cave Man who did the drawings."

"What footprints?"

"The ones left in the mud from last night's rain."

"It didn't rain last night."

Pavements took a long pull from his bottle. He felt the gurgle in his throat.

"I think you did these drawings."

Pavements studied the drawings.

"Did you do these drawings, Pavements?"

Pavements slanted his City Works hat and squinted one eye. "I've researched drawings like these. These are prehistoric drawings depicting ancient legends."

"Did you do these drawings?"

"The blue comes from blueberries from a nearby ancient bog. The red comes from cranberry patches. The fossilized footprints, left in mud and hardened into granite, date these drawings back to Neanderthal times."

"Did you do these drawings?"

"Blueberry juice and cranberry juice. See? Red and blue. Back then, the only job that paid decent money was cave art, which couldn't be washed off, just like this cave art can't be washed off. And crushed minerals. And besides that, it's prehistoric. So I got to seal off the area until I can do more research."

"I think you did these drawings."

Pavements tidied his dinner jacket neatly around him. "Cave art drawings passed on from generation to generation all the way back to the Paleolithic might have been done by a prehistoric Neanderthal, but most likely was done by that species of psychotic Cave Man called the Outreachers, who recently relocated themselves here from Silver City. They're all cousins. They live in groups of cousins. Once they get settled in their territory, that is where they stay and they'll fight to stay there."

"I'm phoning the police."

"You can keep the fence I'm going to put up but you can't remove the drawings."

"I'm phoning the police."

Pavements hustled down the alley until, out of sight behind a garbage can, he settled in the dirt and leaned his back against the wall and took a drink from his bottle. He listened to the liquid gurgling against the glass. He felt the glunk, glunk of liquor in his throat. He wondered how could you drink with that thing in your throat. You'd need a screw-on cap so the homebrew wouldn't leak out.

After capping his bottle and returning it to the bag, Pavements searched through the nearby trash, finally finding a pile of cardboard, no doubt placed there by City Hall to attract the cave artist who did those drawings, originally identified for resettlement counseling and habitat relocation in East Jesus but ending up back here where they came from.

He laid the cardboard on the ground. Leaning against the side of the building, he slid down and settled back against the wall, and drank some more. There was a good butt in the dirt, dropped by one of the Outreachers. He picked it up, careful to close the bottle before he lit up. After his cigarette, he continued along the alley, crossed the sidewalk, and teetered his way through the Sheldon Street traffic to the park. He settled down with the daisies, fresh-picked it looked like.

Pavements drank the same homebrew as the Outreachers. But he didn't live in a tin-and-cardboard shack and he didn't live at the Outreach. He lived at The Daystar, he managed his money and his liquor, always saving a little of both for the next day. Not like Mr. Bones. He found a lottery ticket with enough money on the number to buy a house in the Rose and an SUV and start an investment. Oh boy. But he spent it all on Curveball and Majestic Diner.

Pavements took a gentle pull. He had to be careful with this stuff. He liked Majestic Diner better, brewed from early-spring dandelion leaves, stewed up nice and smooth by Dixie's sister in her restaurant-grade Majestic Diner pressure cooker on the Coca-Cola Reserve. Kawasaki was cooked in car radiators by her cousins in Cape Croker. It was called Kawasaki because of how it worked. First gear gets you started, second gear a bit jerky, but you're in motion and starting to settle into the trip. Third gear you're smoothed out, running not too bad. Fourth gear you're burning on all cylinders and then whoosh, the shift to 747 airborne, riding the wind.

Not too far off, Celia and the three men and some other Jehovah's Witnesses had gathered, giving out their pamphlets to whoever passed by. Afraid she would see him, Pavements snuck out under the shadow of the bridge and climbed the bank to the street. He teetered his way across the bridge to the centre and stood where Caps had stood, one arm on the rail, looking down at Celia and her two friends. Out in the open, the wind was strong; not gusty, but steady, like the wind on your face riding your Kawasaki.

He took another long swallow. He climbed over the rail to stand on the ledge. If he jumped, he would land right on top of Celia, flat on her back, her legs open, like how they used to be in the nice bed they had bought that summer at Bad Bob's.

Looking over the park, Pavements saw the wind in the bushes and in the trees and he knew that the wind in the bushes and the trees was like the Kawasaki in his veins. He couldn't see the wind in the bushes and the trees, but he could see the results of the wind in the bushes and the trees. He couldn't see the Kawasaki but he could feel the results of the Kawasaki in his veins. The Kawasaki had brought Pavements to life and made him move, like how the wind brought the bushes and the trees to life and made them move, soft and gentle and flowing. He took the bottle from his pocket and lifted his right arm and emptied the bottle, and then he lifted his left arm and emptied the bottle again. Teetering on the edge of the rail, arms outstretched, he drifted with the wind through the trees and the bushes. The outstretched left arm of the dinner jacket seemed grey, but it had a pattern of brown and green like the leaves and branches of the bushes beneath the bridge. In his outstretched right arm, he saw that the brown and green of the trees was like the brown and green of the front of his jacket. The inside of the jacket, open to the wind, was grey, and the inside jacket pocket was like little bumps of woven silver.

The wind ceased. The bushes became still and the trees returned rooted to the ground where they belonged. Pavements returned rooted to his brain where he belonged. He climbed down from the rail and away from the ledge where he had not belonged. There was no movement anywhere except for the fingers of Pavements's left hand, nails no longer broken and cracked from laying pavement, reaching into the inside jacket pocket. Then the fingers tips of his left hand, no longer calloused from shoveling asphalt, felt the smooth surface of the paper inside. He opened the envelope. He held the one-hundred-dollar bills up to the sunlight.

"Praise be to Jehovah," said Pavements.

Chapter Thirty-Five

Salty

Six Outreachers had come into The Daystar for lunch. Salty was thinking, they should be staying over in East Jesus instead of sitting with their paper bags in the front yard, two of them falling almost asleep, the other four drinking what even Pavements would say no thank you to. But here they were and Father Sutcliffe had let them in. He wouldn't let them stay the night, but he wouldn't turn anyone away for a meal as long as they didn't cause trouble.

Mr. Bones, who'd been over to East Jesus, explained to Salty, "The ones we get here are the docile ones. There's a lot of fighting over there. All it takes is for one guy to get the swaggers and pretty soon they're all into it."

Donkey Man wandered in and took his seat. "Lunchtime at Hopeless Hotel. Who's going to say grace?"

The four Outreachers were already busy with their ham sandwiches.

"Don't none of you nose-pickers know to say grace before you start to eat? Never mind, I'll say it myself. Thank you for the soup and ham sandwiches."

Donkey Man reached for the water jug and dipped in his comb and combed his hair. Salty watched the snakes slithering along that arm, turning with the twisting of those muscles like water snakes sliding past his boat on a cloudy day. On a sunny day, they'd be on a rock, enjoying the heat. Salty had found one lying in the bottom of Dr. Reed's rowboat. He'd said to Frank, it won't hurt you. It can come along for the ride.

But Frank wouldn't get into the boat with a snake in it. Salty caught it by the tail and threw it up on shore near the path. Too late, he realized, now Frank will be afraid to walk along that path. I should have thrown it into the water. But then Frank would be afraid to go fishing. No matter what Salty did, it seemed to end up wrong.

Donkey Man said, "I found your dog outside wandering loose, dragging his leash. So I tied him to a dumpster."

The snakes reached out for another sandwich. "I hear they serve nice food over there in East Jesus, so why are these Outreach nose-pickers eating our sandwiches?"

The Outreachers were bent over their plates, eyes down. They knew enough to stay clear of the Donkey Man.

"I went over there one day. I know the guy who runs the kitchen. I said, 'Look at all the food here. They're going to have to put these nose-pickers on a diet. They got nothing to do all day but eat and drink like rich people. The government is giving them free cell phones and tablets so they can apply for work, but why work if everything is free? Next thing they'll build a swimming pool and serve them their sandwiches poolside. Maybe serve them those sick-a-boobs on the barbecue. Maybe they'll bring in some nice girls and start having Outreach Rocker Parties.'"

The snakes reached for another sandwich. "I got a bottle of red wine. You want some, Salty? Come and have a drink and I'll tell you the number of the dumpster."

Donkey Man finished his soup.

"Someone said Father Sutcliffe bailed the dog out of the pound. Someone said he told you to keep him on a leash and walk along like Scarlett Johansson with her poodle. Someone said you let the dog wander around dragging his leash instead of you holding it and walking along like in Hollywood. Someone said they seen your poodle in that alley behind the Chinese restaurant. So I went over and first I tied him to a dumpster but he didn't like that so I put him in the dumpster. Come out and have a drink and I'll tell you exactly the number of the dumpster I put your dog in."

Salty and Donkey Man pushed back their chairs. Salty followed him down the hallway to the back door. From behind the garbage can, Donkey Man took a bottle. He sat on the step of the back stoop of The

Daystar and offered the bottle to Salty. Salty shook his head. Even if he did want a drink, he would not drink with the Donkey Man.

Donkey Man tipped the bottle, took a long drink, swished it around between his teeth, swallowed, exhaled loudly, and burped. "Try it. It's better than that homebrew Coca-Cola Reserve goat piss you usually drink."

Salty held the bottle to the light to see through the murky glass. He gave it back.

"I was standing there looking down into the dumpster at the dog wondering if I should tell you. I was thinking, what's the use of having a sheepdog if there are no sheep?"

He tipped the bottle to take a mouthful but took too much and choked, coughing with his mouth closed at first and then doubling over. After a while, coughing done, he wiped his eyes and his face with his shirttail. Drops of red wine hung from the underside of his chin. He lit a cigarette. "The girl I stole the watch from, I told her I was a friend of a porn producer. I'd get her into porn. So I said, 'Get naked for me so I can tell my porn buddy what you look like.' I said, 'He's starting a new magazine called *Outreachers Cock Rocker*. He'll put you in for the Cock Rocker Centrefold.'"

Donkey Man dragged on his cigarette.

"I tried the same story on this other chick a couple of months ago and she believed me. So we played a little spank the monkey and it turns out this match made in heaven was only fifteen."

Donkey Man stared into the dirt, smoking, nodding his head between long pauses. He was stoned on something besides wine, Salty realized.

"I asked her if she wanted to and she said okay. What's the matter with that? That's not rape."

He seemed to drift and then came back. "First of all this chick says I raped her and now she says the kid is mine and now she's talking about playing house with me supporting her so I'm staying out of sight so her brothers can't find me. She got about nine brothers and they're all looking for me."

He dragged on his cigarette. "We better watch Father Sutcliffe doesn't catch us out here drinking. He's worse than that fruitcake

Roger. He used to sit at the desk at the front of the Sally reading books that explain the Bible. Bible stories back in the pyramid days. Roger used to sneak along the street and up and down the alley trying to catch guys drinking, but the cops made him stop doing that. Then he'd go out into the alley to try to catch hookers hooking. That's how he caught guys drinking. I knew him before he got religious and joined the Sally. He should have joined the Mormons. They've got three, four wives and get laid ten times a day."

He swallowed another short slurp from the bottle. "I know a guy who jumped off the bridge the other day. He'd done a run of Kawasaki. It makes you do crazy things. He thought he could fly. We were up on Silver Bridge. The guy's name was... I can't remember. He said, 'You know how I've been telling you I can fly?' and I says yeah, and he says, 'Well I can,' and I says yeah so he starts flapping his arms and jumps. When the ambulance came he was lying on the ground, still flapping his arms like he was flying. Now he wants his cowboy boots back from Mr. Bones."

Salty got to his feet and left.

The dog was not in the park and not at the closed-down Outreach. Maybe, thought Salty, he's at home, on the step, waiting for me.

Salty turned up the laneway behind the Chinese restaurant and headed for the alley leading to his workshop shed. The dog must have recognized his footsteps for, as Salty passed the dumpster, the dog barked.

Salty circled the dumpster twice and called again. The dog answered. Salty circled again, looking for something to climb on. He found a two-by-four and leaned it against the metal side when he noticed the number on the side of the dumpster: 2020.

Salty backed away to the far side of the alley. He sat in the dirt. He watched the flies circling above the open lid, coming out of his mind and circling his head and then flying backward, big as hummingbirds, into the dumpster to crawl in and out of the carpet and fly back towards him to circle and land on the scars on his wrist, their bodies little green bottles in the sunshine. The carpet was green. Him and Lee Ann had gone to the carpet store but Lee Ann couldn't decide between blue or grey. He had wanted blue but he'd wanted her to decide so if she didn't like it, it would be her fault. She chose green. He hated green.

She had trouble making decisions: should she buy this watch or that watch; should she buy this dress or that dress. Just buy a dress, he'd say. Do these pants make me look fat? Do these jeans make me look fat? It's your butt makes you look fat, he'd say.

It used to be he had no trouble making a decision. He did not spend time thinking, should I do this or should I do that? He just did it.

Amos didn't cheat and didn't lie. He was loyal and honest and pure as that five-year-old child from 2002, in his heart still singing that same song, "Long May You Run." But she was older now, this girl Sylvia, and now she could run faster than Salty and now she had caught up to him.

The sunshine in the alley and the traffic along the street and the whimpers of Amos and Sylvia faded away as he directed his path along the alley. Salty was big as a grizzly bear and afraid of no one, but he could not climb into that dumpster.

Chapter Thirty-Six

Sylvia

Sylvia was having her morning coffee in the Rose Starbucks before making her usual trip to the Thorn library. She was reading in the complimentary paper about the homeless hysteria that had taken over Silver Park. Not "homeless;" the politically correct name was "Fringe Dwellers." As an added wrinkle, now there was a First Nations land claim on that portion of the Silver Ravine that ran from the 401 to Lake Ontario. It had been a fur trade route with treaty rights belonging to the Mississaugas. Many of the Fringe Dwellers were First Nations. They were living on land that was theirs, so they couldn't be evicted.

She finished her coffee. She returned the newspaper to the counter. Rather than crossing through the park, she crossed at the bridge. She continued along Bridge Street. She turned in the book and headed home, this time cutting through an alley behind the Soapy Suds Laundry. Passing behind Colonel Wong's, she noticed the dumpster. Then she noticed Salty seated in the dirt, his back to the fence. He is drunk, she thought, coming closer and looking down at him. Now that she had finally decided to have nothing to do with him, she was seeing him not as the father she remembered but as a sad, broken man in a frayed shirt collar and dirty pants. She leaned closer for one last look at the forehead scar hidden in the leather lines of his years of running or hiding or whatever he was doing, which right now was pretending to be asleep.

She said, "I'm sorry I can't help you. But I owe you nothing."

That was the end of it. She was turning away, going home when she noticed that in one hand, he clutched the dog's red ball. She took a few steps back, looking for the dog.

She said, "Where's your dog?"

When she nudged Salty's leg with her foot, the ball dropped from his hand and rolled away. She nudged him again and his eyes blinked open. But he did not look up at her standing over him. He looked away, refusing to acknowledge her presence.

She would have paid no attention to the scratching she thought she heard, except at that moment she noticed that the red ball had rolled across the dirt to come to rest against the dumpster. She hoisted herself up the side and then vaulted over, picked up the dog, and climbed out.

She kicked Salty's leg. "How long has he been in there? What's the matter with you?"

The next kick into the muscle of his thigh brought Salty to his feet. He took the dog. He cradled him against his chest and backed away, confused and frightened.

"What's the matter with you? Why was he in the dumpster?"

They stood face to face. She looked directly at him and he at her. His weathered skin was dry and hard and plowed with determined creases, but his eyes were filled with confusion. He hugged his dog and, like a little kid, hid his face in the fur of its neck so that she could not see his shame, if he felt any, or his thanks, if he had any, or anything, if there was anything other than denial. But what she did see was the nick in the dog's right ear.

She reached out to touch it. "This is Amos. I remember this nick." She held it up, showing him. "How can you not recognize me when this dog can? What is the matter with you?"

The dog in his arms, Salty shambled away, unsteadily at first but gathering momentum, breaking from a trot into a run.

"I remember you killing that chicken," she screamed.

As he disappeared around the corner, he glanced back, first at her then at the dumpster.

"Is it because of my scar? You don't want me because of the scar?"

But Salty was gone.

She returned home. She turned on the television but turned it off after ten minutes. She had a shower. But nothing allowed her to forget the years of remorse that she had seen in Salty's eyes.

Chapter Thirty-Seven

Salty

Salty's knock on Madame Kratz's door was answered by a girl who looked about twelve. "The city health department closed her down because the gas generator she used to pipe the incense into her reading room was a safety hazard."

So, thought Salty, what Madame Kratz had thought was spirits taking shape in her brain, giving her messages and feeding words to her lipstick-caked lips, was carbon monoxide giving her hallucinations.

"Two detectives came here asking about you and she wouldn't tell them, so they reported her to the health department. She'll be back in business as soon as she gets it fixed."

***

No sooner had Salty sat down on the step to feed Amos the bread and meatloaf he had taken from The Daystar than the Donkey Man appeared, coming up the laneway, a baseball bat over his right shoulder, Pavements's City Works baseball hat holding down his long hair. Amos crouched behind Salty's legs.

"How do you like my baseball bat?" Donkey Man hefted his bat. "Any brother comes for me is dead meat." He picked up a stone and hit it down the alley. "I train every day, know that, Salty? Any of those nine brothers come at me, this is what they get." He chopped the air twice, a one-two combination. "I found it in the same dumpster I put your dog. So, this is where you live."

Donkey Man picked up another stone. He rolled it around in his palm. "They told me at The Daystar your dog taught you how to fetch a ball. How'd you like to fetch my stone, Salty?" He tossed it into the air and swung and the stone bounced off a garbage can three garages down the lane.

Salty did not move.

"If you won't fetch my stone, get your dog to fetch it."

Amos slunk away. He glanced back one time before disappearing around the corner.

"Either you fetch it or the dog fetches it. Whichever. I want that stone at my place at The Daystar lunch tomorrow. Same stone."

Donkey Man left. Salty lay down on his couch. Amos would not have gone far; he would be back as soon as he figured it was safe.

Amos did not come back. Salty checked dumpster 2020, not coming too close but calling and whistling. He combed the alleys. He checked with Jake. Amos always waited for Salty by the bicycle stand at St. Luke's. He was not there. He wasn't at St. James's or St. Joe's. Mr. Bones stopped plucking his banjo long enough to remember where he'd last seen the dog: on the old wooden steps of the back stoop of The Daystar.

Salty hurried along Bridge Street to The Daystar.

"Salty," shouted the Donkey Man from the front step. "That dog's got a busted leg."

Salty followed him to the back of The Daystar. With his baseball bat, he pointed under the stoop. Salty crouched to look. Cowering in the dirt up against the back wall of the building, Amos lay on his side, licking his front right foot. When he saw Salty, he struggled up on three legs, but, unable to keep his balance, sank back down. Large red drops fell into the dirt from the mangled paw.

Donkey Man squatted down beside Salty. "See right there?" He pointed with his baseball bat. "That's where it's broke. Right there."

Attempting to move away from the end of the bat, Amos yelped in pain. Salty leaped up and knocked the Donkey Man down. Grabbing the bat, Salty stood back, ready to swing.

The Donkey Man glared up at Salty. The Donkey Man stood and retrieved Pavements's City Works baseball hat, which was upside down in the dirt. He brushed it off, combed through his hair with his fingers, and fastened the hat on his head. He held out his hand. "Give back my baseball bat."

Salty backed away.

"Give it back before I rearrange your face." He stepped forward, but before he could grab the bat, Salty flopped down on his belly and wriggled under the stoop.

Donkey Man crouched in the dirt to swing at him, his fist narrowly missing Salty's face. Finally, he stood and with one boot, kicked the stoop. "I want that stone and that bat by tomorrow lunchtime." He started away. Before he disappeared around the corner and up another alley he shouted, "Remember what I said. I want that stone and that bat delivered by tomorrow."

Salty lay down beside Amos. His tail stirred. He licked Salty's hand. Salty figured he would need a bandage and two sticks for a splint, he knew that much. And something for infection because the cut was filled with dirt. He slid his hands under the dog's belly and rib cage and, holding him against his chest, little by little lifting and dragging, he managed to squirm his way out. The dog cradled in his arms, carrying him carefully but walking quickly, he left The Daystar and started up the street.

"Where's my bat and where are you going with that dog."

Clutching Amos to his chest, Salty hurried on, pretending not to hear.

"Salty. Come back here with that dog."

Salty began to run, clumsily because Amos was frightened and squirming. At Sheldon Street, Donkey Man caught up to him. As he tried to jerk Amos free, the dog squirmed out of Salty's arms and collapsed in a heap on the sidewalk. Then, picking himself up, he lurched on three legs down the street, stumbling several times and falling forward on the broken leg, Donkey Man chasing after him. Halfway along the block, the dog veered to the left onto the street and into the path of a passing car. The driver did not see the dog. The car thwunked-thwunked over Amos and continued without stopping.

Salty waited, staring at Amos stretched out flat on the asphalt, expecting him to get up again. After a while, the Donkey Man said, "You should have left it at The Daystar where I could look after it. I didn't want nothing bad to happen to your dog, Salty."

Turning away, smoothing his hair and adjusting the City Works hat, Donkey Man continued up the street. A car drove by, its tires straddling the motionless black-and-white dog. Another passed. And another. A transport truck with eight double wheels on each side approached. It grew bigger and then with a roar lumbered over the dog, swallowing him up in a twisting funnel of dust.

At first, Salty thought it was the wind moving through the fur. But when Amos lifted his head and looked over at him, Salty rushed into the traffic and dragged the dog back to the sidewalk. As he knelt to feel along his body, Amos's tail wagged faintly and his tongue reached out to Salty's hand. This time when Salty gathered him up, Amos lay quiet in his arms, too weak to struggle. Salty carried him along the street, past the park, and up the lane to the shed. He laid him gently in the cardboard box and sat down beside him and stroked the soft fur of his head. He thought, I'll need gauze and tape to stop the bleeding. I can keep him warm with blankets. I can stay with him so he's not alone.

When Salty ran his hand along the rib cage, he could barely feel the heart beating under his palm. He knew Amos would not last long. The broken front leg was bleeding, and one hind leg seemed crushed. Blood was running from his nose and mouth, and already half a dozen flies had come from somewhere to crawl along the edges of the open wound across his chest. He waved them away but as soon as he lowered his hand they came back, bringing more with them.

"I'm going for bandages," he explained, knowing they'd do no good but needing Amos to think Salty could fix it. He set off for the pharmacy but was in such a rush to get back that he forgot to buy the tape. He hurried down the alley to the drug store, bought the tape, and ran back. Turning up the lane, he noticed that the shed door was open.

Salty removed his jacket. He rolled up his sleeves and opened his shirt. He had worked in construction for years. When he wasn't on construction, he worked as a roofer, laying down bundles of shingles shirtless in the hot sun, the compressor humming and the nail gun snapping. He would like to have a nail gun now.

He saw Sylvia in the shadows of the doorway. He brushed past her, into the shed. "Where is Donkey Man?"

"Not here, that's for sure."

She went over and stood by the box. Amos struggled to get up but could not raise his hindquarters off the cardboard.

"Where did he go?"

"I haven't seen Donkey Man."

Salty came down on his knees and stroked the dog's head and scratched behind his ears, trying to settle him down. As well as the blood from the wound across his chest, more was being lost from the mangled flesh of the hind leg.

"I'm taking him to the vet," she said. "Not the Humane Society. They'll put him down."

She knelt to pat the dog. This time his eyes did not open, nor did his tail stir.

She repeated, "I'm taking him to the vet hospital on Jarvis Street."

For a moment, his eyes met hers. He brought his right hand up to his hair in a useless attempt to smooth away the snarls. He looked down at his clothes. He brought his left hand up to fasten the missing buttons of his shirt. Finally, he shook his head and turned away unable to face her.

But Sylvia took his hand. "Frank never came for me. I went into foster care."

He felt her thin fingers turn over his right arm. She picked up the left arm and turned it to the light so she could examine the scars crisscrossing from his wrist to the elbow and disappearing into the sleeve of his shirt.

"All these years running. It's like the barbs from the barbed wire are still in there, festering. No wonder they're not healed."

He felt the tips of her fingers slide in a zig-zag along the pale skin of his left arm as, one by one, they traced along each scar, the stroke along the first scar un-stitching and re-stitching the fence from gnarled to straight, and then the stroke along the second scar un-stitching and re-stitching the chicken from chopped to un-chopped, and then the stroke along the third scar un-stitching and re-stitching the gun from loaded to unloaded, and then the last stroke along the last scar, un-stitching and re-stitching drunk to sober. Then she knelt down and slipped two hands under the box and picked up the dog and hurried away.

Chapter Thirty-Eight

Salty

Usually this time of day Salty would be sitting on Caps's bench drinking from the neck of an open bottle. Or this time of day he would be on his way to Dixie's Donut Shoppe, having already drunk his first bottle. Returning along Bridge Street, he would not bother to hide his bottle under his jacket or in his pants. He would hold it in his right hand and it would swing at his side, no different from when he crossed the field, stopping for a handshake with Amos before continuing to the big rock where Eli would be waiting.

Some days he would walk across the field, his bottle swinging at his side, to sit with Eli on a hay bale in the barn, out of sight of his wife, who knew they were passing the bottle. But she would say nothing, unlike Lee Ann, who would say plenty when he returned home drunk.

This day Salty was walking across the park, no bottle swinging at his side, no Amos greeting him for a handshake, no sheep grazing in the field, and no Eli waiting at the rock or at the haybale. His knock on Madame Kratz's waiting door was answered by the young girl. "I told you, she's closed until she gets her gas generator fixed."

"But I need to know what to do next."

"I'll go ask her."

The girl came back. "She says to tell you fate has already sealed your destiny."

"What does that mean?"

"I'll go ask her." She disappeared.

She came back. "We're all inkblots, you to them and them to you and you to yourself."

"What does that mean?"

"I'll go ask her."

She returned. "What are the wheels of the mind continually creating? A rose slowly blooming or denials dancing round?"

"What does that mean?"

"I'll go ask her."

She returned. "You made your bed so lie in it."

Salty knew that one.

Pavements was sitting on The Daystar front step, rubbing his hands over his naked head. Behind him, the baseball bat leaned against the Goodwill box on the front porch. Salty motioned for Pavements to follow. Baseball bat over his right shoulder, Salty opened the front door and stepped inside. The Donkey Man was at the dining room table drinking coffee with Father Sutcliffe. Salty reached out and removed Pavements's hat from Donkey Man's head. He held it in his left hand. He did not need two hands for the swing of the baseball bat. In his right arm alone was enough anger to smash Donkey Man's skull like a rotten pumpkin. He ducked and the bat crashed down on his shoulder and crumpled him to the floor.

Father Sutcliffe gripped Salty's arm. "Your dog is going to be all right. I've got a note from Sylvia for you. She'll keep him until he's better."

When Donkey Man moved his arms to get up, Salty crushed his boot into Donkey Man's chest until he gasped for air.

Father Sutcliffe stood close. He leaned over and whispered in Salty's ear. "Sylvia told the detectives you weren't the Salty they're looking for. The police have nothing on you. Keep it that way."

Salty knew that Father Sutcliffe's grip on the muscles of his forearm would be powerless against the second swing that would cave in Donkey Man's forehead.

"That's what she says. Here. Read the note."

Salty did not lift his boot off Donkey Man's chest. Salty motioned for Pavements to hand him the bottle of ketchup sitting on the table. Salty poured the ketchup onto Donkey Man's face. The second bottle he poured into his hair. When he reached for the third bottle, Father Sutcliffe held his arm.

Salty removed his boot from Donkey Man's chest and returned the ketchup to the table. He turned and walked out and sat on The Daystar step. Looking off, remembering, he could see how Sylvia had stood up and had come down Eli's porch steps and had come across the Mennonite field and unrolled herself from the carpet in the pickup and climbed out of the dumpster, the black-and-white sheepdog, Amos, tucked under her arm. Just like that, she had climbed over the side, a little thinner, narrower around the hips, but the same as her mother, and the nose was the same as her mother's. Sylvia had vaulted over the side of that dumpster and had dropped back into now like he knew she eventually would. He saw how she walked when she came up the alley and he saw her up close in the sunlight when she handed him the dog and he saw how her mouth was set and her eyes filled with anger for leaving her in the foster care dumpster back then, and for leaving Amos in the dumpster now. And he saw how her scar had healed with a jog at the end.

Madame Kratz had said, "Let me see your hand, Salty."

She had studied his palm.

"I don't usually read palms, Salty. But this line here with the jog means there is, no, not is, was, yes, I see it: a sharp jog in a path you probably should not have taken."

Then she had pointed to the thin white line in the palm of his right hand. "Do you have any children, Salty?"

"No, I don't deserve to have children."

"Do you have a wife, Salty?"

"No, I don't deserve to have a wife."

"You always deserve what you have, Salty. That's why you have it."

Salty had turned away and he had turned his back and he had gone. But not the chicken. It had picked itself up off the ground and followed him across the yard and up the lane and up the road and across the bridge, all this time wobbling along the broken white lines of those scars, following after him.

Chapter Thirty-Nine

Salty

Salty was sitting on Caps's bench with Celia and the man who'd left his CBC News truck parked on Bridge Street. He was glancing through the pamphlet gave to him by Celia. She was telling him what the pamphlet was saying.

"The bold print title says, 'From life in the street to life in the future.' It explains about the system failures in the Homeless Hub. Silver City is the home of the Fringe Dwellers. But the city is trying to make them homeless by tearing down Silver City."

Celia pointed to Pavements, who was explaining the pamphlets to Juicy, who was going through the garbage can nearest the bridge.

Celia said, "That's the one you want to talk to over there. His street name was Pavements when he was a Fringe Dweller, but now he's a Jehovah's Witness. His real name is Nelson. I told him he has to talk properly for this interview. I told him he's not to say that the Outreachers get into the liquor and then they get the swaggers and then pretty soon the fists get started. That's street talk, so don't talk like that. And don't call them hunters and gatherers without enough brain capacity to get a job, except maybe as scarecrows. Don't talk like that about people less fortunate than yourself."

Pavements had finished with Juicy. He looked around and waved. He looked like he was doing a good job of being Nelson, the Jehovah's Witness, dressed in a blue suit with a matching blue shirt and red bow tie and a sort of English-style Sherlock Nelson Holmes cap. He looked like a Sherlock Jehovah's Nelson.

Celia introduced him to the news reporter, but not to the cameraman who was off to the left. Pavements said, "That woman I was talking to. Her real name is Betty O'Reagan, from Halifax. She goes by the name Juicy. She lives in Silver City."

The reporter said, "The women's shelters are half empty. Why not live there?"

"Because she's not pregnant. All the rooms are reserved for the pregnant ones."

Celia said, "That's what I mean. What's the matter with the system that a woman can't get into a shelter unless she's pregnant?"

Nelson said, "The homeless women get pregnant so they can go into a shelter, but the men refuse to go into the shelters. So, what they should do is put the women who aren't pregnant in the men's shelter and then—"

"Never mind that, Nelson. That sort of street talk is off-putting."

***

A week later, Salty found Pavements standing with his pamphlets by the sundial, talking to a man walking a little white dog. Pavements was wearing a nice suit jacket and tie and a new black wig and a set of new teeth so shiny that Caps could see them from outer space.

Pavements was saying, "It's like you're traveling down a path and you see ahead of you a fork in the path and you don't know which direction to take so you hold out your hand... Hold out your hand."

The man held out his hand.

Pavements put a Watchtower into his hand. "Into your hand comes the direction to take. See here on the front page. The scientists are trying to prove by looking at bones from a million years ago that the first people came from monkeys. The scientists say the bones they've collected belonged to the almost-but-not-quite people who weren't people yet. They could walk on two legs, and had two thumbs, but their brains weren't big enough to learn manners."

Pavements turned the page.

"But see here. The scientists are wrong. Those bones weren't from almost-people. They were ordinary bones from real people. But what made their bones look different was they had rickets. And see this picture here. A complete skeleton only three feet tall that they found in Africa that they said came from millions of years ago and was one stage before man. But the scientists were wrong. Those bones were from ordinary people that didn't get took into the ark that Noah built. Their bones absorbed water while they were floating around in the flood. Then they got dropped down in Africa in the hot sun and shrank down so they looked like smaller almost-people. This proves that God created man, first Adam, then Eve."

The man asked, "Talking about skeletons, what happened to the one who looked like Willie Nelson?"

"The Street Rescue Police came around in a van yesterday and picked him up. I said, 'Where are you taking Mr. Bones?' They said, 'First we get him sober and then if his DNA says he's got no outstandings, we'll take him to Safe Haven.'"

Salty couldn't hear the next question. Pavements held up the pamphlet. "It says right here. The government has created a new Ministry of Relocation, MOR they call it, a bed for the winter and fifty dollars a week if you stay clean, the first fifty in advance just to get you started on your new life."

There was another question and then Pavements answered, "The Lord God is giving them one final chance. But after that, no more. Yesterday I seen the ones they relocated to East Jesus, I seen them all behind The Daystar. They'd spent their homeless allowance at Dixie's and were drinking Curveball and fighting over cardboard boxes to sleep on because it had rained and the ground was wet."

To the next question, Pavements said, "The Lord God should put rat poison in the East Jesus soup. That'd get those rascals off the street. Off the street and into hell, I says."

The next question must have been something like, "Why not just strike them dead on the spot and be done with it?"

Pavements said, "The Lord God gave Adam and Eve and the rest of us freedom of choice. God doesn't send you to hell. You send yourself to hell."

The man nodded, as though he thought Pavements made sense.

Pavements said, "I get worn out some days doing Jehovah's work for him. The other day there was about ten Outreachers hanging out by the sundial so I couldn't get near the fountain. The day before, Beets had his nose stuck right in the water trying to cool it off so I couldn't have a drink. I said to myself, 'I can tell you, Nelson, as far as I'm concerned, if these lazy rascals living in Silver City don't change their ways, they will be punished into eternal damnation along with the Catholics and the child molesters.'"

The man looked like he was glad he was neither.

***

Salty opened the door to his shed to let in the fresh air. He swept the floor, took out the garbage, went through his boxes — junk he did not know he had. He threw it all away. When the shed was finally clean and tidy, he sat down to rest. Maybe I should get some new furniture, he thought. Maybe a new chair and a table. And a new box for Amos.

Hearing a noise outside, he went to the window. Beets was teetering along the alley, walking with the help of a short stick. Someone must have knocked him over, or maybe he had fallen, or maybe he'd been beat up by an Outreacher, whatever had happened, one side of his face was swollen and purple, and one eye was nearly closed. He shambled up the alley, swinging his stick at nothing.

Salty met him at the door. Beets pushed past Salty into the shed and disappeared into one corner. Then he got up and went to the window. From the doorway, Salty watched a cruiser approaching, idling slowly up the alley. Beets headed for the door. But he'd gone only a few feet before the policemen caught up with him.

"Could I talk to you for a minute, Beets?" Officer Hill got out of the cruiser. "What happened to your face? Yeah, I know, fell down the stairs. That's why you should be in this new program we're getting underway."

"I'm not going."

Officer Hill showed Beets the pictures. Salty had already seen them, a low- rise building with studio apartments.

"But we need a name on the application form. Beets is not a name."

Beets leaned against the cruiser and lit a cigarette.

"All we want is a name. It doesn't need to be your real name. It's not like in homeless shelters where they want your birth date and SIN. And there's no line at the bottom that says it's a federal offense to lie on a government form. This is a new program Father Sutcliffe has started. Five new Daystar facilities are now church-affiliated sanctuaries. Since you're already living there, Beets, why not make it official? You've got to be listed as being in a program somewhere, otherwise you're a vagrant. All you have to do is put in a name. Father Sutcliffe doesn't care what your name is, he's giving you sanctuary until he can get you sober. So, find yourself a nice name. Something that kind of fits you, you know, something... you're a quiet kind of guy, thoughtful..."

"Beets," said Beets.

"Beets, well... agrarian. What's for your last name?"

"Beets."

"Beets Beets." Officer Hill smiled. "Hmm. On second thought, I like it. It's a nice play on words. It has a nice beat to it. Good choice."

Officer Hill wrote it down. He said to Salty, "I understand Father Sutcliffe wants you to come with him to work in his new program."

Salty frowned.

"He never mentioned it to you? No, I guess he didn't. He's got some money from the R.C. Church. I'm kind of letting the cat out of the bag. I should let Father Sutcliffe be the one telling you about it. But, since I'm giving out good news, here's more. I went over to Sylvia's place to see how Amos is doing. He's got a sutured gash across his shoulder and a cast on his hind leg. But he's the same old Amos. When I kneeled down, he gave me his paw for the handshake. I said into his ear, 'I'll let you in on a secret. You can sleep easy from now on. Officer Cobbs has gone to 49 Division.'"

Chapter Forty

Sylvia

Sylvia had stopped by The Daystar to tell Salty that Amos was up and around and ready to return to Silver Park. Mr. Bones was sitting on the front step. He said, "Salty's not here. The kill kennel in Montreal phoned to say they had three sheepdogs there, ready for pickup. So, him and Jake went to get them."

Mr. Bones called to the black-and-white sheepdog that had been sniffing along the sidewalk. It came over to lie at his feet.

"Her name is Daisy. Salty found her for me. Him and Staff and Jake are starting this comfort dog program using sheepdogs. Jake's the trainer. It's in a sheepdog's blood to look after whatever needs looking after. Drunks and sheep. The same thing, they both need looking after."

Mr. Bones patted the dog.

"When I go into the Tim Hortons, I have to tie her up outside. So, I go in and look out the window and there she is staring in at me, worrying about if I'm all right, wondering what I'm drinking, and then when I come out, she does a little dance she's so glad to see me. But if she smells alcohol she backs away. I can't stand to see the disappointment in her eyes. I hate it when she backs away like that."

Mr. Bones held out one hand and the dog lifted its paw. "The handshake is important. First thing you do when you meet your dog, you get down on your knees to introduce yourself to your dog with a handshake. Then you get back up on your feet and take the leash and you stand up straight with your shoulders back and your feet pointed straight and you say to the dog, 'You and me, Daisy, one day at a time.'

"We get together at The Daystar every morning with our dogs. It's like a breakfast meeting. We say to the dog: 'Today I will hold my head high; today I will hold my shoulders square upon my back; today I will turn my face towards the sun.'

"You got to talk to your dog. That's the idea. You can tell your dog stuff you can't tell anyone else. You can talk as long as you want. I can sit here patting Daisy's head and I can talk all day and she'll sit there and listen, understanding every word.

"Salty goes around to the kennels and the pound to get them. There's a kill kennel in Ohio that ships them up. But they got to be sheepdogs. And the dogs are called Daisies. Salty says 'I'll pick a Daisy for you now, otherwise, you're going to end up not picking daisies but pushing daisies.'"

Daisy was resting her head on her two front paws, her eyes fastened on Mr. Bones, listening to every word.

"The other day a guy from the government came by. I said, 'When are you going to fix the help hotline on the bridge? Richard still can't speak English.' So, the government guy says they're going to take out the phone and instead spread a net across like at the circus for the high-wire guys, trapeze, you know, what do you call them… Not actors; well, maybe actors. That will stop them from jumping. Father Sutcliffe was there. He says, 'It's not what they're doing; it's why they're doing it. There are many high wires in life. If one falls off, there will always be another waiting in the wings to take his place, net or no net. Our job is to find out what put them on the high wire in the first place.'"

Mr. Bones said, "No one will listen to anything a politician says about the homeless, but they'll listen to Father Sutcliffe. When he goes around raising money, they line up with their chequebooks."

Mr. Bones said, "I seen Pavements the other day. He asked me, 'Do you want to go to heaven, Mr. Bones?' So I said, 'Do they allow dogs in heaven?' He thought about it, looking like Einstein wearing a wig, as though I'd asked some kind of scientific question about molecules. He said, 'No, they don't allow dogs in heaven the same as they don't allow dogs in Tim Hortons.' So I says, 'If Daisy can't get into heaven, I don't want to go.'"

Acknowledgements

My thanks to Adrienne Kerr, freelance editor, for her guidance and encouragement in completing this novel.

CPSIA information can be obtained
at www.ICGtesting.com
Printed in the USA
LVHW032003200521
688023LV00005B/235